Reviews

A bold and engaging read about bullying, love, and explosive reactions reminding us of what it is like to be a teenager today ...

—Nadia Maddy, author of *The Palm Oil Stain*

To have completed a gripping two-hundred-page novel at the age of fourteen is a remarkable achievement. I look forward to reading much more from the pen of this gifted young writer in the years ahead.

—Yema Lucilda Hunter, author of *Her Name Was Aina, Seeking Freedom, Nanna,* and *Joy Came in the Morning*

KEIRA FORDE

Edited by WINSTON FORDE
my Grandfather

authorHOUSE®

AuthorHouse™ UK
1663 Liberty Drive
Bloomington, IN 47403 USA
www.authorhouse.co.uk
Phone: UK TFN: 0800 0148641 (Toll Free inside the UK)
UK Local: 02036 956322 (+44 20 3695 6322 from outside the UK)

© 2021 Keira Forde. All rights reserved.

No part of this book may be reproduced, stored in a retrieval system, or transmitted by any means without the written permission of the author.

Published by AuthorHouse 12/19/2020

ISBN: 978-1-6655-8317-6 (sc)
ISBN: 978-1-6655-8318-3 (hc)
ISBN: 978-1-6655-8316-9 (e)

Print information available on the last page.

Any people depicted in stock imagery provided by Getty Images are models, and such images are being used for illustrative purposes only.
Certain stock imagery © Getty Images.

This book is printed on acid-free paper.

Because of the dynamic nature of the Internet, any web addresses or links contained in this book may have changed since publication and may no longer be valid. The views expressed in this work are solely those of the author and do not necessarily reflect the views of the publisher, and the publisher hereby disclaims any responsibility for them.

Cover Image
Comet Neowise, as seen from Sutton Bank, North Yorkshire, taken by Steven Forde, author's father on July 2020.

To anyone who has a place in my heart. You're one of a kind.

1

Ivy

'"Queen's Central Grammar School,"' I read aloud from the front of the brochure. '"Our prestigious secondary school provides the most state-of-the-art technology to ensure your child has a bright future ahead of him or her." *Pfft, w*hat a load of nonsense.' I toss the brochure over to Mum. She chuckles and places it on the kitchen table.

'Y'know, Ivy, if you concentrated on the positives of the school instead of judging it, you might just have fun there,' Mum advises me, stirring spaghetti hoops in a pan. As if I'm gonna enjoy going to this school. It's a *prestigious* school. *Prestigious* schools are for posh rich kids. I am neither of those things. I am simply Ivy Towers: working-class super dork from Leeds. Now, let me make something crystal clear before we carry on: I am not your stereotypical nerd. I don't sit at home pondering over Shakespeare's poems and reciting the periodic table. (Though don't get me wrong; there is nothing wrong with either.) My life is full of excitement and drama. I am an outgoing introvert—I'll leave you to try to understand that conundrum. Let's just say I'm a brainiac with a big gob.

'Now, remember what we talked about last night?' Mum asks, her voice taking a suddenly serious tone. I nod. 'No one is to know what happened in Leeds,' she orders.

'But what if I make a new best friend whom I can trust with my secrets?' I complain.

She stares at me through darkened eyes. Her voice lowers until it's almost a whisper. 'Ivy, you can't tell a soul. It could ruin your reputation. People might get the wrong end of the stick. No one—and I mean no one—can know what you did. As far as anyone is concerned, you simply got accepted to Queen's due to your high grades, and that's all.'

Even the mention of my past makes my skin crawl. The thought of that cursed night sends my stomach into knots. I'd do anything to reverse my actions—to get rid of the burdens I carry daily. Sometimes I wonder what made me do it—what made me so reckless. Mum is right. My secret must stay a secret if I want any chance of a future. My heart aches for my previous life, my old home, and my grandparents, but I know I can't have them back; my mistake has cost me my happiness.

I mumble to Mum that I'm not hungry and amble upstairs to my new room. I figure I'd better savour these last few minutes by myself before all eight of my siblings get home. Yes, you heard me right—*eight* siblings. Whilst we are on the topic, let me introduce you to them: one-year-old sister Eva, two-year-old brother Archie, three-year-old twins Poppy and Cole, four-year-old sister Coco, six-year-old twins Milly and May, and eighteen-year-old brother Tyler. You're probably wondering how Mum came to have so many children. Let's just say she's had more than a few relationships, and each one ended in a huge fight and a positive pregnancy test. Although I must give credit to my dad, who was responsible for the creation of me and Tyler. He stuck around until I was four, which was three years and eleven months more than any of the other deadbeats.

To take my mind off things, I get my favourite book, *The Angel's Curse*, out of one of my many removal boxes. I begin to read the exotic tales of the mystical angels, and tranquillity washes through my brain. Hours go by, and I find myself nodding off into a peaceful slumber on the floor of my box room.

'Ivy, for God's sake! Get up! Mum needs help in the kitchen!' Tyler's voice hammers through my head like a mallet. He shakes me hard, but finally realizing that trying to get me up is pointless, he ambles back down the stairs, his every footstep echoing through our tiny house.

Just one more minute, I think, but before I can even shut my eyes again, Poppy runs into my room and starts jumping on me as if I'm a bouncy castle. Swiftly, I stand up and spin her around in a circle so she lets out little squeals of delight. I put her down and throw on my new suit. It takes me a while to work out how to perfect the knot on my tie. Being a perfectionist really isn't helpful when you need to get things done quickly. Poppy uses her overpowering puppy eyes, so I end up giving her the piggyback she wanted. 'C'mon, let's go and get breakfast.'

We walk into a room of carnage. Little children race around the kitchen while Mum and Tyler desperately try to feed them. 'Morning, Ivy!' cheer Milly and May. I smile and sit beside my baby sister, Eva. Despite being an infant, she is annoyingly strong. She somehow manages to pull the table off her highchair, so I have to clip it back on.

Whilst both spooning puree into Eva's mouth and eating my own Cheerios, I read the brochure again. Queen's Central Grammar School—it sounds more like a palace than a secondary school for hormonal teenagers. I get lost in the brochure, and when I look up, Eva is covered in apple sauce. *Fantastic,* I think, as I free my sister from her sticky clothes, I glance down at my rusty watch: 8.54. School starts in six minutes. Leaving Eva in her highchair, and Tyler and Mum looking after seven little kids, I run to the door. Just as my fingers rest on the handle, Mum tells me, 'Remember, Ivy: don't tell a single soul what happened.'

Without even turning to face her, I nod and run to the bus stop. Conveniently, the bus arrives two minutes later.

Normally I'm quite a calm and collected person, but today I'm shaking like a leaf. To relieve my throbbing headache, I press my forehead against the cold glass of the bus window. An icy sensation soothes the stabbing pain which had occupied my head. Queen's High is tearing up my brain and pushing out all other thoughts. Could someone ever know about my past? Am I too lower class to be associated with them? Will I be bullied for my dorky personality? Only time will tell, I guess.

2

Eli

Surprisingly, school couldn't come soon enough. Yeah, the summer holidays are relaxing, but my family are driving me insane with all the plans for my wedding. I know what you're thinking: *How are you getting married at such a young age?* Basically, I come from a traditional Arab family, so my parents have always wanted me to marry an Arab girl. To be honest, I was never keen on the idea of dating someone specifically because of her ethnicity. Personality has always been my main priority. But then I met Haila. She is beautiful, she is mine, and I love her to pieces. To cut a long story short, we are getting married this summer. Being back at school is a relief—no more suit shopping or catering planning. I can just play basketball with my best mate, Craig.

'Be Quiet, year eleven! That includes you, Connor! If your conversation is more interesting than listening to me, then I'm sure you'd love to share it with the class,' Mr Cabello exclaims in the usual teacherly fashion. Class begins, but I can't be bothered to concentrate, so I decide to doodle instead. Drawing is one of my few talents, along with basketball and surfing. Mythical dragons and designer skateboards occupy my A4 page instead of notes on primary socialisation.

A chilly breeze enters the stuffy classroom as a small girl with geek glasses and her tie hanging backwards bursts through the door. What a sight she looks: her hair's tangled, her strangely mature business suit is creased, and even her glasses are crooked. I hate to say it, but her peculiar look is oddly satisfying.

Mr Cabello gives her a reassuring smile and turns to the class. 'Class, please give a warm welcome to Ivy Towers! She has travelled all the way from Leeds to Dover to join our school.' Mr Cabello has a strangely warm and affectionate tone to his voice. It almost seems as though he shares a special connection with Ivy. Despite Mr Cabello's best efforts to end the glares and whispers, the whole class stares deep into her soul, observing her unusual choice of dress and most likely judging her. Mr Cabello scans the room for a spare seat until his eyes rest on the one next to Martha Jones. It's quite ironic, considering Martha is the oddest person I've ever met. She has no friends, and that doesn't surprise me. She dresses almost exactly the same as Ivy, and she is smart and mature. All I ever see her do is read and sit alone in the library. Martha doesn't deserve friends.

Mr Cabello directs Ivy to her seat, and with a hesitant nod she traipses awkwardly towards her desk. *Time for me to put some life into this bad excuse of a lesson.*

Carefully, I edge my foot into the aisle between the desks, and as Ivy walks past, she trips on my foot and goes flying. A rumble of laughter spreads like wildfire around the classroom. Craig high-fives me from his desk, cackling and slamming his hand down on the table.

'Nice one, Eli!'

Ivy's bag spews its contents all over the floor, so Martha stands up to help her. Of course Martha would help; she's such a goody two shoes. They stoop to pick up pens, pencils, books, and a variety of girly stuff.

I observe the items, and my eyes land unexpectedly on one in particular: her *period plugs*. Whilst pretending to help her pick up her belongings, I pick one up and remove the plastic case.

Feeling quite pleased with my find, I hoist myself up and shout, 'Good thing you brought these to school! Wouldn't wanna get blood on your pretty little pinafore now, would we?'

Her face goes as red as fresh blood, and so does Cabello's. His body quakes with anger; the whole class falls into an awkward silence. He's ready to explode.

'Eli Bishara. Isolation. Now.' These are the only words he can manage to release. Smugly, I toss the tampon at Ivy; she dodges it like it's some sort of bullet. Laughing at her strange reflexes, I pick up my bag and saunter out of the classroom. For good measure, I wink at Ivy as I leave. Ashamed, she moves her gaze to the wooden desk in front of her.

I focus my eyes on the blank wall in front of me. On either side of my desk are two more walls. I swear this whole isolation thing should be illegal. I'd decided to try and concentrate on my work, but all I can think about is Ivy. *I wonder where she came from. Probably some poor area. It's easy to tell she is trying to hide how poor she is under that weird suit. Well, she isn't fooling me.* Poor people don't belong at Queen's. If it were up to me, poor people wouldn't even be allowed through the front door, but it's all about equality nowadays. *Well, I guess all I can do is make sure that Ivy knows she isn't wanted here. Not by anyone.*

— 3

Ivy

I'm so embarrassed. Normally I'm not one to hold a grudge, but Eli Bishara had better watch his back. To be honest, he should know better. Has he never heard the phrase 'Quiet people have the loudest minds'?

I try as hard as I can to concentrate on my work, but I can literally feel people staring daggers through me from across the classroom. A part of me feels as though they all know what I did back in Leeds, but I push that thought out of my head. Of course no one knows. They are simply staring at me because I am the strange new girl. I've got to stop being so paranoid.

As far as I'm concerned, everyone in this class, except one girl, appears to be what I call a 'default'. 'But what is a default?' one might ask. Let me explain. There are two types of default: (1) Failure to do something, or a flaw in something, and (2) the way that something will happen, or appear automatically, if you do not make any choices. I'm referring to the latter. In my eyes, someone who is a default has made no attempt at originality, personality, or lifestyle speaking. For example, a default teenager most likely wears ridiculously priced tracksuits, follows the crowd, and strives to live according to what social media tells them to do. At a young age, I decided that I would do everything in my power not to be a default. As Oscar Wilde once said, 'Be yourself, everyone else is already taken.' I couldn't agree more. Why follow the crowd like a blind sheep when you can be exotic and proud of your personality?

The one person in this classroom that doesn't seem to be a default is Martha. She is wearing smart yet colourful clothing and vintage boots which, I have to say, really suit her. Just from looking at her, I can tell that the girl doesn't care about what others think about her; she loves herself for who she is.

As I scan the sea of new faces, my eyes fixate on the one particular boy sitting next to me. There's something about him that I recognise. The tall, buff structure; curly perm cut; and small grey eyes are all too familiar. Craning my neck discreetly, I read the name on his exercise book: Craig Wilson. *Where have I heard that name before?* Then it clicks. I know him; and more to the point, he knows me. What a coincidence. I hope he doesn't notice who I am; that could ruin everything.

As soon as the bell goes, I find myself sprinting to the door. But before I can reach for the handle, Mr Cabello softly puts his hand on my shoulder.

'Ivy, may I speak to you for a minute?' My mind is screaming, 'No you can't, you old man; *I have better things to do,*' but instead I reluctantly nod. We wait for the swarm of sixteen-year-olds to exit the classroom before we begin talking.

'Ivy, are you okay?' 'Of course I'm not okay!' I want to scream.

'Yes, I'm fine,' I reply, in the hope of making this awkward conversation end quickly.

'I know that Eli may seem a bit of a … bully, so if you ever need help, just come to me, okay? I'm here for you.' His aqua-blue eyes search around my sluggish brown eyes. This man is way too close for comfort. He doesn't realize that Eli's prank isn't causing me discomfort; Craig's the problem. He has the chance to ruin me if he realizes who I am. For some reason, I can't form any words, so I just nod and spin on my heels in an attempt to leave.

Again I feel his large warm hand hold on to my bony shoulder; he's a little firmer this time. The teacher spins me around to face him.

'Promise me you will tell me if Mr Bishara says anything unkind to you?'

'Y-yes, I promise, sir,' I eventually manage to say.

'Okay,' he utters in a low, unnerving tone. Cabello releases my tense shoulder, so I sprint out of the classroom as fast as possible.

It's such a relief to get out of that dreaded classroom. It felt as if I were being choked. The hallways are almost completely empty. *Am I really that late out of sociology? My timetable says that I have history next.*

Fabulous. Using the blurry map in my planner, I slowly but surely make my way to the history block. Instead of bursting through the door as I did in my first lesson, I gently push it open and walk calmly into the room, hoping to attract minimum attention.

Fail.

The entire class is glaring at me as though I just shot a fairy. They seem to treat tardiness like an almighty sin at this school. Or maybe it's just me. I guess I am just the new geeky freakazoid that had a tampon flung at her within the first five minutes of arrival. A tall and slender man is leaning against his desk and talking about the Great Fire of London. *Seriously? I'm in year eleven and we're still learning about such a basic subject?* Luckily Craig isn't in this lesson, so my shoulders relax slightly. I make a mental note to breathe and start talking calmly.

'H-hi sir. I'm Ivy Towers, transfer student from L-Leeds.' The class all giggle when I say the name of my hometown, a northern city. What snobs! The teacher gives a warning look to them all and turns to me.

'Welcome to year elven history, Ivy. My name is Mr Batch. I'm sure you'll fit right in.' At that, the kids giggle again. I feel a sudden urge to knock out every single one of these idiots with a heavy-duty metal pan, but I shake that thought out of my head. Instead of scuttling over to my desk, I casually strut over to the empty seat at the back. Apparently cool kids sit at the back of the classroom, and I guessed that by doing so, I would climb a few rungs up the social ladder. Maybe.

Whilst Mr Batch explains the possible causes of the 1666 fire, I study his features intensely. Every strand of his hair is ruffled up into a messy yet immaculate mop of curls on top of his head. His jawlines are strong and well defined, and he has a tanned olive complexion, which has always been a dream of mine. His brows are thick and neatly shaped and are perched perfectly above his mysterious, dark hazel eyes. Every once in a while, he licks his thin pink lips, and I calculate that, on average, every 33.7 seconds he ruffles up his curls.

'This may come as a shock to you, but there were only six deaths in the Great Fire of London!'

'Wrong,' I say, shocking both myself and everyone present. Mr Batch squints his eyes and nods at me to explain.

'You are right in that there were only six reported deaths in the fire, but they obviously didn't search around the ruins of the peasant villages.

Peasants were irrelevant in society and were often frowned upon, so the government wouldn't have taken it upon themselves to go hunting for the corpses of perished peasants, would they? Life in Tudor Britain was cruel and run by hierarchy, so it's remarkable that we still go by these evidently spurious figures.'

By the time I've finished ranting, the whole class, including Mr Batch, is staring at me in pure wonder. My sheer braveness comes as a shock to me too, if I'm honest. I didn't think I'd ever get my confidence back after the 'incident', but here I am. Mr Batch's lips crack into a pleasing smile.

'Looks like we have a budding historian on our hands!' he says, slapping his palms together. Many of my classmates roll their eyes or mumble that I'm a know-it-all, or whatever, but it doesn't bother me. I like being smart, so smart is what I'm gonna be. The rest of the lesson flies by, and before I know it, we are all streaming out of the door to our next lesson.

When it finally reaches lunchtime, I feel so relieved. My brain is completely shattered from listening to so many idiots all at once. I didn't bother to put my hand up unless everyone was being so incredibly stupid that they couldn't work out such basic answers. Some people go off to the cafeteria, and some go outside, so I opt for the lunch hall. I get only an apple and orange juice because the school food looks rancid. Clutching my apple, I come to a devastating realisation. I have no friends here.

Back in Leeds, I would've sat with Cass, Sydney, and Simon, but I can't now. Cass and Sydney are still in Leeds, and Simon—well, I'll save the story about Simon for another time. Right now my only priority is working out where the hell I'm gonna sit. Every table has a different genre of people. It kinda reminds me of those cliché American high school movies where all the jocks sit at one table and the cheerleaders at another. Instead of taking my chances sitting next to any old person, I venture out of the cafeteria and into the school field outside.

A beautiful oak tree is planted right in the middle of the field, so I sit under it and begin reading *The Angel's Curse*. To be completely honest, I've read this book three times over already, but it is simply the best thing ever created. You have to read it to understand. The book vaporises all my worries as I lean against the old oak tree. Calming rays of sunshine beam down on me and warm up my skin. The oak bark from the tree sticks to my skin, and the scent of freshly cut grass and ancient trees dances in the air. I'm snapped out of my bookworm trance when a pair of retro boots appears in front of me. I look up, and standing there is Martha. She smiles and slumps down beside me.

'What ya readin'?' she asks, peering at the front cover. Her eyes bug out when she reads the title. 'Oh ... my ... sweet ... Jesus!' she squeals.

My brows knit profusely. 'What?'

'You're reading *The Angel's Curse!* That book is my life!' Never-ending squeals come flying out of my mouth, and we end up hugging in a weird mutual-fan frenzy.

'We have so much to discuss! Plus, we have last period off. Oh, this day just gets better and better!'

It's official. Martha Jones is my spirit animal. For the next hour and a half, I discuss everything about the book under the summer sun with my new-found friend. Turns out we are both crazy about the mansion master and super-hot vampire, Pablo Sinfara. Some may find it weird to fangirl over a character that isn't even illustrated in the book but, honestly, you have to read it to understand. After what seems like five minutes, the shrill bell rings and we are forced to part ways and go home.

On arrival, I close the door behind me and watch the chaos unfold before my eyes. Children of all ages are scattered about the room, doing various things: eating, playing, and watching *Peppa Pig*. It's at times like this that I wish Dad hadn't walked out when I was four. He could have been helping Mum right now. We could have been happy. Leaving my duffel bag on a chair, I help Tyler clean up the meatballs that have just been flung on the floor. Sometimes I dread the days when I finish school. Tyler goes to sixth form, but he spends his free periods assisting mum with the little ones.

'Good day?' I tease, trying to lighten the mood. He glares at me, so I stop talking and continue scooping up the puddle of spaghetti. Once the remains of the meaty mess have been cleaned up, I attempt to head straight to my room, but before I make it to the staircase, Mum calls, 'How was your first day, Ivy?' I'm not in the mood for a conversation, so I simply reply with, 'It was all right. Could've been better.' I know it may seem ungrateful, considering I had caused my whole family to move across England because of my unfortunate mistake, but I'm just too tired to have a long conversation.

I fling myself onto my bed and open my laptop. The tedious FaceTime ringtone sounds until Martha finally answers.

'Hey!'

'Hi! I thought that since our reading session was cut short, we could continue on here?'

We spend hours discussing *The Angel's Curse*. Who could have imagined that a book could create such long conversations? During a heated debate with Martha on who is the best character, a Facebook notification pops up on the corner of my screen:

Eli Bishara wants to be friends.

Yeh, right. Even though the irony of the notification irritates me, I press the Accept button. Almost straight after I accept, he sends me a message:

Hey cotton! Today was great! Your face was priceless ;)
can't wait for tomorrow. This is just the beginning.

The message pierces me like a million needles. Tears begin to well up in my eyes.

'Ivy ... *Ivy, what's wrong*?' Martha yells. I snap out of whatever emotional trance I was in and weakly reply, 'Eli is sending me messages ...'

'Don't let him get to you. He's not worthy of your time or energy. Now c'mon; we have so much more to discuss about Gareth, the evil undertaker!' Martha really is a perfect friend.

☙❧

Despite knowing me for all of about two days, Martha has noticed that I'm not my normal confident self. To be completely honest, I haven't really been myself since the incident, which was a year ago.

Being the amazing friend that she is, Martha knows just how to cheer me up, so after school on Wednesday we get the train to the Kensington Central Library. My nose tingles as I breathe in the scent of ageing books and immortal fantasies. I sink into a large armchair in the 'quiet corner' and breathe out a huge sigh of relief; Martha mimics me, dramatically falling into her chair, huffing loudly.

'Martha! Shhh. This is supposed to be the "quiet corner",' I hiss, making quotation marks with my fingers. She giggles but stops immediately when a thought pops into her mind.

'Okay, Ivy. I need you to try to stay calm.' A sinking feeling fills my stomach, just as on the night of the incident. The look on Martha's face confirms that bad news is coming my way. She slowly reaches into her beige Kanken bag and pulls out a small parcel.

'Martha, what's that?'

'Open it and see.' She tries to mask the excitement, but her voice cracks midway through speaking. That's what I love about Martha—she can't stay serious for longer than a second. I take the parcel and break the seal. My hand reaches inside, and I pull out two identical books. I read the cover:

The Angel's Curse 2: Demons' Karma

My mouth hangs open in utter shock.

'How did you get this? I mean *how!* It hasn't even come out yet!' I exclaim, forgetting I'm in the quiet corner. A passing librarian shushes me, but I dismiss her completely.

'My dad is best friends with the writer, Thomas Lead,' she exclaims, clearly very pleased with my reaction.

'Martha Jones, you really are the best person I have ever met.'

Encouraged by the inviting atmosphere of the library, my best friend, and a perfect story waiting to be read, I open the book to the first page. I look up at Martha to see her nose already in the book. With a cheesy smile plastered on my face, I begin reading. All my worries evaporate, just like the night before my first day at school, and tranquillity washes through my brain as I read the exotic tales of the mystical angels.

'Don't you just wish *The Angel's Curse* was illustrated?'

'Oh my gosh, yes! I bet Pablo is really cute!' Martha squeals. All eyes are on us as we walk down the school halls, but I honestly couldn't care less; I am with Martha, and that's all that matters.

'We should totally work on our own illustrations for the book and send them to Thomas Lead. He might make a new illustrated edition!'

'That would be so cool! We'd be famou—' My voice trails off. 'Martha, why are there so many people at my locker?' I find myself sprinting to my locker, pushing people out of the way. Getting through this crowd is like wading through water. After a lot of shoving, I reach my locker. Stuck to the door is a packet of tampons, staring me right in the face. I tear the pack off my locker and tear off the note that's stuck to it. It reads,

> To our dearest Ivy,
>
> We wanted to make sure you had enough supplies to last you, so we got you a jumbo pack! Don't use them all at once.
>
> Lots of love,
> Eli and Haila xxx

The devilish duo appear among the laughing crowd surrounding me. I wonder why Haila should laugh at me for having tampons in my bag. She's a girl too. Surely she should understand.

'Turn that frown upside down!' Haila says, poking me hard in the jaw.

Martha watches helplessly, paralysed with fear.

'Why would you do this? I didn't do anything to you. I—'

'Oh save your breath, Cotton. You should be grateful. We got you an expensive brand and all,' Eli scoffs.

'Well, say thank you then!' Haila grabs my collar, holding me up against the lockers. 'Go on! Say thank you! Ungrateful cow.' Spittle flies out of her mouth and lands right on my forehead.

'Th ... thank you,' I whisper. What's happened to me? I'm normally so confident, and here I am, thanking my own bullies for publicly embarrassing me.

'Louder so everyone can hear you!' she barks at me like an army sergeant.

'Thank you!' I yell, my voice still trembling.

'Good girl!' she coos, releasing my collar, and she saunters off, arm in arm with Eli. The small crowd follow after them, cheering and laughing.

I sit in a huddled ball on the floor, weeping into my blazer sleeves.

Martha runs over to me and wraps her long arms around my quivering body.

'I'm sorry, Ivy. I should've stepped in. I should've told them to stop.'

'Too right you should've! You just stood there! Thanks a lot, Martha. Good to know I can count on you for support the next time they humiliate me.' I shove her arms off me and charge down the corridor.

My eyes look deep into those of the girl staring at me through the grubby school bathroom mirror.

'What have you become, Ivy? I don't know you anymore.' My tone changes from soft to angry.

'Why didn't you stick up for yourself? What is wrong with you? Sort yourself out! Sort yourself out!' I scream and scream till my voice goes croaky. My voice returns to a whisper. 'Get it together, Ivy. This isn't who you used to be. You used to be fun and charismatic, and now look at you. Don't let them hurt you, Ivy. You are worth more than that.'

'She's right, Ivy.' Martha appears in the bathroom doorway, smiling at me. Bitter feelings for Martha still loom in my heart.

'What do you want?'

'Ivy, I can't tell you how sorry I really am. Please, let's be friends again.' Even though my heart aches for our friendship, Martha has only proved to me that I can't rely on her. 'C'mon Ivy. If we aren't mates, who am I gonna have nerdy conversations with? What do you say … friends?' The smile that I tried so desperately to hide spreads across my face. I run to Martha and hold her tight, crying into her blazer.

'You're the best, Martha.'

'I know.'

'Hey, mum! Sorry I'm late back,' I say as I amble through the door at 8.54 p.m. 'I went over to Martha's house …' Mum and Tyler are sitting side by side at the kitchen table. Mum looks awful; her eyes are raw from tears, and she's still in the same PJs she was wearing when I left this morning.

'Mum? What's wrong?'

'Come and sit, darling. We need to have a chat.' I sit beside Mum, holding her hands in mine.

'We are in a lot of debt, Ivy. The bills just keep coming, and between the nine kids and the mortgage, I don't know if I can keep on top of it all. We need more money.' She hangs her head in shame. My heart aches for her. It hurts to see my mum so ashamed.

'Don't worry, Mum. We can use my savings to pay the bills.'

Mum's head lifts. 'Really? You'd do that?'

'Of course I would.'

'Oh Ivy, I don't deserve you.' I let her cry on my shoulder till she has no tears left. It's the least I can do, considering all she's going through.

'Is Mummy okay?' a small, tender voice asks from the stairs. Standing there in Thomas The Tank Engine PJs is Cole, my three-year-old brother.

'Mummy's fine, Cole,' Tyler tells him.

'But Mummy's crying. Crying means she's sad!' Cole says, pleased with his cute little analysis. We all chuckle, but the laughter dies away as quickly as it started.

Tyler walks over to Cole and swings him onto his hip. 'Everybody has to cry sometimes. Now c'mon; it's way past your bedtime.' Tyler climbs up the stairs, Cole clinging to him and his old teddy bear.

It really does warm my heart to see Tyler acting like a father to the younger ones—and sometimes to me as well. We'd all love for Dad to come home, but it's obvious that if it were to happen, it's a long way down future lane.

'I think I'm gonna hit the hay too,' Mum mumbles, wiping tears away with the back of her hand. She begins to stand up, but I hold her arm.

'Mum, promise me you won't be too hard on yourself. This isn't your fault, okay?' Although she nods in agreement, I know my mother. She's really gonna take this whole situation hard, and knowing that I can do little to help really hurts. But we'll sort it out. The Towers always do.

4

Eli

'Dude, don't tell me you're even considering missing out on the best party Queen's has ever seen?'

Craig seems almost offended that I'd turned down this invitation. Some guy called Kirk Jones is one of the most popular year-twelves in school, and for some reason, he has decided to invite me and Craig to his September house party. Yes, he has a monthly house party. This is a pure example of just how sad some people are. They somehow feel the need to be partying every day.

'I dunno, Craig. It's on a Thursday. Is it really a good idea to party on a school night?' I ask, raising my eyebrows at him.

Craig scoffs, rolling his eyes so dramatically that I'm surprised his eyeballs don't get stuck inside his head. 'Since when were you such a goody-goody?' he snarls.

'That's not the point. The point is—'

'The point is, this is a massive party! There'll be year-twelves there. Good music, cute girls, and finger foods! I know how much you love those little cheese ball things,' Craig teases.

'All right, fine, but this is a bad idea and I know it.'

✥

'Why is the music so loud?' I shout over the mix of screaming kids and awful dubstep music. Haila and I bob awkwardly to the beat of the music while Craig goes all out, throwing his hands in the air and attempting to moonwalk. Despite the fact that Kirk's house is huge, the place is packed. Everyone and their mothers seem to be at this party.

'Hey! You're Eli, right?' a girl asks me. She has curly blonde hair and obviously fake eyelashes. She's one of those weird Wotsits-coloured girls that strut around school with their fake designer bags.

'That's my name. What do you want?' I pick my words carefully because Haila is right next to me, staring intensely at both of us.

'I'm Kasey, Emma's mate.' Emma's my ex. Let's just say we had a messy breakup and she has despised me ever since. I really couldn't care less. We lasted only a week. To be completely honest, I haven't really thought about her since we broke up.

'Yeh, I've heard about you. Why are you talkin' to me?' I keep my tone cold to keep Haila warm, if you know what I mean. You know what they say: 'Happy wifey, easy lifey.' Yep, I cringed too.

'Well, you and Emma didn't work out, so I guess you're single. I'm free tonight.' She winks at me with her massive camel-like eyelashes.

'Take a step back, you little cheese puff,' Haila interrupts. 'He's mine, and he always will be. Got that?' Kasey doesn't even answer. She simply flicks her blonde locks in Haila's face and storms off.

'Creep,' Haila mutters.

'Oi, Eli! Let's go get some drinks from the bar!' Craig yells. We push our way through to the bar until the drinks are finally in sight.

'This kid is rich!' I say, looking at the pristine bar, complete with every type of alcohol to exist.

Craig rolls his eyes at me. 'Dude, you can't say anything. Your house is a mini mansion.' He scoffs.

'Yeh, a *mini* mansion. This is a mega mansion.'

He laughs and asks the bartender for a Coke and vodka for him and a mock tail for me. This guy is obviously not a licensed bartender; he doesn't even ask for ID.

5

Ivy

'Martha,' I hiss. 'Martha, look to your right.' Martha follows my gaze. On the other end of the bar are Eli and Craig.

'Ugh. This is gonna be a fun party. I can feel it in my kneecaps,' she giggles.

'Enough with the old people talk. Now keep a low profile; I'm not trying to get bullied tonight. It's torture enough you dragging me to this lame party.' Martha smiles. We make small talk whilst Martha sips her martini. She offered to get me one, but I swore I'd never touch alcohol again—not after last time. I haven't touched a drop since the incident. I know nothing will happen, but it's only a harsh reminder of my past life.

Me and Martha are way too awkward to make conversation with other people; Socializing is my idea of literal torture.

'I can't believe Tyler is cool with you going to a year-twelve party,' Martha exclaims.

'As far as my brother is concerned, we are having a quiet study session at your house, got it? Not a word to him or I will end you,' I threaten jokily. We carry on talking, but my only focus is on Martha's drink. How I long to have some, but I can't. It can't happen again. 'Do your parents know about this party?' I ask.

'Nah. Not like they care anyway. I haven't seen them in months. If they aren't on some business trip, they are relaxing on some tropical island. They don't give a toss what Kirk and I are doing. I could die and it would be months before they even realized I had gone.' Martha stares into her drink.

'At least you have two parents,' I muse.

'It wouldn't make a difference if I had one or two! Zero even. Not like they care about me,' she mumbles. 'Are you sure I can't get you a drink?'

As much as I want to say yes, I can't. 'Nah, I'm good.'

'Suit yourself,' Martha says before taking a sip of her martini. Her drink is taunting me, but I must hold back; I must control myself. I'm not taking any chances.

'What the hell are you doing here?' Eli yells, walking over to us. *Oh, fantastic. My one chance of having a little bit of fun at this sad excuse of a party is officially out of the window.*

'Uhm, we are partying. What does it look like, Sherlock?' I remark.

'What I mean is how on earth did you get an invite to Kirk Jones's party?'

'Because Kirk wanted us here, dummy.'

Martha chimes in. 'If you must know, Kirk is my brother. You got a problem with that?' Eli looks stunned, as if he's been shot.

'Kirk Jones is *your* brother?' he jeers. Craig and Haila appear behind him, their arms crossed.

'Yeah? Why's that so surprising?' Martha asks, starting to seem agitated.

'Well I just can't believe your parents have had one good-looking kid and one that looks like a mutated turtle.' Martha flings herself at Eli before he can hurl any more insults in her direction.

'You wanna fight? 'Cause I will take you down in a heartbeat, you little rat!' she screams, pouncing on him. They scrap about on the floor like animals. The alcohol has clearly gotten to Martha's head. A sober Martha wouldn't hurt a fly. A feeling inside me tells me to intervene, but I'm not looking to mess up my pinafore that I spent so long ironing. Kirk fights through the crowd of onlookers and pulls Martha off of Eli. They both stand up, brushing themselves down and untangling bits of crushed crisps from their hair. Kirk is tall and buff. He has his hair in a brunette man bun and is wearing a tight grey T-shirt which outlines the pattern of his six pack.

'Oi, stop it now!' he barks. Kirk looks them both up and down. 'Don't you dare touch my sister!'

'Your little sister went at me firs—'

'Does it look like I care?' he screams in Eli's face. 'You don't hurt girls.

Now scram before I throw you out myself!'. Spit flies all over Eli and lands about his face. This is pure gold!

Eli, Craig, and Haila shuffle out of the room, ashamed and embarrassed. The murmur of voices becomes louder and louder until the party is back in full swing.

'Nice one, Kirk!' Martha cheers, going for a high five. He forces her hand back down beside her.

'What the hell is wrong with you, picking fights with guys like that? Just go upstairs, get out—I don't care. Just stay out of my way and stop damaging my reputation!' He pushes past her.

Martha turns away from me, though I see her wiping a tear away. She doesn't like it when people see her being upset.

'C'mon; let's go get you cleaned up.' She lets me guide her upstairs and towards her room. I sit on Martha's king-size bed, while she takes a hot shower. The normal Martha would be singing her heart out to *Hey There Delilah* and using the showerhead as a makeshift microphone, but today's Martha doesn't utter a single word. The only noise to be heard is the water slamming against the shower floor and the occasional muffled cry from my best friend. It genuinely hurts to see her like this. After about ten minutes, Martha emerges from her en-suite bathroom sporting Miffy PJs and bunny slippers. She walks over to her chest of drawers and rummages through the bottom drawer.

'What are you looking for?' I ask. She doesn't answer but continues to search through her cluttered belongings. Eventually she stands up holding two big bottles of vodka and a set of crystal shot glasses.

'Martha, what are you doing with those?' I ask, though her intentions are pretty obvious.

'I don't know about you, but I'm getting hammered.' she says through a big, cheesy grin. 'I'm done with holding back.'

'Pass me a bottle.'

'I thought you'd never ask.'

⊛

'Three … two … one …' we both down our tenth vodka shots, grimacing afterwards.

'Wooo!' I yell. I haven't had this much of a buzz since last year. What a lonely year it's been. We look at each other and end up giggling freely for no reason. Alcohol does funny things to you.

'I know; let's c-call myy bwover Ty Ty!'

'H-hell yeahhh!' Martha says between hiccups. With trembling hands, I get my phone out and call Tyler. The phone beeps until my brother answers.

'T-tyyleerrrr is thattt youuuuu?' I say, putting my hand over Martha's mouth to muffle her giggling.

'Ivy, what the hell are you doing?' Tyler roars.

'I'mmmm taaaaalkin' to youuu, what does it sound liiiiike?' I snarl. Martha slaps her knee and explodes in laughter.

'Wait ... Don't move a muscle. I'm coming over right now.' My brother hangs up on me. Martha and I roll on the floor, cackling with laughter.

'Th-that was *epic!*' Martha screeches. We continue to drink and laugh until the door flings open and Kirk and Tyler storm in.

'Martha!'

'Ivy!'.

Kirk helps Martha up and onto her bed, whilst Tyler tries to get me to stand up, though my legs are too weak to support my body weight. He eventually gives up and throws me over his shoulder.

'Bye, Kirk,' Tyler says as he carries my limp body through the door, my head colliding with the doorframe as we go.

'Ow! My noggin!' I protest.

'Oh shut up,' Tyler orders.

As he carries me through their house, I notice that everyone has gone. *Wow, it really must be late.* Instead of placing me in the car gently, Tyler practically chucks me onto the back seat and slams the door.

'What is your problem, Ivy? Sneaking off to a party and getting drunk? After last time! Are you *nuts?*' he screams.

'I didn't dwink d-dat much,' I drawl.

'Ivy, you're absolutely pickled! I have half a mind to leave you to walk home by yourself!'

A sudden wave of emotion floods over me. 'Pwease don't leave me. Everybody leaves me.' I start to blubber, wiping my nose on my sleeve. I look in the mirror to see Tyler's face soften.

'Oh, Ivy, I'm not gonna leave you, okay?' he says gently.

'How did you know w-where I was?' I mumble.

'Kirk's one of my best mates. I told him what you were up to, so he gave me his address. Let's go home and get you to bed. We can talk in the morning.' I don't have to be sober to know that our 'talk' in the morning will be more yelling and less quiet conversation.

❧❦

'Ivy, I'm going to work early, so you and Tyler are in charge, all right?' Mum says the next morning as she fumbles through her purse, looking for a lipstick.

'Mum, I can't, school starts in twenty minutes!' I say, grabbing a pair of sharp scissors from Coco. 'Where did you even find them?' I ask my four-year-old sister.

'I found them on Tyler's bedside table!' she says innocently. I roll my eyes and chuck them on the kitchen table.

'I'm sorry, darlin', but you're gonna have to be late for school. Tyler really needs a hand with these monsters. Besides, it's the least you can do after getting wasted last night.' She sloppily applies a crimson lipstick and throws it back into her bag.

'Get a babysitter or somethin',' I suggest.

'Oh, sweetheart, you know we can't afford that,' she says. 'See you later, kids!' Mum blows a half-hearted kiss to baby Eva and walks out, not even bothering to shut the door behind her. I walk over and close the door for her.

'Tyler!' I yell. The sound of my own voice pains me. Hangovers are the worst, especially when you have seven screaming kids and an angry brother in tow.

Tyler walks downstairs, buttoning up his shirt. He walks straight past me and sits next to our six-year-old twin sisters, Milly and May.

'Tyler, can you quit leaving scissors on your bedside table? Coco nearly sliced herself with them!' He doesn't even acknowledge me. 'Oh, so we are doing this, are we?'

'Ty Ty, can you help me with my maths?' Milly asks, tugging at his sleeve.

'Sure, Mills.' He helps her with basic multiplication and occasionally steals a look at me. I pretend I'm focused on playing trains with Archie on the living room floor, but I'm waiting for Tyler to say something.

I eventually get fed up with waiting.

'Tyler, cut it out and talk to me,' I command, standing up and walking over to him.

'Hey, Ivy, you still have my choo-choo train!' Archie shouts. I throw it to him and turn back to Tyler.

'I dunno what you're on about,' he says, not even looking up to talk to me.

'You said we'd talk in the morning, so let's talk.'

'I can't be bothered to argue with you, Ivy,' he mumbles. 'I'm booking you in for rehab, by the way.' He says this as if it's not a big deal.

'Like hell you are!' I shout.

'Will you shut your trap; the kids are here,' he says, sounding as cool as ever.

'Tyler, I'm not going to rehab! I don't need it!'

'Ivy, you got completely mullered last night. It's for the safety of you and the kids. We don't need a repeat of Simon.'

'Don't you dare bring Simon into this!' Tears start streaming down my cheeks, staining my white blouse.

'Ivy, you are going to rehab whether you like it or not.'

I grab my bag and storm over to the door. 'Keep dreaming, Tyler. Keep dreaming!' I slam the door and storm down the street, tears still flowing out of my eyes. According to the bus timetable, the next bus doesn't come for half an hour. *Fabulous.* I'm thankful that the bus journey to school is short, and within minutes of getting on the bus, I'm at school, walking through the shiny corridors. It doesn't really bother me that I'm late. My only concern is that Tyler is booking me in for rehab. Yes, I got drunk last night, but it was only once. He's just being paranoid like normal. I check my timetable: sociology. *Ugh! This day just gets better and better.*

I walk casually into class and sit in my seat.

'Miss Towers, thank you for gracing us with your presence,' Mr Cabello says sarcastically.

'No problem, sir,' I reply. There's a low sound of giggling, but Cabello's death stare stops that immediately.

'Care to explain why you are'—he looks at the clock on the wall—'thirty-four minutes late?'

'I was babysitting my siblings,' I reply coldly.

'Again? I'd be more likely to believe you if you didn't use the same excuse every day,' he snarls.

'I ain't lying', Mr Cabello.'

'Yes you are.'

I get up from my seat and walk right over to him, staring him deep in his eyes. 'I said I'm not lying,' I say through gritted teeth.

Instead of looking intimidated, he reaches for his walkie-talkie and says, 'A member of the pastoral team to my classroom. Ivy Towers is using threatening behaviour.' The whole class lets out a simultaneous 'Oooooo', and some start laughing.

'Threatening behaviour? You're kidding me.'

'Does it look like I'm kidding? Now sit back in your seat till someone comes. You don't want to make it worse for yourself, now do you?'

Fair play, Cabello. You got me.

He continues his lesson on racism until Mr Kilt knocks on the door.

'I'm here for Ivy Towers,' he says, looking around for me. I've never met him before, but rumour has it that he's an absolute demon.

'Ah yes. She's just over there.' Cabello points to me.

'C'mon then, kid,' Kilt says, motioning for me to follow him. He waits for me outside while I pack my stuff up. I start to walk out, but I trip on Haila's foot, which she obviously stuck out as I was approaching. I leap off the floor and spring at her.

'Don't even start with me, 'cause I will end you!' I yell.

'Enough! Ivy, just get out!' Cabello screeches. Instead of arguing back, I figure there's no point making things any worse.

As I walk out, various people shout, 'Good luck, Cotton!' and 'Brace yourself, Towers!' As soon as I'm out of the door, Mr Kilt starts questioning me as if I'm some sort of hardened criminal.

'What are you playing at?' he asks.

'Me? Cabello's the one being a numskull!' I argue.

'I find that hard to believe.'

'Believe what you like! He's got it in for me; I know it!'

'Quit being dramatic, Miss Towers,' Mr Kilt says, combing his fingers through his fawn-coloured locks. 'Now, what are we gonna do about this little kerfuffle?'

"Kerfuffle?" Is he being serious? 'Let me guess, isolation?' I say, folding my arms and leaning against the wall.

He chuckles. 'Yes, but that's not all I'm here for.' I look up at him, raising my left brow. 'The pastoral team have noticed that you've been struggling in your first weeks, so from Monday I am going to become your mentor. I'll check up on you regularly in order to help you through your school life.' I try my best to seem annoyed, but I'm fighting the urge to smile. Mr Kilt seems to be a bearable guy. He can't be a day over twenty-five, so he must be able to relate to my childhood trauma that is modern education.

'Fabulous,' I say, trying to sound sarcastic. Mr Kilt simply smiles and starts walking down the corridor, so I follow him. I have to run to keep up with his long strides.

We walk up, what seem like endless stairs until we reach isolation—or 'Internal Exclusion,' as it reads on the door.

'Booth number three,' he says. I nod and walk over to the third booth, throwing my bag down and slumping in the chair. Unlike most days, there is no one else in here. *I suppose it is only the first lesson; I'm sure there are more outcasts to come.*

'I'll get someone to bring you some work,' he says before reaching for the door. As he leaves, he turns back to me and says, 'You're a good kid, Ivy. I can tell. See you on Monday.'

After that 'kerfuffle,' he calls me a good kid. He really must have some faith in me. My eyes study the originally all-white booth. Graffiti is spread across the walls. I enjoy reading the various comments and remarks about teachers and kids that have been scribbled in the booth. After what seems like an age, the door swings open and Eli walks over to me.

'Nice one, nerd,' he grumbles, tossing me a social studies textbook. Eli tries his best not to look impressed, but he clearly has some admiration for me. 'I didn't know you had it in ya.'

'There's a lot of things you don't know about me,' I reply, not even looking at him.

'Whatever,' he says, and he walks away, closing the door lightly behind him. Just like that, I'm all alone again. It isn't as bad as I thought it would be. Martha said it's like being incarcerated, but I feel as free as a bird. There's no one else in here and no one else to stop me doing what I like. I open *The Angel's Curse: Demons' Karma* and let the story consume me.

6

Eli

'Oh, come on, Haila! You can't seriously think that One Direction are a decent band?' For being such an intelligent person, Haila has awful taste in music.

'How can you not like them? Especially Harry! Have you seen his eyes?' she squeals.

'I really thought you were different, but you really are just a typical fangirl,' I tease as we amble down the pristine pavement until we reach my front door.

'I am not that! I simply have a passion for inspirational music.'

An enthusiastic smile invades my face and stretches from ear to ear. 'Oh, is that so?'

'Oh, 'tis so!' I pick Haila up and passionately kiss her soft lips. I hold her close to me for what seems like forever. I breathe in her soft passion fruit scent. The whole world becomes a blur, and all that matters to me is my girlfriend.

'Eli Bishara, stop canoodling with Haila and come inside! We have a wedding to plan!' my mum exclaims. Haila and I simultaneously roll our eyes. I slip my hand into hers, and we follow my mum inside. I hang our bags on the silver coat rack in the cloakroom. When I return to the living room, the planning group is sitting around the table, discussing our seating arrangements.

'Eli, do you think Aunt Dana should sit near Uncle Youssef, even though they are divorced?' I shrug and sit next to Haila, sliding my hand into hers. The smooth texture of her small fingers sends sparks down my arms. We try to concentrate carefully on the plan, but all we can hear is my mum pounding the *aseed* with a *mihwash* in the kitchen. *Bang, Bang, Bang, Bang!* Eventually the noise stops and my mum strolls into the room, proudly bearing a big bowl of aseed.

'Dinner!' she announces.

We all sit around our food mat on the floor of the living room.

'Bismillah!' we all say before tucking into the aseed along with samosas and *saltah*, my favourite.

'So,' Haila's mum says between mouthfuls, 'how's school going, you two?' We smile at each other. All that's occupied our week is Ivy. I wouldn't really call it bullying, but Haila and I are making sure she knows her place, which is right at the bottom of the school hierarchy with all the other nerds. It isn't bullying. We simply occasionally slip a note to her during class or trip her up—nothing major. That's not who I am.

'Oh, school's good at the moment, Miss Adil. A new girl, called Ivy, has joined,' I explain. We stay on the topic of Ivy for quite a while. I can see Haila staring at me as I explain Ivy's features in way too much detail. She pulls at her hijab, a classic sign that Haila is unhappy about something.

'You know her well!' Haila exclaims bitterly.

'Yeh, I sit near her in most lessons. You get to know her appearance when she's there everywhere you turn.' I reply carefully. The adults all chuckle.

Haila's face develops an uneasy expression. 'I guess you're right,' she says. 'Just don't end up falling for the nerd or anything like that, because that could ruin this whole marriage.' Sarcasm drips from her every word. The laughter and jokes come to an abrupt end, and a noticeably awkward silence hangs in the air. Everyone looks from person to person, not knowing if it's appropriate to speak. This is the worst type of silence. Everyone wants to speak, to break the tension, but nobody can. Something is holding everyone back.

'Eli and I had better go upstairs and do our homework,' Haila mumbles. She forcefully pulls me to my feet, and we walk out of the room. I turn on my flat screen 3D TV and begin scrolling through *Netflix*.

'I'm sorry I went on that little rant about you liking Ivy,' my fiancée apologises as she slips into one of my many hoodies. 'Of course you don't like her. She's a freak. It was stupid of me.'

'Don't worry. It's cute how protective you are of me. It shows you care,'

I reply. She slides into my bed next to me, and we settle on watching *The Good Place*. Like a little girl with her father, Haila curls up in my arms, and we watch the entertaining tales of the not-so-perfect Eleanor Shellstrop. After a couple of hours of laughing and joking, Haila nods off to sleep. I lightly kiss her burgundy hijab and cuddle with her. It's moments like these that I wish could last forever.

The next Monday, I walk hand in hand with Haila, together with Craig. We stride confidently down the polished white corridors and make our way to our first class, sociology. Once everyone is in place, Cabello starts the lesson.

'Today our topic is recreational drugs.' Cabello turns on a DVD about ecstasy and its effects. Midway through the film, Ivy bursts into the classroom. It's like déjà vu; her clothes are rumpled, her limp brown hair is in a tangle, and the bags under her eyes take up most of her face.

'S ... sorry I'm late, sir. I was—'

Cabello interrupts her. 'I've had enough of your excuses. Let me guess—your mum needed help with your siblings?'

'Y-yes, Mr Cabello. I wasn't lying.' Her face is helpless. She looks over at Martha, who offers a sympathetic smile.

'Just go and sit down, Miss Towers,' Cabello says with a melodramatic sigh. Embarrassed, Ivy scuttles to her desk, which is a row in front of mine. She focuses on the drug documentary, and things carry on as normal. It surprises me that she doesn't fight with Cabello again. I guess she doesn't want a repeat of last weeks' events. I tear a piece of scrap paper out of my notebook, roll it into a spitball dispenser, and shoot small saliva bullets into the back of her hair. It takes a while for her to notice, but when she does, her hazel eyes search desperately for the culprit until they rest on me.

Anger boils through her like piping hot water. Hysterically, she leaps out of her chair and yells, 'You know what? I've had it with you. Do the world a favour and go die in a hole, Eli!' The class falls quiet; some snicker, and some gasp. Cabello's entire body trembles with rage.

'Towers. Bishara. See me after class. And Ivy, sit down!' he barks. *Fantastic*. She shoots me a victorious smile and sits back in her seat. *What a snake*. Ivy reaches into her bag and gets out her *Angel's Curse* book, and instead of watching the documentary, she buries herself in the text. For the first time, I begin to realize some of her rather complimentary features:

she has a set of strong dimples, a strangely cute style, and small, glossy red lips. Don't get me wrong, she is such a nerd, but I applaud her ability to look like a sort of stylish dork.

The rest of the lesson goes by normally until the shrill bell sounds and people begin to exit the classroom. Craig gives me an angry look as he leaves the classroom, and Martha glares over at Ivy as they both leave. No doubt they are both gonna stand outside and try to listen in. Ivy's smug expression still hangs about on her face. We walk forwards awkwardly to Cabello's desk.

'I don't know what's going on between you two, but it ends now,' he demands. 'I know you are behind all of this drama, Eli.'

'That's not tru—' I begin to protest, but he stares creepily at me, so I refrain.

'I have an idea that may help both of you to … bond.' We don't need to bond; we need Ivy to go back to wherever she came from, which is far from here.

'I'm setting a project for the whole class to make presentations in pairs on important parts of modern society. The rest of the class will pick their partners, but I'm putting both of you together. I would like you to do the topic of teen pregnancy.' *You've got to be kidding me*, I think. 'Do you understand?' We both nod. 'Off you go, then. You have one week. Don't screw this up.' He turns to his computer and starts to e-mail someone. As we turn to leave, the faces of Martha and Craig watch us worriedly through the window.

7

Martha

My patience is wearing thin, and although I may seem quiet and timid, Eli has hit a last nerve. He's always getting Ivy into bad situations, and I won't take it anymore. Watching Ivy look so aggravated while talking to Cabello has given me a feeling of anger that I've never felt before. Eli Bishara had better sleep with one eye open.

8

Craig

I'm sick of dumb girls getting Eli into trouble. Before Ivy came along, Eli was never in hot water, and now look at him! Ivy will wish she'd never been born, once I'm finished with her, and I have the perfect idea to make sure karma comes back to bite her. Eli and Ivy both walk out of the classroom. Martha entwines her arm in Ivy's, and they are about to walk off when Eli calls, 'What's the matter, Cotton? Never been in trouble before?'

She sarcastically replies with, 'No, I haven't, and I don't intend to just because some steroid-induced popular can't keep his flap shut!' Martha giggles pathetically. When Eli can't form an answer, I pull him along the corridor, towards the basketball courts. He begins to protest that we have to get to English class, but I give him a look so he knows there is no way of changing my mind.

To let off some steam, we skip class to shoot some hoops. No one else is around. Awkwardly, we play in silence. I dribble the ball past him and toss it into the basket.

'Nice one,' he praises. He walks to his duffel bag and takes out a bottle of water. While I stand there watching, Eli takes a swig of Volvic. *Glug, glug, glug.* Neither of us knows what to say. Tension is jammed in my throat, preventing me from talking. Eventually I pluck up the courage to spout out, 'Why don't we just forget basketball and chat like old times?' Eli simply nods and sits down on the bench, so I sit beside him.

— 9

Eli

'Eli. I can't do this anymore.' Craig can't even look at me. His eyes stare at the shiny court floor. 'We used to do everything together. We used to be a team.' Something must be wrong with him; I've never heard him speak in such a clichéd manner before.

'I know. I've just been really busy; that's all. We are still mates, Craig. We always will be. Craig, what is happening to us? We sound so cringey.' A smile forms on his originally pouted lips. 'To make it up to you, let's go to the alleyway and shoot some hoops, for old times' sake.' Craig nods. I can tell he is trying to contain his excitement. 'Okay, we'll drive there after school. Now let's get to class before Miss Coral notices we are gone.'

— 10 —

Ivy

'C'mon in, Ivy!' Mr Kilt shouts from his office. I walk in sheepishly and sit in one of his plush armchairs.

'I heard that something happened between you and Eli Bishara today.' Kilt raises his eyebrows and twiddles a biro between his fingers.

'Mmm hmm,' I mumble.

'Come on, then. What happened? You can tell me. I won't be mad,' he says, although he knows that I don't care whether he's angry or not.

'I don't wanna talk about it,' I mutter.

'Ivy, this is only going to work if you open up to me.' A streak of light peeks through the curtain and shines on Kilt's iris, highlighting his moss-green eyes.

'It's Eli. He's always bothering me,' I explain.

'And how do you react when he "bothers" you?' Kilt asks. This is why I hate this counselling type of conversation; he knows the answer, he just wants to hear me say it.

'I lash out at him, okay? Can you blame me? The guy's a waste of precious oxygen!' I exclaim. Mr Kilt smiles to himself with perfect pearly teeth.

'Bullies want a reaction from you. They want to see you retaliate. Don't give him the satisfaction, all right?'

'Fine.'

'If you ever need advice, you come straight to my office—got it?' I nod. 'Good. Chocolate?' he offers, holding a large *Quality Street* box in front of me.

I take a toffee penny, my favourite. 'Thanks.'

'No problemo. How's the rest of your day been so far?' Normal counsellors would ask this question without a smidgen of interest, but Kilt seems to genuinely care. I'd normally decide not to bore them with the facts, but it looks like he can take it.

'Truth be told, it's been awful! So far I've passed precisely nine "couples" biting each other's faces off in the corridors. On 16th July 1439, King Henry VI banned kissing in England, as it was the cause of many diseases, and although this occurred around the same time as his mental breakdown over his wife, Margaret of Anjou, I still think the old guy had it spot on. I mean, does nobody know that a ten-second French kiss exchanges about eighty billion germs between the partners? I dare call them partners! Attention-seeking snobs seems more suitab … Why are you smiling at me like that? I find it rather discomforting, if I'm completely honest.' Kilt appears to have his arms folded loosely, and he seems really pleased, if a bit stunned at the same time.

'You are something special, Ivy Towers,' he says whilst tapping his pen against his head.

'Don't ever forget it,' I say, tilting my head ever so slightly.

'Now remind me. What are you going to do if Eli starts troubling you?' he asks.

'Ignore him,' I say, rolling my eyes.

'I think you've got it, kiddo!' he goes for a fist bump, but I don't return it. The mentor glares at me humorously. I find fist bumps rather unnecessary and slightly painful. Since when did colliding knuckles become cool?

'Don't leave me hanging. You're not leaving this room till you pound it!' I give up and fist bump him just to get him off my case.

'Can I go now?' I moan, although secretly I'd rather stay.

'All right. Have a good day, kiddo. Stay out of trouble. I don't want any more complaints about you. Is that clear?' Mr Kilt says in a mildly serious tone.

'Crystal,' I say, making my way out of the office. As I reach for the handle, I turn to Kilt and ask him, 'Why are you so nice to me? Everyone says you're a nightmare.'

He laughs to himself. 'I can be mean if I want to be, so watch yer back, all right? Now get to class before my devil side takes over.'

Satisfied with his answer, I leave the office and make my way to food tech.

11

Eli

We make small talk for a bit whilst sitting on our basketballs. After a while, we run out of things to talk about. Normally we talk for hours on end, but times have changed; our bond has changed. We end up in a heated discussion on who is the best at hook shots, which is obviously me.

'Eli, you have only been interested in basketball since you met me. How long's that, a year? I've played for my entire life. Do you really think you can outplay me?'

'Just because you've played longer doesn't mean you are better!' I argue.

'Practice makes perfect.' Craig insists. It's time to settle this once and for all.

'All right then, Craig. If you are so confident that you are better at hook shots than me, let's compete. We'll film both our shots on my GoPro, and we'll get my mum to decide the winner. Her word is final.' Regret is written all over his face. Everyone knows that I am the king of hook shots. Being the confident lad that he is, he accepts my offer graciously. I go over to my bag and grab my GoPro, excited to show off my kit.

When I return, Craig is doing weird stretches, pretending he is preparing himself to win.

'Show me what you've got then, Eli.' Craig persists, placing the GoPro in a hole in the wall where a brick should be. He motions for me to start. Concentrating hard, I gently throw the ball with a soft sweeping motion and follow through with my arms suspended above my head. Craig seems both impressed and intimidated at the same time.

'Hmm. Not bad for a novice,' Is the closest he can get to a compliment. As Craig is gearing himself up for his turn, my mum texts me.

Habibi, where on earth are you? You must get home now. We have the Adils over to help us make table decorations. Mum xxx

'Mate, I'm sorry, but I gotta go. Haila's family are over again.'

Craig's face falls. 'Oh, ok. We'll play some other time, or something.' As much as he tries to hide it, I can see the disappointment in his expression.

'I'm so sorry.'

'Nah, don't sweat it. Fiancées come first.' I want to disagree with him, but it is sort of true. This wedding gets in the way of my normal life. I hate to say it, but I just want to marry Haila and get on with my life.

⁂

'Okay, class. Today we are looking at teamwork! Teamwork is essential in everyday life, so to show you this, we are going to do a little exercise.' Mr Cabello has a real passion for team exercises; I don't know why though. It's so much effort. We're standing in a freezing school field, while massive balls of hail are raining down from the sky. It's surprising that somebody hasn't got a concussion yet.

'Sir, its freezing out here!' Haila complains, shivering dramatically. For some reason, wearing coats is against our school rules, so we all stand there feeling almost naked.

'Oh, don't be such a drama queen, Haila. It's actually quite warm out here!' Cabello replies, wearing two thermal sweaters and a jacket. I wouldn't be surprised if he was hiding a cashmere onesie under all those layers. 'You are going to be split into three teams. The aim of the game is to make your pile of sticks and a cloth into a teepee.' Everybody stares at Cabello as if he's nuts.

'That's well easy,' someone scoffs.

Ivy rolls her eyes as if in disbelief of how dumb everyone is. 'Guys, there's obviously a catch,' she says so matter-of-factly that I want to strangle her.

'Guys, there's obviously a catch,' Haila mimics in a funny voice. Cabello raises his brow at her.

'Laugh all you like, Miss Adil, but Ivy is correct. The catch is … you'll all be blindfolded!' He pulls out a bag full of blindfolds and begins handing them out to people. 'Here you go! Now, time to split you into teams!' We all begin to group ourselves, but Cabello clearly has other plans.

'I'll be picking the teams, thank you very much.' Why do teachers have to be so lame? Any chance we get in school to actually make our own decisions gets snatched away by a teacher. Mr Cabello takes out a wrinkled piece of paper and begins reading from it. He squints his eyes, trying to make out his own handwriting, which I find quite funny.

'Okay! Team one is Daniel, Mimi, Ewan, Rick, Katie, Lola, and Martha!' Martha walks towards her teammates, making a crying gesture to Ivy as she goes.

'Team two is Zoe, Taylor, Paisley, Milly, Tristan, Conrad, and Zack!'

Oh no ... that can only mean one thing.

'And last, but certainly not least, team three is Tilly, Nate, Craig, Emma, Eli, Saskia, and Ivy!'

'Lord, help me,' Ivy murmurs. I decide that, with Ivy, I have to pick my battles, and this just isn't worthy of my time.

'I object,' I say, folding my arms, dismissing Ivy's snarky comment.

'I'm afraid, Eli, this isn't a court. You can't object, so man up and get on with it,' Cabello orders.

'Fine ...'

Once we all have our blindfolds on, we stand in a line, waiting to start.

'Three ... two ... one ... go!' Everyone rushes over to our small pile of resources, frantically trying to make some sort of structure. My hands reach for a stick. The warm hand of Ivy land on mine. We stand there awkwardly, neither of us knowing what to do. She snatches her hand away, and I feel the wind as she walks off. Thank goodness everyone was blindfolded; I wouldn't want anyone to have seen that. Slowly but surely, our pile of wood begins to look more like a tepee—well, at least I think it does. It's hard to tell when you can't see a thing.

Haila has assumed the role of team captain, and for once, she is driving me insane.

'Whoever has just put that stick there, you need to move it now! You've put it in the wrong place! I bet it was you, Ivy!' Haila yells.

'I'll be putting that stick somewhere else if you don't shut it,' Ivy remarks.

'Watch your mouth, Miss Towers,' Mr Cabello chimes in. I can almost feel Ivy's sarcasm radiating off of her, and I love it. A high-pitched scream sounds right next to me.

'Haila, you cow!' Ivy cries. 'You've just put that stick in my arm. Oh hell, I'm bleeding! I'm bleeding!' No one can resist the drama, and within seconds everyone's blindfolds are off. It seems as though both Haila and Ivy have had their blindfolds off for a while.

'Okay, calm down, Ivy.' Mr Cabello says, putting a teepee cloth over her wound.

'Do you know how much bacteria's on that thing? Get it off!' she yells. The whole class bursts into laughter. Ivy manages to be a know-it-all even when she's hurt.

'Miss Towers! Just because you are injured doesn't mean you can be so disrespectful!' Mr Cabello says, his fun, bouncy tone disappearing in an instant.

'Oh, I'm sorry! Are you the one with a deep hole in your arm? I don't think so!' she shouts.

'That's it! You'll be spending your lunchtime with me.' Mr Cabello says.

'Does it look like I give a toss?! There is blood seeping out of my arm!' Cabello rolls his eyes.

'Haila, take her to Medical, please.'

'If I must.'

12

Ivy

As we are walking in, she leans in close to me, her hair tickling my neck.

'That wasn't an accident, y'know, and I'm just getting started, so don't mess with me, Ivy Towers. You have no idea just what I'm capable of.' My mouth can barely form a reply, so I just nod.

Daily messages from Eli have been popping up on my phone just to remind me of how ugly I am, as if I didn't already know. These messages are like pins. A prick from one pin barely hurts, but the more pins I'm poked with, the more pain it causes. This is like the hundredth message he's sent me. It doesn't seem long till I, metaphorically, bleed to death. Plus there's the occasional text from Haila telling me to stay away from her man. As if I'd want a single thing to do with her "man". It beats me why she's so bothered by my existence.

'Hey, sis, I gotta go pick up Cole, Archie, and Poppy from that kid's club thing. Wanna come with me?' Tyler asks, standing up from the couch. He proposes it as a question, but I can tell by the way he is looking at me that I have no choice.

'All right.' I mutter, barely looking up from my phone. He walks over and snatches it.

'I'm sick of you staring at that thing all day! Who are you even talking to—' His eyes glare at Eli's message, as if he is in disbelief of what he's reading. He stands there reading the message over and over again. In my opinion, he is overreacting. The message simply says 'You're a waste of oxygen'. It's hardly an original insult, but Tyler seems to think otherwise.

'Get in the car now,' he growls.

'Oh come on, Tyler! You're being ridiculous. Just give me my phon—'

'I said get in the car now!' he repeats, throwing his arms in the air. To stop me from doing something I regret, I follow his order.

I watch the geese fly by from the car window. They fly in a group of about ten. It's cool how they stay close to their family and make formations together. Five minutes later, Tyler joins me in the car.

'Sorry, Ivy. I wasn't mad at you; I just wasn't thinking—'

'Tyler, stop rambling. I get it. Now can you just drive. The kids will be waiting for us.' He grins at me, knowing that was my way of accepting an apology. Needless to say, my social skills aren't great.

We pull up at the kids' club thing that Mum signed them up to. I read the sign: 'Mud Pies Organic Childcare Centre'.

'What the hell does it mean by "organic"?' I ask, squinting my eyes to make sure I hadn't misread it.

'Dunno. Maybe they make the kids drink kale smoothies and do yoga,' Tyler suggests, wetting his lips and running his hands through his hair. He makes weird posey faces in the mirror when he thinks I'm not looking. My brother really does love himself. That's the great thing about Tyler. He does think a lot of himself, but at the same time, he's so selfless and caring.

'Right, let's go inside,' I say, realising just how late we are. The car park is completely empty except for our car and another—which I assume is owned by the teacher.

Sure enough, when we walk inside, the only people there are our siblings and a tall woman in a top reading, 'Life is like a box of chocolates: full of chemicals and not all it's cracked up to be.' She wears tight Lycra leggings and a sweatband.

Archie and Poppy waddle over to us, but Cole stays by the teacher, his head hanging low.

'What's up, buddy?' Tyler walks over to him, crouching down to his level.

'Cole pushed another child over today,' the woman explains. Tyler's mouth drops open. 'Don't worry; the girl is fine—just a few scratches here and there,' she assures us, though it's pretty obvious that Tyler doesn't give a toss about the welfare of that kid.

'Cole, for goodness' sake! We've talked about this before,' Tyler says, cautious not to lose his patience. If you get angry with Cole, he'll kick off, and Lord knows we don't need that meltdown displayed in public. My little brother's always been a little hot-headed. Tyler is convinced that he has some sort of disorder, but Mum refuses to get him checked out. She always says, 'I'm not having my dear baby prodded by some poncy doctors! There is nothing wrong with him. He simply has a very big character.' Mum's obviously in denial, though we don't like to point it out. Tyler leads all the kids to the car, and Cole walks slowly behind, dragging his feet and kicking at stray pebbles.

'Sorry about him. He's always been a bit of a character.' I curse myself in my head for using mum's lame excuse.

'No worries. He's a good kid at heart. I can tell he has a bright spirit. Something about him just confirms that he has a beautiful soul!' she says, using her hands for emphasis as she speaks. I nod and smile, pretending to be touched by what she's saying, when really I couldn't care less. 'You have a lovely son, you know. Don't ever doubt that!' It takes me a while to work out if she is having me on. *This woman seriously thinks I'm a mother. Do I really look that old?* I try my best not to be insulted.

'Umm yeah, thanks. See you soon.' I turn and bolt out of the door. I see her in the crazy fun mirror on the wall, giving me a sidewards glance as I leave.

As soon as I'm in the car, Tyler starts driving, pressing on the gas pedal way too hard. I really want to tell him to calm down, but it'll only make it worse. He managed to contain his anger at the daycare, but I don't think he can hold on much longer. We go on in silence for a few more minutes. The only noise to be heard is the slight sound of Peppa Pig's voice playing through Poppy's cheap headphones.

'What on earth were you thinking?' Tyler eventually blurts out. 'We've talked about this, haven't we? Cole, are you listening?' Cole stares out the window, wearing his earphones, pretending he can't hear Tyler. I can see the anger building up inside of Tyler, so I whisper to him, 'Ty, calm down. If you get mad, he'll get upset. We don't need another meltdown.' He nods, although I know my words have just gone straight over his head. His hands tremble on the steering wheel. It's obvious that he hasn't had a good day; Tyler's never this aggressive with the younger ones.

'Cole, will you take those stupid earphones out!' he barks. Cole instantly sits upright, taking out his headphones. His eyes are full of fear and remorse.

'Why would you push someone—a girl as well!' he yells. Poppy and Archie both shift about in their booster seats, clearly very uncomfortable.

'Sh-she took my teddy, s- so—'

He doesn't even let Cole finish his sentence. 'So you thought you'd just push the kid?'

'Will you let the poor thing speak?' I murmur under my breath.

'No. I'm sick of him and his antics,' Tyler says. I look in the rearview mirror to see Cole. He's completely still, staring right at Tyler's seat. He looks so terrified it makes me angry. His expression starts to change; his lips begin to tremble. Cole lets out a massive wail and starts having a hissy fit.

'Now look what you've done,' I hiss, elbowing Tyler.

'Let him cry. Get it outta his system.'

I roll my eyes, completely shocked by Tyler's sudden change in mood. The rest of the journey home is cold and uncomfortable.

When we arrive home, instead of helping me get the kids out, Tyler walks straight inside. I know there must be something seriously wrong with my brother; he never acts so aggressively. Mum quickly drops the other kids home and hurries off to work. She blows me a kiss as she hops into her rusty red convertible. I set all seven of the little kids in front of the TV to watch *Monsters, Inc.* so I can talk to Tyler privately.

I go to his room and knock on the door. When he doesn't answer, I gently push the door open and sit beside him on his hard mattress.

'Ty Ty, what's up? Tell your little Petal what's wrong,' I coo, making him crack a smile. When we were young, our family had a small rose bush in the corner of the garden. One day we were having a barbecue, but I was so hungry that I couldn't wait for the burgers to cook. I went over to the rose bush and took a big bite out of the rose flowers. Tyler started to call me Petal, and the name stuck.

He looks at me intently, obviously trying to work out what to say and how to say it.

'You don't have to hide anything from me, y'know.'

'I know. I just ... I feel like such a let-down.'

'Why, Tyler? Talk to me.' I move closer to him, resting my hands in his.

'I'm getting really bad grades in my coursework. If I don't do well in sixth form, who knows where I'll end up next. All my life I've wanted a job … to support Mum. But now my dreams are slipping away from me, and I can't stop it—' His voice breaks, and my brother falls apart. I hold him close to me, rubbing his back with a flat palm.

'Shhh. Hey, it's all right; we all have our off days, okay? Look at me.' He lifts his tear-covered face to meet my gaze with hopeless eyes. 'You are the reason our family is still in one piece. You're like a second dad to all of us. Without you, I'd be failing maths right now. Without you, how would May have learnt to do a forwards roll, or Cole to build a sandcastle? You are the furthest you can get from a failure, okay?' He nods unconvincingly. 'I said, okay?' He nods again but with more confidence. I smile and pull him back into a hug.

'Is Ty Ty okay?' a little voice asks from the doorway. Cole stands there, playing with his hair nervously.

'Come here, kid,' Tyler says, opening his arms for Cole. Cole runs—well, toddles—to him and falls into his strong arms.

'Listen, buddy. Ty Ty's sorry about earlier, okay? I shouldn't have yelled at you. But you mustn't push people.'

'I must not push people,' Cole concurs, as if he is trying hard to remember Tyler's basic instructions.

'Hey, Cole, I think we should leave Ty Ty alone so he can go to sleep,' I suggest, picking Cole up off Tyler.

'Okay. Nighty night!' Cole says as I carry him out. He rests his head on my shoulder.

'Good night, Tyler,' I say, smiling at Tyler. He wipes the tears off his face and lies on his bed, staring at the plain ceiling.

After a couple of hours of chaos, I manage to get everyone fast asleep. My footsteps are light as I creep across the corridor, not daring to wake anyone up.

I slide into my bed and turn off the lamp on my bedside table. For the next few hours, I'm going to drown out the world with my snoring.

❧❦

After a relaxing session of reading with Martha in the library, I arrive home. I wearily close the front door and sit down beside Tyler. The whole family is already having dinner. There isn't much energy left in me; even eating seems to require a great deal of effort. I roll the peas about my plate with my shiny fork that we got from Disneyland that time we went with Dad. I wish I could remember what he looks like. I was so young when he left.

'How was school?' Mum asks me half-heartedly: she is too busy trying to get my brother Archie to eat his broccoli. How do I answer that? It's so much easier to sugar-coat things, but I feel like she deserves to be told the truth.

'School was fine, Mum, all good,' I lie. Tyler rolls his eyes.

'Please, she is obviously lying,' Tyler scoffs.

Mum turns to me. 'Is that true, Ivy?'

There's no point lying anymore. 'Fine. If you must know, there's this boy called Eli. He's ... picking on me, and now we are paired up for a class project so we can "bond", but I can handle it. Don't worry, you have enough on your plate.'

Tyler goes a worrying deep red colour as he clenches his hands into tight fists. 'Where does he live? I swear, when I find the little monster, I'll ...I'll ...' He struggles to get his words out. 'I'll crush his tiny pea brain into a ball and kick it to Antarctica.'

'You will do no such thing, Tyler,' Mum cautions. 'Bullies get bored after a while, honey. Don't let him get under your skin.' I nod, unconvinced. Archie is putting his arms in the air, evidently wanting to get out of his seat, so I swing him on my back and trudge up the carpeted stairs. Carefully, I swing my brother around and lay him down on his car-shaped toddler bed.

'Nighty night,' he mumbles before nodding off to sleep. Grateful to finally be home, I slide into my bed and get my phone out.

Me:

We need to meet up so we can start our project.

Eli:

Sure, Cotton. What about Saturday 8pm at my house?

Me:

Uhh yeh sure. Send me your address. Goodnight, Eli.

Eli:

night Cotton ;)

Whoever said 'Sticks and stones may break my bones, but words will never hurt me,' was clearly in denial.

※

Mum didn't come home Monday night. Mind you, it doesn't surprise me. Life is starting to take its toll on her, and there's nothing she can do to stop it, so she turns to alcohol. There's a long line of drunks in our family, and I'm starting to worry that Mum may become one of them.

However, I doubt that will happen. My mother knows better than that. In 2017, there were 9,214 alcohol-related deaths in the UK, and I'll do everything in my power to make sure my mum doesn't share a similar fate.

Mum's inconvenient disappearing act has left me and Tyler feeding the small ones their breakfast. This is almost an impossible task because these brats are so fussy! 'I don't like this; I don't like that' is all I hear, and it's starting to drive me up the wall. We eventually settle on pancakes because everyone likes pancakes. It's a known fact.

'For the last time, Coco. Sugar!' Tyler holds up the sugar shaker. 'Salt!' He holds up the salt shaker and shakes it like a maraca. Coco giggles and takes the sugar. She tips, like, half the jar on her pancakes, causing me to switch to mum mode.

'Lawd, Coco! Are you eating for the whole of England?' I say, taking the sugar from her. She looks up at me with innocent eyes and starts licking the sugar off her pancakes.

'You'd think that my sky-high IQ would've rubbed off on this lot, but clearly not,' Tyler mumbles.

'No, it looks like your IQ really has rubbed off on them,' I say, pointing to May, who is trying to squirt out honey when it still has the safety seal on it. He chuckles and throws a tea towel at me, which I bat away with my hand.

A slamming noise echoes through the house as the front door is forced open. Both Tyler and I sprint to the scene, leaving our seven clueless siblings to munch on their crêpes. Mum is flopped against the wall, three beer bottles lodged between her fingers. She takes a swig of all of them at the same time, which I have to say is quite impressive. Instead of sympathising with Mum, I feel intense anger swimming inside me and running through my arteries.

'Mum, are you out of your mind? Gimme those!' I snatch the bottles out of her hands and chuck them against the wall.

'Ivy, y-you stupid ch-child! Clean that ... clean that up nowww!' She stutters. Tyler glares over at me as if to say 'Just do it', but I'm not taking orders from a woman who is absolutely mullered, mother or not.

'Do it yourself! I hate you!' I shriek. I break between both of them, grab my school bag, and stomp down the street. I've never dared to tell my mum I hate her, regardless of the situation. It's never felt right, no matter how much of an idiot she is being. As I dramatically plod down the street, a black moped pulls up beside me. I nearly jump out of my skin, and I quickly engage my ninja reflexes. I can barely imagine how stupid I look clenching my fists and scanning my surroundings with such paranoia. My eyes squint to see who's inside the helmet only to discover my best friend, Martha, sitting in the driver's seat.

'What the hell, Martha! You scared the living daylights outta me!' I say. My legs feel weak and my whole body resists but I manage to force myself sonto the passenger seat.

She smirks and passes me a helmet. 'I saw you walking to the bus stop and thought you might like a lift,' she says, as cool as ever.

'You do know that mopeds are incredibly dangerous.'

She simply nods and starts driving.

Oh no. I can feel the flashbacks. They are coming. The blinding light. The fearful eyes. The horror. The darkness.

'M-Martha, pull over ... I said pull over!' I scream over the noise of the road.

'All right all right!' She pulls over into a lay-by. 'Ivy, what's wrong?'

My whole body is trembling, and I can't stop it. I can feel it. I know what I need to do.

'Martha … I need to tell you something.' *I'm going to do it. I'm going to tell Martha about my past.*

'Okay, go on.'

'Basically, something happened. Something awful. And I wish I could take it ba—'

'Oh no, look at the time! We are so late. Can we talk later?'

I just nod. I was ready. I was ready to finally open up about my sins, and now I have to wait. It's like secrecy is my God-given destiny.

⊛

'Tax,' Mr Cabello says. He writes the word in large letters on the board and encircles it with a sloppy bubble. 'Today we are going to have a debate. The statement is "The more you earn, the more tax you should pay." If you agree with the statement, go to the left side of the room; and if you don't, go to the right side of the room.' Martha and I head straight to the left side of the room, while Eli goes to the right. We chat amongst our team members and start discussing our debating techniques. This is one of my favourite tasks. I love to make my point, to make my voice heard. Emma goes up as our first speaker.

'You have thirty seconds to make a point. Off you go,' Cabello says, pressing the start button on a stopwatch.

'People with a high income should pay more tax because you should be helping your community to thrive, if you have the money to do so, instead of keeping it to yourself. Why should the country deteriorate whilst the rich people buy themselves a fancy new golf course? People in bad financial situations shouldn't have to be paying the same taxes as people who are earning six-figure salaries.'

'Time's up! Nice one, Emma.' Mr Cabello scribbles on a notepad. We all cheer and high five Emma as she walks back to our corner.

'Eli, you're up!' Eli struts to the front and clears his throat.

'Thirty seconds … go!'

'I think people with less money should pay the same tax as rich people because why should we have to cop out for them while they sit on their backsides doing nothing but buying alcohol and snorting crack—'

I push past my teammates and storm over to Eli. 'You do know that poor people have to work hard too? Sometimes they work harder than you toffs!'

'Ivy, pipe down,' Mr Cabello orders.

'No, I won't pipe down! This rat seriously thinks he can degrade people in poverty like that!' I scream at Cabello. He sighs and sits back in his chair. This man is smart enough to know that once I get started, there is no stopping me.

'Ivy, you're just jealous because you know you couldn't even afford to lick the dirt off my shoes.'

'Shut up or I'll kick you right where it hurts.'

'Purr-lease, you don't have the guts to do tha—'

I kick him square in the crotch with all the power I can muster. He crumples into a heap on the floor and cries out in pain. I flee from the room before Cabello has a chance to shout at me, because God knows what I'll do to him if he tries to start on me. I catch my breath outside and start kicking hard against the wall. It looks like those self-defence classes that Mum forced me to take have finally paid off. To my inconvenience, just as I'm about to go back in, I see a silhouette charging towards me. The black figure starts to look more and more like a distinct person until I realise who it is. Instead of coming right over to me, he stops in his tracks and motions for me to follow him. I can't believe Cabello already snitched on me!

Instead of offering me a soft armchair as usual, he slams the door behind him and stands behind his desk.

'What in God's name were you thinking?' Mr Kilt says, his voice rising as he speaks.

'Keep your voice down; there are lessons going on,' I mumble, smirking at him. I chuck my bag on the floor. The teacher shakes his head and purses his lips hard. His jawline clenches.

'Every time I give you guidance, you just brush it off! It's like you are incapable of good behaviour!'

'Now you're just being harsh!' I say.

'It's like you don't care about doing well in sociology! Never mind your complete disregard for anyone's feelings but your own!'

'You're supposed to be my mentor, not a frickin' prosecutor!' I wave my arms around hysterically.

'Well, maybe if you got your act together, we wouldn't be having this conversation!' His face softens, and he draws a deep breath. 'Listen, Ivy. You're a bright kid—'

'Oh don't give me the "you're a bright kid and you have loads of potential" lecture! That's the last thing I need!'

'But you really are bright, Ivy. You really are, and I'd hate to see such talent go to waste.' He falls into his office chair and stares at me, biting his lower lip.

'Oh, so now you're calling me a waste of talent?' I begin.

'Ivy, you know that isn't what I meant,' he mumbles.

'No … no, it's fine! That's what everyone thinks of me, isn't it? That I'm a waste of space!' I shout. My voice is hoarse from my emotional outburst. 'I'm sure my mum would agree with you!' Tears start spilling out of my eyes. The anger that has grown inside me from this morning is starting to overspill, and I don't know how to control it. See, this is what Mr Kilt should be talking to me about. He should be helping me make my way through life. Instead he is acting like some sort of stalker, ready to pounce on my every wrongdoing.

'Ivy, I can't get through to you when you are angry like this—'

'Me, angry? Oh, that's rich coming from the man who nearly ripped my face off ten seconds ago!' I interrupt.

'Look, I'd like you to go and spend some time up in isolation to calm down.' Mr Kilt genuinely seems to have good intentions, but I'm not in the mood to be rational about things.

'Oh, so now you're trying to cart me off to isolation because you can't cope? You know what? Fine, I'll go!' I grab my bag and make for the door, but before I can leave, Kilt calls out, 'All right, if you wanna be all sarky, I'll see you in detention tonight.' When I turn to face him, he has a smirk dancing on his face. I open my mouth. Then I close it. Then I open it again. My brain can't seem to formulate a witty response, so I end up shouting 'Fine!' as I walk out of the office. I know that he likes to have his door shut, so I leave it swinging open.

I feel genuine shame about being in detention. It's not because I 'know better than this' or because I'm a 'bright kid'. No, I feel ashamed because this is where defaults go. They all like to think they're 'hard' for being late or arguing with a teacher, when I, on the other hand, genuinely can't help it; it's how I'm hardwired. Me and my big mouth get me into all kinds of situations, but not these kids. They all do it on purpose because, for some reason, being an absolute pain is deemed 'cool' nowadays. I look around me and notice that Eli doesn't seem to be in here, which is a total injustice, considering he's the opinionated rat that got me into this mess.

I've got one hour to kill, so I decide not to let it go to waste. Mr Kilt is on detention duty, so I study him and start to draw a funny cartoon of him. I'm supposed to be writing out the school rules, but that takes way too much effort. I'm not gonna say how I've drawn him in the picture, because it's pretty rude, but you get the point. I try to mask my giggles as I admire my artwork, but Kilt notices. His forehead wrinkles as he tries to work out what I'm doing, but he decides it's an argument not worth having.

When the bell goes, the others take their time packing up, but I attempt to sprint out. Before I can make it to the door, Kilt blocks my path.

'Off you go, everyone. I don't wanna see any of you in here again. Ivy, hang back for a moment, will ya?' He gives me a victorious look and hops on his desk. I huff but decide to comply. I slump back in my seat, holding my masterpiece beneath the desk.

'Lemme see that,' he says, motioning to my drawing.

'No way. It's personal.'

He hops off the table. 'If you ever wanna leave this school on the bell ever again, I suggest you hand it over right now, Miss Towers.'

'All right all right!' I pass him the paper and brace myself for his outburst. Kilt studies the picture and, instead of doing his nut, he laughs to himself.

'You're a good little artist, y'know. Maybe if you utilised your talents better, you could get into an art school,' he suggests.

'Mmm ... no thanks. Art's a waste of time. I only did it because you stuck me in here.' I get out of my chair and attempt to take my drawing back, but he swipes it away quickly.

'Nuh uh.' He points to the picture. 'This is staying with me.' He folds it and slips it into his blazer pocket.

'Whatever,' I mumble, and I pick up my bag. As I go to leave the room, he calls after me, 'See you back here tomorrow!' I turn around to glare at him. He simply smiles and says, 'Nobody draws me in that light and gets away with it, Miss Towers. Oi! If you don't smarten up, I'm gonna take those rolling eyes and use them for marbles.' That last comment gets me speeding out of the door before you can say 'Mr Kilt is a creep.'

On my short bus journey, I make the decision that Tyler is not finding out why I'm so late getting home. The last thing I need is him breathing down my neck like an angry dragon. Being in detention has really opened up my eyes to the life of a default. Gawd, it must be so horrible being so unoriginal. Though it must be easier; instead of thinking for themselves, they just follow everyone else like blind sheep.

13

Craig

I haven't hung out properly with Eli since Ivy joined our school because he's too busy getting into hot water for all his 'pranks' on her. Before she joined, basketball was his main priority. Next thing you know, the only thing he cares about is buying flour to booby-trap Ivy's locker. I decide to text Eli:

> **It's been a while since we hung out. Wanna go to the cinema and watch a horror film?**

Immediately he texts back:

> **Sorry, I can't. Ivy's coming over to study on Saturday, so I need to go buy snacks and stuff. Another time?**

I text back a passive-aggressive 'OK' and chuck my phone onto my bed. Ivy is getting in the way of what I want. Soon the little neat freak will regret her existence, and I know exactly what to do to push her over the edge. I know things about her that she doesn't want released, but if she's not careful, these little secrets might just get put out there for all the world to hear.

14

Ivy

'Kirk was being such a pig yesterday! Basically, when I got home I went to his room to ask for some Sellotape and accidentally stood on one of his PS4 game CD thingies—I dunno what they are called. He went all stir crazy and tried to lock me out the house! I mean, does he seriously think …'

Welcome to one of Martha's daily rants about Kirk. This one was the Wednesday lunchtime edition. Hearing about Kirk really makes me grateful for Tyler. It's as if we bought lottery scratch cards and I got the sixty-million-pound prize and Martha got the fiver. Most of what Martha is saying is going straight over my head. All my concentration is settled on the unfolding drama going on across the field. Some year-seven kid is trying to square up to Eli, which I have to admit is the funniest thing I've ever seen, but it looks like Eli is having none of it. I can't help feeling bad for that kid; he has no idea what he's letting himself in for.

'Ivy? Ivy, can you quit zoning out all the time?' Martha shrieks right into my ear.

'I wasn't zoning out!' I say, pushing her away from my ringing eardrum.

'As I was saying, before you rudely started ignoring me—'

'Martha, look!' I leap off the bench and sprint over to the scene. Believe me, this is the first time I've run in years, apart from when I'm being forced to run in PE. The last time I ran properly was to catch a bus.

It takes me ages to get to them, but when I do, I dive right in. I swear the kids at this school are brain dead; Eli is practically beating this poor kid to a pulp, and the only thing their tiny brains tell them to do is chant 'Fight!'. Fists are flying everywhere, but there are no teachers around, so I don't hold back. I try my best to pull the tiny kid out from beneath Eli, but he's just too strong. All the chanting is drowned out by the familiar screaming and wailing from Haila. She's such a drama queen.

'Eli, let him go! Just stop!' I scream. Nothing I do or say stops Eli from pulverising this child. Even in my wildest days of 2017, I wouldn't have gotten into a scrap with an eleven-year-old. Turns out this school really is nothing like how I imagined. I was expecting posh kids and etiquette lessons, but it's the polar opposite here at Queen's. The only thing posh about this place is the building and the high income of most students.

Blood is smeared over my hands, and at first I think it's my own, but then I realise it's the blood of the year seven victim. Fury overtakes me, and I yank the child out from Eli's grasp. The poor thing is crying his eyes out, and Grace, some girl in my form, tries to help him. She gives him tissues, but the blood is pouring quicker than she can mop it up.

Haila runs over and pulls Eli close to her. 'C'mon, baby; let's go get this blood off you,' she whispers, taking his hand but releasing it when he cries out in pain.

'You're not going anywhere, Mr Bishara,' Mr Kimberley says.

Oh great, the head teacher! Things literally couldn't be worse.

'Grace, take Tommy to Medical. We'll talk later, Mr Fraiser.' The year-seven nods and follows Grace inside. 'Eli, come with me; and Ivy, go to Mr Kilt's office now.' You have got to be kidding me. So I'm guessing my cuts and bruises aren't enough to get me sent to Medical. Martha gives me a look and follows the rest of the crowd to lessons. Fantastic! I'm not only going to get a lecture from Kilt, but from Martha too. This day just can't get any worse …

Instead of his usual 'C'mon in, Ivy!' Mr Kilt simply says, 'Enter,' in the bluntest voice I've ever heard. Sometimes, I wonder why I get myself into these situations. I guess living in rough areas has taught me to fight well.

Before I've even made it fully into the room, Kilt starts having a go.

'Do my clear instructions mean nothing to you, Ivy Towers?'

'Hmm … yeh I suppose they don't,' I say, trying to lighten the mood. It goes down like a lead balloon.

'Miss Towers, this isn't the time for you to get smart. Just on Monday I told you to not retaliate, and now look what you go and do!' He waves his arms around like a madman, which looks hilarious, considering his mildly out-of-proportion limbs.

'Hold on a second, Kilt, I didn't retaliate to anything! Eli was beating up some weedy little kid, so I came in and saved the day!' He doesn't even crack a smile. *Wow, this man really is a hard case.*

'Don't try to sugar-coat it. The point is, you got into a scrap when I specifically told you not to! It's like you do this just to wind me up!'

'Maybe I do,' I murmur—not quietly enough. The mentor death-stares me. I'm beginning to worry that the guy might pull his hair out. 'Look, what did you want me to do—just let Eli throttle the kid?'

'No! You should've got a teacher to step in! You don't need to go wading in yourself,' he exclaims, writing down notes in some file.

'Oh, I'm sorry I'm not exactly an angel sent from heaven! Wait … what are you writing?'

'This is your file. At the end of term, I'm giving this to your mum so she can see your progress over the weeks.'

'So you can snitch on me, more like! You're supposed to be my mentor, not my mum's private investigator!'

At that a small smile does crack at the corner of his mouth. 'Ivy, this is all about progress. I want your mum to share your achievements with you and to understand how you overcome your day-to-day challenges.'

'This is absolute bull,' I remark.

'Oi, watch your language,' he says, not even looking up from the paper. *I bet you anything he's writing a detailed log of every sentence I say.*

'Now I want a written apology by the end of tomorrow.'

'An apology to whom?'

'To me, for ignoring my instructions.'

'Now you're just taking the pi—' He glares at me, so I don't dare finish my sentence. 'Fine, but don't be expecting a massive letter from me grovelling to you.' I'm not going to write a whole essay on what I did wrong, when I was clearly doing the right thing.

Kilt finishes his sentence with an exaggerated full stop and puts the file in a rusting silver cabinet. 'Just go to your next lesson,' he orders before sipping a grey cup of tea.

'Oh, but I've got maths. I'd rather listen to you bang on than go to that torture chamber.'

He chuckles and gently leans back in his chair, stretching his arms and letting out a mahoosive yawn. 'All right then. I'll give you two choices.

Either go to lessons like I've told you to, or you can come here during lunch and clip my toenails.' I know he is kidding, but even the mention of his rank toenails anywhere near me has me out the door at the speed of light.

'Bye, sir.'

'Bye, Ivy.'

※

Detention is slightly less tedious than the other day because instead of Mr Kilt, Mr Batch is on duty. Batch has grown to be my favourite teacher, and he seemed mildly surprised when I walked into the room. But he didn't seem completely shocked, seemingly as I've kinda got myself a mildly poor reputation amongst the teachers. I think I'm known as the one who is 'too smart for her own good', which doesn't really bother me. In fact, I embrace it. Who said being smart was a bad thing? Instead of drawing Mr Batch, I draw Mr Kimberley as a three-headed monster. I don't think Batch deserves to be drawn in such an unflattering guise. The teacher leans back in his black office chair and reads a book called *The Art of Being a Perfect Teacher.*

I like observing people when they think no one's watching; that's when you see what type of person they really are. Occasionally my history teacher glances around the room, but after that, his head is straight back in the book. One of his black curls has fallen out of place and droops down his forehead, which makes him look intentionally scruffy. He looks up and catches me off guard, staring at him with great interest. Instead of holding an awkward stare, the teacher smirks and looks back down at his book. *Nice one, Ivy.*

Both my mentor and my history teacher tend to help me a great deal these days. However, I favour Mr Batch more than Mr Kilt because Batch supports me and has a sweet personality. Kilt is all helpful but is a complete pain to be with. Looking around now, I realise that there is only one other kid in the room—a tall, buff teen with broad shoulders and slicked-back hair. Craig. An email pops up on Batch's computer; he looks at it and smiles. He starts typing a reply, grinning the entire time. I spend the next few minutes trying to work out who could possibly make a man gleam like that.

After half an hour, Mr Batch looks at the clock.

'You can go now, Craig. Have a good night.' Craig turns to smirk at me and saunters through the doorway. *What the hell?!* You're not supposed to talk for the whole hour, but I'm sorry, this is totally unjust.

'Why does he get to leave, but I can't?' I challenge dolefully. Mr Batch looks up from his book and smiles. He gets out a burgundy bookmark and slides it into the novel before gently placing it on the table. I really admire his respect for books. There have been numerous occasions when I've had full-blown arguments with people for folding the corner of a page. In a literal manner, that is book abuse, and if I were prime minister, I'd make it strictly illegal.

Mr Batch walks round his desk and hops up onto it, swinging his legs gently and smiling at me, just as Kilt did yesterday.

'Special request from Mr Kilt,' he replies. Oh, how I hate that man.

'What a pillock,' I mutter. Mr Batch chuckles instead of telling me off, which kinda takes me by surprise.

'Why do you say that?' he asks, combing his slender fingers through his mop of unruly black curls.

'He's supposed to be my mentor or whatever, but all he does is shout at me and stick me in here or isolation. What's the point in that? I expected a proper counsellor, but instead I got lumbered with Mr Shout-A-Lot.'

At that, Batch lets out a deep belly laugh, which I'm surprised doesn't make the whole room tremble. 'Ivy, you really are an incredibly smart kid, but I do think that you create a wrong impression of your true character. If you try to seem less ... arrogant'—wow that cut deep—'then maybe you'd get on better with the teachers.'

'Yeh, I suppose you're right, but why should I have to keep my thoughts quiet when it's perfectly permitted for you lot to tell me exactly what you think of me?' He doesn't have an answer to that.

'What are you even in here for? I can't imagine you causing trouble.' This guy really must be living under a rock.

'Mr Kilt was already all up in arms about me stopping Eli from pulverising some weedy little kid; then he completely lost the plot when I started arguing back.' He gives me a look as if to say, 'See, you are too cocky!'

'Just try being less ... loud and see how that goes, all right?' I nod, although we both know that will last all of about five seconds before I'm correcting teachers again. I just can't help it. Some teachers are so brain dead it actually hurts.

Mr Batch slides off his desk, walks over to the door, pulls it open, and ruffles his hair for the billionth time in the past forty-five minutes.

'Go on. I won't tell Kilt you left a couple minutes early.' Batch beams a smile in my direction and holds the door for me. Throwing my backpack over my shoulder, I speed walk over to the door before the teacher has a chance to change his mind. As I'm leaving, he grabs my drawing of the head teacher out of my hands and smiles. Its like deja-vu.

'I watched you draw this. It was fascinating,' he teases, holding it high in the air as I jump to try to retrieve it.

'Give it back!' I whine. He has a serious height advantage, so I don't stand a chance against his giraffe-like structure.

'Nah. You can have this back if you go a whole lesson next week without correcting me or anyone else.'

'We both know that's impossible,' I say, giggling. Gosh, I never giggle. Being silent for an hour must've gotten to my head.

'Well, if you fail to meet my challenge, this'—he waves the paper in my face—'goes to Mr Kimberley's pigeon hole straight away,' he says, with a victorious smirk at the corner of his lips.

'You wouldn't dare,' I hiss.

'Watch me.' And with that, he closes the door in my face. It doesn't upset me, because he was just messing around, but I'm gonna have to tape my mouth shut with several layers of duct tape if I stand a chance of getting that picture back. Good luck to me.

I'm gonna need it.

※

On Friday, I am strolling across the PE field next to Martha when Miss Greenly calls from across the field, 'Ivy Towers! Martha Jones! Get those legs moving or do two more laps!' We simultaneously stick our tongues out and continue walking our way around the field.

I know it's quite a childish reaction, but it seems suitable, considering the circumstances.

Damp, icy air swirls around us and blows my hair in all directions. Leafless trees lined on either side of the field droop sorrowfully, casting a gloomy shadow over the PE field. Around thirty other girls are, for some reason, trying to get a good time on the running test, but Martha and I put in very little effort. This run isn't worth our time or energy.

At first I had considered refusing to run at all, but God forbid Mr Kilt should find out; he'd rip my head off—literally.

Miss Greenly jogs over to us.

'Oh Lawd, here we go,' I mutter to Martha. She smiles.

'Towers! Jones! Run!' We both look at her and continue our slow amble across the muddy lagoon that lies before us. Miss Greenly picks up her whistle and blows it right in my ear.

'*Argh!*' Martha yelps.

'That's gotta be child abuse!' I shout at her. She mumbles something under her breath, which sounds something along the lines of 'Why didn't I go into primary school teaching?'

'Actually, Miss Towers, it isn't child abuse, considering I didn't even touch you.'

Our mouths both drop open in disbelief. We reply in unison, 'Child abuse can be verbal and physical.'

'Don't get smart with me,' she eventually replies. Still we continue to walk.

'Should I get my walkie-talkie to summon Mr Kilt down here? Don't you think for one moment that I won't.' As soon as she mentions his name, I start running as fast as I can, which forces Martha to chase after me. All the teachers know that I'm being mentored, and they seem to be using it against me. It's seriously starting to get on my nerves.

❦

'I still can't believe Cabello paired me up with Eli,' I complain before slurping at the last few drops of my iced coffee through a straw. The bustling of the cafe is messing with my head. Families with noisy children and excitable groups of friends surround us. Baristas in brown aprons hurry around the room, serving an array of sugar-filled beverages.

Martha smiles. 'I think it'll be good for you. You can get some answers.

Find out why he treats you like this,' Martha suggests, excitement creeping into her voice. I admire Martha's ability to turn everything into a game.

'Martha, imagine being alone with Eli in his room! He'll probably choke me to death!'

'He won't be the problem. Haila will be your problem if she finds you've been in his room.'

'Haila? Why would she care?'

Martha bursts into laughter. 'Have you never noticed that she's always hanging around him?'

I nod. 'She's just a silly girlfriend though, isn't she?'

Martha shakes her head. 'Oh, innocent little Ivy. She isn't "just a silly girlfriend". She's his wife-to-be! Eli and Haila are planning to get married.' Everything makes sense now. 'Ooo. Speak of the devil.' Martha looks over at the door of the coffee shop. Eli and Haila stroll in, arm in arm.

'All of a sudden, it smells like wet dog in here,' I say, hoping they hear me.

'Shhh, not so loud, Ivy. They might hear us!' Martha hisses.

'Oh, c'mon. Lighten up,' I tease. As the duo saunter past us, Haila purposely knocks Martha's drink off the table. However, the drink tips backwards and spills all down Haila's overpriced branded leggings.

Martha and I are in fits of laughter, while Eli runs off to get some tissues.

'Shut it, creeps!' Haila demands, but we just can't stop laughing.

'Looks like karma really does exist!' Martha cries happily. With an exaggerated sigh, Haila storms off to find Eli. He emerges from the men's bathroom and begins to help her clean up.

'I can do it myself!' she shouts, snatching the tissue out of his hand. All eyes are on them. I know it's stooping down to their level, but it's so satisfying to watch them get a taste of their own medicine.

Haila storms out of the cafe, and Eli runs frantically after her. Just before he reaches the door, Eli turns around and mouths 'sorry' to Martha. Martha's mouth drops open. For the first time since I met her, Martha is speechless.

'D-did he just … did Eli Bishara just say sorry!' she stutters.

'He must be ill or something!' I say, laughing. My phone vibrates in my back pocket, so I take it out. It's a message from Craig.

> **I'm sick of you, Ivy. Seeing you start your life over has made me realise just how much I hate you. I was on board with keeping your little secret, but it can't go on any more. The world needs to know what you are. For Simon's sake.**

I read the text over and over again. I'm not sure if my eyes are deceiving me. Craig wants to expose my secret? He promised he'd take it to the grave. I look up to see Martha staring at me curiously.

'Who's that from?' Martha leans over the table to look at my phone. I quickly press my phone to my chest.

'It's none of your business, Martha!' I blurt out, immediately regretting it afterwards. The hurt shows in her eyes. 'I'm sorry, Martha. I didn't mean it …'

She dismisses my apology. 'Don't worry; I have to go anyway.' She picks up her backpack and storms out of the cafe, the door swinging behind her, creating a chilling breeze throughout the room.

As much as I feel bad for Martha, I don't have time to worry about that now. Craig knows my secret. If he releases it, I may have to move again. Once I've managed to calm down, I respond:

> **What secret?**

I manage to convince myself that Craig is talking about something else. Maybe he's talking about the extra mayonnaise I took from the cafeteria or the library book I've lost. My phone sounds again. I snatch up my mobile and read the reply:

> **Stop playing dumb, Ivy. That night is engraved in both our minds, and soon enough everyone will know what a monster you really are.**

It really is true. Craig is ready to break the silence, and if he does, my life will be well and truly ruined.

I lie awake, staring at the crusty cream wallpaper above my head. It feels as if the world is just telling me not to sleep. The noise of revving engines goes on and on for hours outside my window. There is obviously some illegal racing going on down my street again. Mind you, it isn't uncommon around these parts. Sometimes I wish I lived in Eli's area, though I swore I'd never live with the likes of those toffs. I bet he doesn't hear drug dealing going on outside his bedroom window.

As well as all the loud noises, another thing is stopping me from sleeping: Craig. It's like he can control me even when I'm not with him. All I ever worry about is Craig because he knows. He knows what I did. As much as I try to hold it back, guilt always overcomes me and Craig is the epicentre of my guilt. I can only imagine what he could do with my secrets—how he could ruin my life. I'd lose everything; I'd lose Martha.

Tears start spilling from my eyes quicker than I can wipe them away, and before I know it, I'm bawling my eyes out. I try to muffle my wailing by burying my face in a pillow, but it makes no difference. A streak of light stretches across my room from the doorway. Tyler walks over to my bed and sits on the edge, making the mattress dip heavily.

'Hey, Petal,' he whispers, pulling me into his arms. I end up lying in his lap, as though I'm three again. 'Shhhh, Petal. It's okay. Has someone hurt you? Do you want me to go beat them up for ya? 'Cause you know I will.' My wailing softens until I can breathe again. I eventually manage to calm down so I can sit up cross-legged on my bed.

'Now you gonna tell me who made my petal cry?' he asks.

'Tyler, you can keep a secret, right?'

'Yeh, course I can,' he says. Tyler stares at me with a stern yet worried expression. I take a deep breath.

'Y-you remember the Wilsons, right ...'

'The Wilsons ...?' He pauses for a few seconds. 'Oh ... you mean the Wilson Wilsons ... the ones who ...' I don't even let him finish the sentence. It'll only start me crying again.

'Yeah, those ones. Well, it turns out that Craig Wilson goes to my school. In fact ... he's in my class.' Tyler's face doesn't change; he just stares at the wall behind me. His eyes twitch slightly. His mouth opens and closes over and over again. He's trying to find the words but can't.

'He ... he hasn't done anything to you, has he?'

'Nah, it's all good. I don't even think he remembers me. After all, I did change my hair colour and everything.' I'm lying through my teeth, and I hate it.

'You hesitated, Ivy.' I should've known better than to try to fool Tyler. He knows me too well.

'All right, fine, just ... just promise you won't tell Mum.'

'Tell her what? Ivy, quit playing around and tell me,' he orders.

'Well ... long story short, he's threatening to reveal my secret ... to everyone.' My face crumples, and I begin crying again. Instead of comforting me, Tyler just stares into thin air. He can't seem to comprehend what I said, and it's starting to worry me. Just like Cole, Tyler can kick off at any given moment. I suppose that's where my little brother gets it from.

'Tyler, please say something,' I beg. I shake his arm, but my brother still continues to stare.

'I'm gonna kill him,' he eventually whispers.

'No, Tyler, please ...'

'Go to sleep, Ivy,' Tyler whispers. Still he stares at the wall, looking completely emotionless.

'Oh, but Tyler—'

'I said sleep!' My brother charges out of the room and slams the door behind him.

I spend another hour crying. I cry and cry and cry until there are no tears left in my body and my eyes are raw. Although I know Tyler isn't angry at me, it still shakes me to the core when he shouts. It's surprising that no one woke up when he yelled. Everyone's probably fast asleep. But not me. This is one of the many nights that my eyes won't close and my body won't rest. What can I expect? That's my life now: sleepless nights and immortal regret. I guess I'll just have to learn to live with it.

⚭

My appearance has never been a major concern to me. But for some reason on this cold, Saturday night I feel a lot of pressure to at least make sure I look decent for going to Eli's house. Although it'll be difficult, I've decided to push Craig out my mind briefly. Tonight is all about me, Eli, and the project. Knowing that it is now after 6.45 p.m, I search frantically through my tiny wardrobe.

'There must be something decent that I can wear!' I cry, throwing yet another jumpsuit on the floor. I don't know why I care so much. I'm only going to Eli's house. After about thirty minutes, I choose a black skater skirt and a tight blue T-shirt. Sitting at my second-hand vanity table, I attempt winged eyeliner; it goes horribly wrong. *Ugh, why am I such a failure?* Deciding that winged eyeliner is only for pretty people, I wipe it off and apply a crimson lipstick. *All this for a study session,* I think to myself. I really am being dramatic. Using a comb, I rake out the many knots in my brunette mane. One last time, I check myself in the grubby wall mirror to make sure I look somewhat average.

Grabbing my denim jacket, I tiptoe down the stairs so as not to wake up my younger siblings. As I reach for the door handle, the low, rumbling voice of my older brother asks, 'Where do you think you're going?'

I spin round to find Tyler standing there, arms folded.

'If you must know, I'm going to a friend's house to study,' I say, which isn't a complete lie. I am going to someone's house to study, but he doesn't even come close to a friend. Tyler studies my outfit.

'Looks like you're trying to impress whoever it is,' Tyler says, raising his bushy eyebrows slightly. He's right. Why am I trying so hard to impress Eli? I hate him, after all.

'Listen. It's none of your business. Now, I've gotta go, all right?' I say, folding my arms.

'Okay, but I want you home by no later than ten thirty,' he orders in a patronising tone that angers me slightly.

'What are you, my dad?' We both fall silent. The word 'dad' has, sort of, become a taboo in our family. Even mentioning him sends Mum into a flood of tears.

'Sorry ... I didn't mean to ...' I mutter.

Tyler embraces me in his long arms. 'It's okay. It's hard for you too. Now go; I don't want you to be late for your study session. I won't tell Mum that you're out late, okay?' Nodding, I open the door and let it close lightly behind me.

I'm about to hop into Mum's rusty convertible when all the memories flood back. How I wish I could take back that dreaded night. The angst is too much, so I decide against driving. Luckily, the bus is at the bus stop just as I arrive.

Not to my surprise, Eli's house is right on the other side of town to mine; he lives on the richer side. I walk slowly down his street, reading the names of each house—Stable Close, Kings Chase, Rose Cottage—until I finally come to his house, the Ivory Lodge. Jeez, he really is well off. Apprehensively, I walk towards his mansion.

Walking up the long path towards the double-doored entrance, I mentally prepare myself to meet Eli. After taking a deep breath, I knock on the door using the lion-shaped knocker hanging from the mahogany frame. Anxiousness circulates through my veins as I await an answer. A pattering of feet grows louder and louder, until the door swings open and standing there is Eli.

'Hi,' he says dryly.

'Hi,' I reply with an equal lack of affection. An awkward silence lasts for what seems like forever until I say, 'I brought Doritos.' With a smile, he motions me inside.

Eli's house is huge! Impressive chandeliers hang down from the marble white ceiling, detailed paintings of women in exotic dresses are arranged about the home, and a light vanilla smell delights my senses. We walk up an elegant staircase and into a large blue room. It's a typical boy's bedroom, complete with various basketball and guitar posters. A popcorn machine and a mini fridge stand side by side in the corner of this huge room. I stare in awe at his luxuries.

'So you like it then?' he asks, sitting down on his king-size bed. With a weary smile, I sit down beside him. 'So … on to teen pregnancy,' he begins. I smile and open my old laptop.

15

Eli

As we do research on teen pregnancy statistics, I watch Ivy with fascination. She has such a calm yet confident aura about her. Tucking a stray hair behind her ear, she reads out a fact: 'The UK has the highest teen pregnancy and abortion rate in the whole of Western Europe.'

'Wow. There are some real idiots in this country,' I mumble. I look up from my notepad and see that Ivy is staring at me in utter disbelief. 'What's up?' I ask.

'My parents had my brother as teens. Are you calling them idiots?'

I feel so stupid. Why do I always mess up? 'I'm sorry. I didn't know ...' My voice trails off. For the first time in my life, I actually feel remorse for my actions towards Ivy.

Her face grows into a pleased smile. 'Am I making you nervous?' she teases, nudging me playfully.

My voice grows strong and sturdy. 'Of course you aren't making me nervous. Narcissistic brainiacs like you don't scare me.' The words escape from my mouth before I can take them back. Ivy stares deeply into my eyes. The colour of her iris dilutes as the murky tears appear.

'Ivy. I didn't mean it ...'

'Just forget it, Eli,' she responds, her voice breaking from emotion. 'I kidded myself. For a split second, I thought you were changing. Becoming a better person. It seems you really are just stuck in your ways.' Ivy throws her denim jacket on, puts her laptop in her bag and storms out of my room.

'Ivy, wait!' I call, sprinting after her.

'Just save it, Eli.' For being a self-occupied bookworm, who never seems to exercise, she really is quite fast.

As we race down the hall, my mum comes round the corner and bumps into Ivy.

'Why hello, dear. Eli didn't tell me he had a friend round! Please stay for some tea!' my mum presses politely.

Whilst still running, Ivy replies, 'I'm not Eli's friend. He is my study partner and nothing more. I must get home. Bye, Mrs Bishara.' And with that she's gone.

Mum glares at me. 'What did you do to that poor girl? It's like you attacked her or something!' she cries.

'Nothing happened, Mum. She's just in a hurry. I'm off to bed.' I retreat to my room and start watching *Top Gear*. Why should I chase after her? It isn't my fault that she can't take a joke.

— 16 —

Ivy

I just need to get home. I can't take this anymore.

Before I change my mind, I find myself charging down the street. I observe my surroundings, noticing how the air is cool and clean, the stars sharp and defined. Violent gusts of wind fling my hair in all directions. Turning the corner, I begin to make my way down the dark alleyway, towards the bus stop. Silence surrounds and suffocates me.

The sinister atmosphere of the alleyway has me walking faster and faster, my intolerable heels clacking against the floor. *Click clack click clack.* At the end of the alleyway, dull street lights cast spotlights upon the rain puddles that lie below them. *I'm almost there. A couple more metres and I'll be on the main road.* Just as this heavily reassuring thought enters my mind, I feel a cold yet muscular hand grab my arm and pull me to the ground. Before I can let out a scream, the hand is over my mouth, muffling all noises. Mounting me like a helpless horse, my assailant begins to punch me in the face, causing a never-ending nosebleed. I try to escape, but it's no use; the aggressor is just too strong. I frantically thrash around, trying to free myself from this nightmare. In the most patronising tone possible, the person hushes me repeatedly. A hint of a smile stretches across the imperceptible face.

I see the glimmer of a knife blade in the hand covering my mouth. I can feel my heart palpitating in my throat. Beads of sweat cover my pale forehead and dribble into my pulsating eyes, causing even more torment. Mercilessly, the person pounds at my chest with a tightly closed fist, making breathing almost impossible. I try to beg for the assailant to stop, but the person shows no mercy. Shockwaves of pain surge through my helpless body. When the assailant accidentally lets the hand slip from my mouth, I release the loudest scream possible. Instead of helping my situation, as I had intended, it does the exact opposite. It aggravates the aggressor to a level that I've never seen before.

The person attacking me slices down my right arm with the knife, causing me excruciating agony—more than I have ever endured in my life. I watch as scarlet leaks out of my system. Instead of screaming, I cry. I cry and cry and cry until my eyes are raw. I'm too weak to scream. I know my time is over. I've never believed in any sort of God, but I find myself praying in my head. *Lord, I know I've never taken notice of you before, but please, have mercy on me.* My mum has always been a devout Christian, but she never managed to get me to join the faith. It seemed too illogical for me to follow. I desperately try to think of some of the hymns mum sings. One pops into my head, so I repeat it over and over again, through my mind. *'You are the way, the truth and the light, we live by faith and not by sight for you, we are living all for you.'*

The nightmare continues. The aggressor punches me hard in the neck, making my throat throb and burn. The alleyway becomes a blur. I try hard to identify the person's features, but a black hoodie is pulled down over the culprit's face. The person holds my neck tight, cutting off my oxygen. Every time I try to get away, the attacker cuts small slits in my stomach until it feels as though I'm in danger of death. I want to scream again, but I know that will only worsen the situation. However, I find that I cannot scream, as the assailant seems to have a hand firmly on my neck. Floods of tears escape my bloodshot eyes. By now I don't know if I can cling onto life for much longer. The realization that my life could slip out of my hands any minute now sends me into a fit of distress. I look up and desperately try to see the attacker's face. When I finally realize who it is, I wish I hadn't. Just as I begin to hold on to life, he slams my head into the ground. I'm trying to cling on, but my minutes are numbered.

17

Eli

Just as the thrilling events of *Top Gear* begin to push Ivy out of my brain, a shrill scream echoes through the valley. I wonder if anyone else had heard it. *Was it just my imagination?* Another high-pitched scream sounds. It's coming from the alleyway. Grabbing my leather jacket, I sprint down the stairs and out of the front door. Without thinking, I charge down the alleyway. What I see horrifies me. A man is stabbing Ivy. A river of crimson blood trickles down the passage.

'Hey! Get off her! I'm calling the police!' I bark, racing towards the crime scene. The criminal leaps off of Ivy and sprints away. I attempt to run after him, but it's no good. He's obviously a very athletic person. I turn to Ivy; she's lying on the floor, weeping in a pool of her own carmine blood. I lie next to her, holding her lightly to my chest.

'H-he attacked … Can't … breathe …' she cries into my shirt.

I hold her hand tighter, softly smoothing her hair. 'Did you see who did it? Ivy, stay with me,' I ask, trying to appear composed. With a great amount of effort she manages to lift her head up, revealing her mascara-ridden face.

'I-it was Craig. Craig attacked …' she manages to whisper before falling unconscious.

I feel the blood drain out of my face. *Craig. My best friend.* The one person on this planet whom I have trusted for a year stabbed an innocent girl. Tears begin to well up in my eyes, but I blink them away. I must be strong for Ivy.

I put my jacket on the floor and carefully lay her on it. 'Don't move, okay. I'm calling an ambulance,' I order in an authoritative voice that I've never used before. She doesn't reply.

Within eight minutes, an ambulance appears at the end of the street. The passage is too small for the vehicle to get down, so they place Ivy on a stretcher and carry her to the ambulance. I follow them into the back of the ambulance and sit on the chair beside her. She is unconscious, and I can't tell whether she's breathing or not. I remember a trick my mum taught me when I was little to tell whether someone is breathing. I place my cheek near Ivy's mouth and look at her chest for signs of movement, while feeling for breath against my own cheek. Warm air smothers my face; my muscles relax slightly. She'll be okay. I know she will.

Although the hospital is miles from my estate, we arrive there in a matter of minutes, with the assistance of lights and sirens. As soon as the ambulance stops, at the trauma centre, the doctors spring into action. A young female paramedic in their distinctive bottle-green uniform swiftly wheels Ivy into the hospital on a trolley, and a man begins asking me for details. I can't form any words. My eyes just follow Ivy's stretcher; I need to be with her.

'Sir? *Sir!*' I snap out of my daze and look over to the person asking me questions. Before me stands a male staff member wearing scrubs that look similar to the clothing worn in an operating theatre; he has a well-trimmed ivory beard and a moustache to match.

'Sir, I know you are in shock, but we need answers. Please come with me.' He begins to walk inside, but I stay glued to the ground, paralysed with anxiety.

'Please let me go with Ivy. She needs me! She doesn't have anyone else here!' I plead, crying and spluttering.

The man has a pitiful expression on his face. 'Sir, she has gone in for an emergency blood supply. She lost a lot of blood. Now I need you to come. We need to get in contact with her parents, and we need information. The only way you can possibly help her at this point is by helping me understand what has happened.' Eventually I give in and follow him.

We walk down many corridors until we reach an office. He types in a combination code, and the door swings open.

We sit at the table, and I tell him everything—everything but the fact that Craig is the perpetrator.

After the interview, we sit in an awkward silence. An icy blast flings papers off the table as someone enters the room. There are two people standing in the doorway: a young man and a slightly older woman. The lady looks most distraught. Her face is as white as chalk, her clothes clearly haven't made contact with an iron for a while and her hair is damp.

'Where is my baby? I want to see her now!' she demands, slamming her hands down on the doctor's desk.

'Mrs Towers, Ivy has gone in for emergency resuscitation. This can involve blood transfusions, a trip to the CT or MRI scanner, assessments by surgeons, and procedures carried out in the emergency department. Your daughter has been stabbed in the chest and may well need to have a tube drain inserted through the chest wall,' he replies in a monotone voice. 'I'm afraid you won't be able to see her for at least two hours. In the meantime, would you like some coffee?' The doctor doesn't hold any information back from these next of kin, realising that Ivy's mum could potentially lose her baby. And that's all he has to say.

'Stuff your stupid coffee! I want to see Ivy *right now!*' Her anger simmers down until she falls to the ground and bursts into tears.

'Now look what you've done!' the boy barks.

'Excuse me for asking, but who are you?' the doctor asks.

'I'm Ivy's brother, Tyler. We want to see our Ivy now!' The doctor nods. Once Ivy's mum has regained some composure, we follow him down many corridors at a brisk pace until we reach a large room, white and clean.

Instead of letting us go into the resuscitation room, he motions to an observation window in the wall between us and Ivy. It takes every bit of my strength to look through that window. There are several spacious patient bays, each with monitors for blood pressure and other vital signs mounted on the wall, trolleys, oxygen masks, intravenous drips and mobile X-ray machines. I see a staff base with notes, telephones, and computers. A lot of people are bustling around—not just doctors, nurses, and porters, but even a couple of policemen keeping their distance and watching what is going on in Ivy's bay.

Nausea overcomes my quivering body. Despite the many doctors around her, I manage to catch a glimpse of someone dressing her chest wound, and one particular cut catches my eye; a long incision has been made down her right arm. A whole array of emotions course through my body at once: anger, confusion, upset, and even hurt. How could Craig do this, and more importantly, why? Yes, Ivy is sometimes arrogant and nerdy, but that can't have been his motive. Small whimpers of pain escape Mrs Towers's mouth. Other than that, she shows no emotion.

We stand there. Watching. Waiting. Time slows down. Life becomes a blur.

'I'll leave you to it. My mum will realise I'm gone by now,' I whisper.

Mrs Towers can offer only a weak nod.

'Thank you, Eli. Without you, Ivy could've … you know …' tears fill Tyler's eyes and spill down his cheeks.

'She'll be okay, y'know. The doctors are doing everything they can. We'll get her back.'

Just as I'm about to walk off, Tyler's eyes go cold. He stares at me. His breathing becomes quick; his shoulders, tense.

'I knew I recognised your name from somewhere.'

Before I can make sense of what's happening, he charges at me, grabbing my collar. Tyler pulls me down the corridor until we are out of the view of his mum. He holds me against the wall.

'Ivy's told me about your little pranks.'

'I'm so sorry.'

'How pathetic can you get? Picking on the new girl! Now I'm gonna show you what it's like to feel small.' He throws a punch at me, his fist landing right between my eyes. My legs give way, leaving me to crumble to the floor. I hold my face, trying to stop the blood from spilling out. Tyler crouches beside me.

'Now listen here, you little rat. You touch my sister again, and I'll finish you. Got it?' I nod, too frightened to fight back.

'Good.' He stands up and walks back towards his mum.

※

There's no chance I'm sleeping tonight. I lie awake, staring at the shining stars through my ceiling window. Mum questioned me about the scar—the one that Tyler planted on my face—but I just told her that I tripped on the curb and hit my face. She made an awful fuss about it, but I felt bad about being pampered by my mum, given Ivy's current circumstances. My mind is in turmoil with all these unanswered questions. *How do I confront Craig? Is going against your best mate easier said than done?*

When the pressure of these questions becomes too much, I open my phone and scroll through my contacts until I reach Craig.

My fingers tremble over the keys before I begin typing. It takes me at least ten minutes to work out what to say, but I eventually come up with…

Why did you do that to Ivy? She's unconscious. She nearly died! Are you crazy?

I know it's quite a bland text, but what else am I supposed to say—'Congratulations, you're officially a knife-wielding criminal'? Anxiously, I lie there, awaiting a reply. After five minutes, my phone lights up, illuminating my caliginous room. Without hesitating, I snatch up my mobile and read his reply:

Why would I care if she's unconscious? She deserves it. I know things about her that you don't. Besides, she is getting in the way of our friendship. We were gonna do all our projects together, but stupid Ivy had to come in and ruin everything. This'll teach her to stay away.

Eli:

I'm gonna tell everyone what you did. The whole world will know just how twisted you really are.

Craig:

See, the thing is, you won't tell anyone.

Eli:

you wanna bet?

Craig:

If you tell anyone what happened, I go to the school about you bullying Ivy. You could get excluded, and

> **I'm sure you can't become a doctor like your mum wants if you have a bad school record. Plus if you tell the police that I attacked her, I'll tell them that you were in on it and that you got Ivy to leave your house at a certain time so I could be waiting in the alleyway for her, and BOOM … bye bye, Ivy. It's my word against yours. Pick your fate.**

Eli:

> **You make me sick.**

Craig:

> **Trust me, Eli. The feeling's mutual.**

Unconsciously, I sit bolt upright. I can't believe my eyes. The reason he decided to make her life hell, the reason he decided to almost steal the life of an innocent girl, was all out of jealousy? By now I'm shaking with anger. Unintentionally, my palpitating fingers curl into compact fists, dropping my phone in the process. My mobile shatters into millions of shards of glass whilst somehow barely making a sound.

For the first time since my brother, Khalid, died, I surge into a flood of uncontrollable tears. The realisation of what I've put Ivy through hits me like a truck.

I need to fix this. I must help Ivy.

※

Mum drives me to the hospital in the early hours of Saturday morning. Although the sun has barely risen yet, I have decided I need to see Ivy as soon as possible, thinking she is probably well enough for us to talk now. Before mum has even parked the car properly, I hop out of the passenger seat and run to Ivy's room.

'Excuse me. Are you Eli?' a mellow voice asks me. I turn around to see a small woman staring at me with cold, dark eyes.

'Yes, I'm Eli. Can I help you?'

'I'm afraid we have some bad news about your friend Ivy.'

'What? Has she ...'—I can barely bring myself to finish the sentence—'died?'

'Oh no, nothing like that. I'm afraid Ivy is in a coma. We have been able to work out that the culprit strangled her for just under three minutes. I'm surprised she survived, to be honest. She may not wake up for weeks.'

'N-no. She can't be. She has to wake up!'

I run into Ivy's room, where I kneel beside her, holding her cold hands. My voice lowers to a whisper. 'Ivy, they've got it wrong. You aren't in a coma. Just wake up.' I shake her gently. The nurse watches me from the corner of the room.

'Try to refrain from touching the patient,' she mumbles, with not a hint of affection.

When Ivy doesn't stir, I begin to feel an intense rage tremble through my body.

'Ivy ... Ivy, wake up! You're not in a coma. You have to wake up. You're scaring me. Wake up. Wake up. *Wake up!*' I shake her hard, crying and wailing hysterically. I don't know what's come over me, but whatever it is, I can't and I won't control it. The nurse runs over, pulling me away from Ivy.

'What did I say about touching the patient?' I shove her off of me and storm out of the room, tears still flowing. My pace quickens until I'm running down the corridors, dodging various doctors and elderly people.

I reach the waiting room and begin searching frantically for Mum. My eyes rest on her. She is seated in the far corner of the room, reading an Arab fashion magazine.

'Ma, we need to go now,' I instruct between sobs.

'Habibi, what happened?'

My body collapses in her arms, and my tears stain her rose-patterned dress. 'Sh ... she's in a coma. What if she's asleep for too long and they turn off her life support?' My crying turns into howling; everyone in the room is watching my manic episode unfold.

'Shhh, my love, she will be okay. The doctors will do everything they can.'

'But what if they can't do enough? This is all my fault!'

She caresses my back, holding me tight. Her tone grows serious. 'None of this is your fault.'

'She's right,' a voice says from behind us. I lift my head up from Mum's shoulder, and standing there is Tyler.

'I'll leave you two to talk,' Mum says, heading towards the canteen.

'Let's take a walk.'

We take a stroll around the hospital gardens. I take a deep breath of the clean morning air. The scent of blossoming flowers delights my lungs. Violent rays of scorching sun heat beat down on my head.

'Tyler, I'm so sorry. I'd do anything to take back what I did to your sister.'

'Don't worry. I have to admit, I haven't got the best track record when it comes to bullying. Anyways, that isn't why I wanted to talk. I need to ask you something.'

'Oh, okay. Fire away.'

'Do you know who stabbed Ivy? The police have no idea who it could be.'

I don't know what to say. 'I wish I could help, but no, I have no idea.' My gaze moves to a lilac butterfly; it flutters from flower to flower. A stray cat stares at the butterfly, licking its lips. Discreetly, it tiptoes behind the innocent insect, and with a swift motion, it opens its mouth and clamps it over the butterfly.

'Eli, please. If you know something, the police need to know.'

'Don't you get it? I don't know!' I snap. 'Sorry. I didn't mean to rip into you.'

'Forget it, Eli. You really are just a bully.' And with that he is gone. Why do I always mess up? It's like I'm pathologically incapable of being kind.

⁂

Monday offers a cold English afternoon. Gusts of wind surge through the building, throwing doors open, causing alarm to unsuspecting year sevens. Rain hammers down on the windows, thrashing and pounding, trying to break the fragile glass panes. The tempest dampens my mood, although unlike normal, I am thankful for this storm. If this thunder and lightning hadn't arrived, it would've been outdoor basketball practice at lunch today, which would've meant seeing Craig. It's been three days since the attack, yet I still can't bring myself to speak to him face-to-face. If anything, I dread to think what I'll do to him when we are eventually made to talk. Haila and I are in the cafeteria, sitting on the windowsill.

'Hey, Eli, could I maybe copy your maths homework? I don't understand it, and it's due tomorrow.'

'Sure,' I mumble, taking my geometry book out of my bag and tossing it at her.

'Baby, what's up?' Haila asks, pulling on my jumper sleeve like a toddler.

'I'm fine,' I reply bluntly.

'Eli, we never keep secrets from each other.' My eyes stay fixated on the flailing tree outside. 'Baby, please. Talk to me.'

'Haila, I said I'm fine. Will you just stop banging on?' I snarl, shoving her off my sleeve, an instant sense of regret settling in the pit of my stomach. 'Sorry. I'm not feeling too good at the moment.'

'Yeah, I can tell,' she replies coldly.

'Oh, c'mon Haila. Don't be like that.' I pull her close to me, kissing her pouted lips. She gives in, sinking into my arms, holding me close. Our romantic moment ends when the bell rings.

'We'd better get to music,' I say, gently pushing her off me. Hand in hand, we make our way through the herd of sweaty, hormonal teenagers.

The minute we enter the classroom, my eyes begin to search for Craig. These past couple of days, I've automatically scanned my surroundings for him. I can tell by the way he acts Craig knows I'm onto him. I spot him in the far corner of the room, so I sit near the front, far from him. He catches my eye and smirks an aggravating smirk.

Good morning, year eleven!' Miss Farrow chimes. When nobody replies, she says, in an even more high-pitched voice, 'I said good morning, year eleven!'

'Good morning, Miss Farrow,' we all grumble, with not a hint of enthusiasm. Everything about Miss Farrow annoys me: her exaggerated grin, hypnotising patterned dresses, and even her perfectly straight white teeth. But the most irritating thing about this teacher is that she is so nice I feel bad for hating her.

'Now, class! On today's agenda we have ... drum roll please!' The room is so quiet one could hear a pin drop. 'Oh, okay. Well, today's lesson is … rhythm and rhyme!'

The entire class lets out a simultaneous groan.

'Oh, c'mon, you negative Nellies! One at a time, I'm going to call you to the front so you can share the tongue-twisters you made up over the weekend! Nina, you first!'

Nitty Nina, as I like to call her, stumbles up to the front, head hanging low. She had a large infestation of nits when we were in year seven, and even though the bugs have gone, the embarrassment has stuck with her ever since. She clears her throat, slightly lifting her head to read the words on the crumpled piece of paper she holds.

'Cool cats cut cucumbers crookedly,' she mumbles.

'Marvellous, Nina! Simply wonderful! I think that deserves two merits!' Miss Farrow squeals.

'Now, who's next?' Her dark green eyes search for a victim. I look away from her, so as not to make eye contact. 'Craig! Come on up, darling!' It takes every bit of my willpower not to burst out laughing. To my surprise, instead of looking mad, he looks happy—cunning even. *What is he planning?*

Craig struts to the front.

Confidently he clears his throat and says, 'How many girls can a knife stab if a knife blade could stab girls!' I pounce at him, pulling him to the ground with me.

Not having been able to find nail clippers for weeks has done me a favour. I scratch his face with my overgrown claws, causing him to look as if he's been attacked by an aggressive kitten. Miss Farrow tries to step in, but I shove her off—just a little too hard. She falls back clutching her stomach, where I elbowed her. The rest of the class watches in awe. Some begin chanting my name. Miss Farrow reaches for her walkie-talkie.

'Pastoral team to classroom 2 of the music department immediately. A fight has broken out between Eli Bishara and Craig Wilson. Over.' We continue to scrap on the floor until two teachers manage to tear us apart.

'Mr Kimberley's office now!' Miss Farrow yells in a stern voice I've never heard her use before. Mr Kimberley is our head teacher. Despite his stout and majestic appearance, he doesn't really scare me. My mum, however, will go nuts when she finds out about all of this. But the most aggravating part is that I can't tell Mr Kimberley why we were really fighting. Craig could ruin my life if I tell them the devastating truth.

Mr Kimberley is at a meeting, so Craig and I sit alone in his office, awaiting his arrival. Apart from the noise of lessons going on down the hall, the only sound I can hear is the ticking of the standard white school clock hanging above the door frame.

Craig looks over towards me and smirks. 'I knew you'd cave in. Your face left me in no doubt as I read out my tongue twister.' I stare out the window, not daring to look at his smug face. 'Ouch. The silent treatment. You're almost as silent as Ivy was when I went to visit her in the hospital. At least now she's in a coma and I won't have to listen to her dumb voice drone on and on.'

My emotions spill over. 'Don't you dare talk about her like that!' I snap, looking him deep in the eye, daring him to make one more gabby remark. The smirk remains on his face.

'I knew you'd crumble eventually. That's how you work. You act all hard, but deep down inside you are crying out for help.'

'You are so sick and twisted it's unbelievable. Ivy could die, and you're here making jokes about it!' I cry, launching spit cannonballs at him.

Still he wears a smile—a cold, heartless smile.

Again I lunge at him.

'All right, break it up,' Mr Kimberley orders, walking in and sitting in his large plush office chair. He twiddles a pen between his fingers, looking us both up and down. 'Oh, Eli. What have you done this time?' He tuts, shaking his head and writing down seemingly pointless notes in his notepad.

'I haven't done anything. It's him.' I point to the poisonous cow sitting next to me.

Mr Kimberley grins. 'From what I understand, Mr Wilson here didn't provoke the fight. As far as I'm concerned, you were the one who lunged at him. Were you not?'

'Well, yeh, but …'

'So doesn't that make this your fault, Mr Bishara?' I try to think of a witty reply, but my brain lets me down.

'Yeah, I suppose so,' I mumble. Craig shoots me a victorious look.

Craig chimes in. 'Sir, it was a completely unprovoked attack. I don't know what came over him! I was just reading out my tongue-twister, and he lunged at me! He's an absolute nutcase.'

'We both know that isn't what happened,' I mutter.

Mr Kimberley looks intrigued. He leans closer to us, his warm, cheesy breath smothering my face. I discreetly lean back, taking gulps of fresh air.

'Go on then, Eli; enlighten me. What really happened?' It takes everything in me not to tell Mr Kimberley what he did. The whole world needs to know, for Ivy's sake. All I want is for Craig to rot in prison and for Ivy to get her life back. It's what she deserves. I look over at Craig, and he smiles at me. English lessons finally come into use; although Craig looks kind on the outside, I can infer that he will literally destroy me if I don't keep my trap shut.

'Nothing happened, sir ... I'm just having a bad day.'

'Right, well in that case, Eli, go to isolation; and Craig, go back to music.' We both nod speechlessly, me because I can't believe the injustice, and Craig probably because he can't believe his luck.

Craig struts out, and I trudge behind, purposely dragging my feet. We stand outside the office.

'I can't believe you, Craig. I really thought I knew you. I really thought you were a decent person.'

'Oh, come off it, Eli,' he scoffs. 'You're no better than me.' How can he seriously compare me to the likes of him, a knife-wielding psycho.

'Craig, I am nothing like you. Do I terrorise people with knives? Do I put people in hospitals? No, no I don't, so don't even go there.'

He laughs an evil laugh I didn't even think he had in him. It irritates me how well he takes on the role of criminal mastermind. 'You may not carry a knife or put people in hospitals, but you are a bully—a cruel, arrogant bully.'

'I haven't scarred Ivy; you have! You certainly have! I mean, look at her!' Craig simply smiles. 'What's so funny?' I growl.

'Don't you get it?' He steps closer to me so I can feel his warm breath on my neck. 'You like to act like you haven't hurt Ivy—like you're some sort of superhero. You may not have physically scarred Ivy, but emotionally you have wrecked her. Do you remember the charismatic girl that she used to be? You've killed her lively spirit. You and your strange girlfriend have destroyed her confidence. Me and you? We are just as bad as each other.'

Craig strides off towards music class while I stand there watching him. As much as I hate to admit it, he's right. I really am just a bully.

⁂

Mum went absolutely ballistic when she found out about me and Craig's fight. How I wish I could tell her why it all happened, but she'd only worry herself sick and go to the police. I want to wait till Ivy wakes up before I say anything to the police. I want to make sure I tell them only what she wants them to know. This is her business, not mine. Unbelievably, the police haven't even gotten round to questioning me yet! I thought they would be onto the case straight away, but it seems they have bigger fish to fry.

⁂

'When Ravi told me what Lillah had done, I was so mad. How could she be such an interfering brat!' Haila gossips at me on Tuesday, waving her hands everywhere. I'm really not listening, though. Craig's words have cut me deep, and I probably shouldn't be making jokes about cuts, considering Ivy's current state. We are seated on the floor of Haila's pink bedroom, 'doing homework'—as far as our parents are concerned. Though there are exercise books all over the floor, we haven't even picked up a pen yet. All I want is for Ivy to wake up and for me to give her a big hug and tell her everything will be okay, but I can't. Craig's snatched my dreams away from me.

'Eli … Eli, are you listening to me?' Haila asks. Her stunning green eyes are staring right at me, her eyebrows raised slightly.

'Y-yes, I'm listening. You were saying something about Ravi.'

'Eli, that was ages ago. Baby, what is going on with you? You've been so distracted recently,' she says, sliding closer to me.

'Haila, I've told you before! Nothing's wrong,' I say, trying to convince her, but there is no fooling Haila.

'Eli. The more you lie, the worse it's gonna get. Just tell me.'

'All right, fine. Ivy's gone into a coma. She was attacked down the alleyway near my street …' I try to carry on talking, but my voice cracks from emotion. My expectation was that Haila would be sympathetic, but being the cynical person she is, her facial expression doesn't change.

'Eli, why are you crying? This is perfect! She'll be out of our way for a bit, and when she wakes up, we can carry on hassling her! Oh, baby, this is great!' she squeals. I can't tell if my ears are deceiving me. Instead of replying, I simply stare at her with cold, emotionless eyes. 'What's up with you?' she teases.

My breathing becomes fast, and my body begins to tremble. I try to hold in my anger, but it's just too difficult.

'Are you actually so twisted that you are enjoying this? What if she dies? You'll still be happy then, won't you? You're a heartless psycho, and I hate you.' I push past her, storming down the stairs. My parents are downstairs, having tea with Haila's mum and dad.

'We are going,' I say coldly, tears still flowing.

'What's going on, my love?' Mum calls after me.

My legs carry me outside, not giving me a chance to change my mind. It's beyond me how Haila can be so heartless. I take deep breaths of the cold English air; the icy sensation tantalises my lungs.

Dad appears in the doorframe, a stern look painted on his face. 'Eli, what on earth are you playing at?' he snaps.

'Haila's being awful. I don't want to be here anymore; can we just go?' Dad's about to protest when he notices my puffy red eyes.

'Get in the car, son,' he says softly. 'I'll get your mother.'

18

Tyler

'Milly, give it back to her!' I order on Wednesday evening. She clutches the Barbie doll tightly and shakes her head. Why do little kids have to be so defiant?

'May's been playing with her for ages! It's my turn now!' Milly whines. May makes a sly attempt at grabbing the doll from her twin, but Milly turns away from her.

'You guys have thousands of dolls to play with. Just use a different one, like this one.' I grab a random blue-haired rocker chic doll and thrust it at Milly. She grabs it and throws it on the floor.

'Milly! You know what!' I snatch the Barbie doll and put it on top of the fridge. Both of them stare in horror, as if I'd killed someone. 'Now both of you go and play upstairs before I take all your princess dolls and put them through a shredder,' I say.

'Fine!' they yell simultaneously, and they storm up the stairs. I can hear them mumbling to each other as they leave. These kids are six going on sixteen.

I check the time: 7.54 p.m. *Where's Mum? I'd best get the small ones ready for bed. Mum doesn't need to come home to madness.* I'm trying to keep it together for mum and the kids, but my heart is aching. All I can think about is Ivy. Mum insisted on staying with Ivy at the hospital, but the doctors managed to convince her that there is no point. the prognosis is that Ivy is unlikely to wake up for at least a week. I don't think the reality of the situation has sunk in yet. My baby sister, my best friend, may never wake up. She may never recover. I fight back the tears just as I have done continually during the past couple of days.

'Right. Cole, Coco, Archie, and Poppy, it's bath time.' They all clap their hands in excitement. Poppy, Coco, and Cole eagerly climb up the stairs, and I carry Eva and Archie on my hip. Sometimes I really do feel like a full-time dad. I help them all undress and put Eva to sleep in her baby pink cot. The poor kid has had a long day, so within seconds she's fast asleep, making cute little sniffles once in a while.

Despite our bathtub being absolutely tiny, they all manage to squeeze in side by side. My siblings splash about in the water for as long as they wish. I decide to let them get all their energy out now so they'll fall asleep straight afterwards, even if that does mean that the walls are covered in bubbles and water marks.

Eventually they start to calm down, so I get them all out and dressed in record time. Poppy and Cole waddle off to their room, and Archie toddles next to me, his soft small hand entwined in mine. When we make it to their room, he climbs into his car-shaped bed and instantly drifts off to sleep. See, I really do have a magic touch. I tiptoe across the landing and into Milly and May's room. They are both fast asleep on the top of their bunk bed, clutching two Barbie dolls.

Just as I'm about to go to my room, I hear the door rattle as it closes. My first assumption is that there's an intruder, so I reach for a hockey stick that's propped up on the wall, but then I realise who it is. I race down the stairs, and leaning against the front door, beer bottle in hand, is Mum.

'Oh, Mum, what have you done to yourself?' I walk over and gently take the bottle out of her hand, placing it on the coffee table.

'T-Tywer. I-I want my bwaby back.' Mum bursts into tears and falls into my arms. I help her upstairs and into bed; she weeps the whole way. She blows her nose into her cardigan sleeve and lies on the bed.

'S-she's gone, Tywer,' Mum mumbles.

'No, Mum, she hasn't. We aren't giving up on her,' I reply. Tears start spilling out of my eyes, but I wipe them away before Mum sees.

'We don't have any luck, baby. Between Simon and your Dad … we don't stand a chance with Ivy. Sh-she's gone.' Her harsh words set me off wailing myself. I know that she is wrong, but it still hurts to see that she's given up. I mumble goodnight and walk out of her room, slamming the door behind me. I don't care if the kids wake up; I don't care if I upset Mum even more. Nothing's ever about me anymore. I only ever do things for other people, and I'm sick of it. I run to my room and fling myself onto my bed. I grab a cigarette from my bedside drawer and let the fumes burn away my problems. I swore I'd never go back to smoking, but I need this. I need the comfort.

19

Eli

Mum and Dad have both tried to get me to tell them what happened between me and Haila on Tuesday, but there's no way I'm telling them. They wouldn't cancel the wedding if they found out; it'd just be an uncomfortable and forced marriage. Haila and I can work this out by ourselves. Besides, it's not like they'd understand. In the olden days, people chucked little pebbles at windows to get attention or asked others out face-to-face! It certainly doesn't work like that anymore. The one thing that's always cheered me up is video games, so Thursday after school, I slide onto my big gaming chair and let the adventures of *Call of Duty: Black Ops* push out my worries. My hand–eye coordination is amazing if I do say so myself, so every game I play ends in a win.

'Nobody stands a chance against Eli The Great!' I profess. I do a cheesy air punch with one hand; the other continues shooting the enemy with my Xbox controller. Deciding that playing against computerised people is boring, I switch to Xbox Live.

I join a server and wait to begin. I pick up my cup and take a gulp of my caffè latte. Names pop up on my screen:

DruggedFrog224 joined the server.

LokoForCocoPops101 joined the server.

!TinyTimothy! joined the server.

CraigWilson16 joined the server.

Without hesitation, I click the Exit button and throw my controller on my bed. It feels as if Craig is there, everywhere I turn, watching and waiting. I've tried my best to shut out the images of that cold Saturday night, but I can't. I try to run away from my emotions, but they all come crashing over me like a huge ocean wave, drowning me—choking me. I stand up and grab my coat, heading down the stairs and out through the door. I shout, 'I'm going out, Mum!' and slam the door behind me. My legs carry me to my moped and I speed down the street.

I sprint straight to Ivy's room and gently push open the door. There's a chair by her bedside, so I sit in it. She looks so peaceful. Her hair is draped on either side of her shoulders, and her lips are still stained a crimson colour from Saturday night. My mouth opens and closes as I try to find the perfect words to say. In doing so, I realise that no words can express my feelings right now. It's just me and Ivy in the room, so I feel free to say anything to get this bulky weight off my shoulders.

'Hi ... how's ... how's the coma?' I stutter. *How's the coma? Seriously Eli? Think!* 'I ... I miss you, okay! I wish you weren't asleep, and I ... I really want you to wake up ... ' Silence. 'You're looking really pretty today, y'know? I know your favourite colour is red, so I ... I brought you this.' I slide a red hair clip into her hair. Admittedly, I found it in the bottom of my mum's makeup bag, but it suits her perfectly.

'That's really sweet of you, Eli,' a voice says from behind me. I turn around to find that, standing there, watching me, is Tyler. His face breaks, and I run over to him, hugging him tight. He weeps into my jumper, clutching me close. Waterworks of my own start flooding out of my eyes. I cry not only for Ivy but also for my brother, Khalid. All of this is only making me realise just how hard life can be.

'I'm so sorry,' I wail. 'Please forgive me.' I gasp for air and continue crying.

Tyler's cries soften. He lifts his head and stares deep into my eyes. 'It's ... okay. I forgive you.' He looks over at Ivy. 'We need to be strong ... for Ivy. She needs us.'

I nod. 'Can I get you a coffee or something?' I offer between sniffles.

'I'd love to, but I've gotta go look after my siblings. Thanks for the offer though.' We both smile, wiping tears from our faces. 'We can meet up some other time though. Set some things straight?'

'Sure.'

He walks out of the room.

'Get better soon, Ivy. We all need you,' I whisper. A single tear falls from her eyes and runs slowly down her cheek, but her expression stays untouched. *She can hear me?* Knowing that she understands us is enough to reassure me that she'll be okay, so I leave the room and close the door behind me.

❦

Upon seeing Tyler yesterday, I noticed how all this stress is affecting him. The bags under is eyes are as big as ever, and he has this constant expression on his face as if to say, 'I haven't slept in days, please help.' I've decided that the least I can do is go over and help with their little siblings. Apparently they have seven little brothers and sisters and no dad, which must be such tedious work.

When I knock on the door, he looks so relieved to see me. Tyler graciously accepts my offer to babysit and plods up the stairs to go to bed. Sure enough, scattered about the living room are seven small kids. *Ugh, this is gonna be one hell of a day.*

❦

'Who's that trip-trapping over my bridge!' I yell from under the park's wobbly wooden bridge. All of the kids squeal in equal excitement and terror. One of the six-year-olds, I've forgotten her name, yells, 'It is only me, the smallest billy goat Gruff, and I'm going up the hill to make myself fat!' They all cackle with laughter.

'Now I'm coming to gobble you up!' They all scram from the bridge, darting off in all directions. I run after Coco, swooping her up in my arms and pretending to eat her. 'Gotcha!' I say, pretending to take a bite out of her stomach. Coco squirms around until I let her go, and she runs after Archie. Eva watches from her buggy, clapping her hands and giggling in delight. I'd always disliked little kids; they just seemed like disgusting brats. But I have to admit, it is so much fun to play with them. I guess you could say I've taken a liking to Ivy's siblings. Thankfully, my dad has many cars, so I borrowed his minivan. I know its illegal but my dad taught me to drive over the summer. Police don't really patrol around here so driving has become a habit of mine. I round up the kids like a border collie herding sheep. After a couple minutes of struggling to fasten excitable kids into car seats, I eventually manage to get going. I cautiously drive through town and back to Ivy's house.

Every single one of them is absolutely knackered, so I get them all into the living room to watch a film. Within minutes of the film starting, every single one of them is asleep, including Eva, who is snuggled on my chest and gripping my grey shirt with her tiny fingers. I find myself nodding off to sleep but force my eyes open. I feel a great responsibility to make sure they are all safe.

Halfway through the film, Tyler comes down the stairs, covering his mouth, which is opened widely in a huge yawn. A smile spreads across his face, and he whispers, 'You, Eli Bishara, are incredible.' Tyler's words give me a sense of pride that I've never felt before. Tyler reaches into his pocket and thrusts a fiver at me.

'No, it's okay. I really enjoyed today. Being with this cute bunch was payment enough,' I say. Tyler thanks me wholeheartedly, and I tell him I'd love to babysit anytime. After placing Eva carefully in her cot, I say goodbye to Tyler and make my way home. I'd never wanted kids before, but today has slightly changed my opinion.

— 20

Ivy

I can hear them. I can hear them wishing me well and telling me about their days. I can feel them. I can feel their warm hands holding mine. I can see the light through my eyelids when the switches are flicked. On. Off. On. Off. I can feel the breeze when the nurses open the windows for some fresh air. But I can't talk to them. I can't tell them that I'm okay. I can't tell them that I miss them too or that I am proud of them for passing the exam they tell me about. I can't move. I can't squeeze their hands back or give them a hug. I'm in a white room. I'm waiting, but I don't know what for. This blank abyss is consuming me, and I can't escape. I am trapped.

21

Eli

My phone is placed right in front of me, but I can't bring myself to pick it up. The all-too-familiar text ringtone has just rung, but I don't dare to reply. I know it's from Haila, and I just don't feel ready. *C'mon, Eli; just man up and text her! It's only Haila; what's she gonna do to you?* After taking a deep breath, I pick up my phone. Sure enough, I've received a text from Haila:

Please can we talk? Xxx

What do I reply to that? After about five minutes of pondering, I reply with a simple…

There's nothing to talk about. You messed up.

I purposely don't put kisses on the end, just to rub it in. Instead of being sarky and rude, she says,

Babe, I'm sorry. Come over and I'll explain Xxx

All right, fine. You'd better have a good explanation.

I wish I didn't give in so easily to her. Haila has me wrapped around her little finger.

I rap my knuckles on her polished white door. Haila pulls open the door.

'Hey, babe. Come in.' She takes me by the hand and leads me to her bedroom, not even giving me a chance to take off my shoes. I have to dodge various Lego blocks on the stairs, helpfully left there by her eight-year-old brother, Mathew. Haila bounces onto her bed.

I place myself next to her. I must stay firm if I want any chance of regaining some control in this relationship, because right now Haila is wearing the trousers.

'About the other day … I'm sorry, all right? I didn't know that little gremlin meant so much to you.' I swear Haila is incapable of being kind to Ivy.

'She doesn't mean anything to me,' I whisper.

'Well how come you got all hysterical when I laughed at her?'

I quickly fire back, 'Because laughing at a dying girl isn't okay. Whether we love her or loathe her, she doesn't deserve this. No one does.' My voice comes across stronger than I'd expected. Haila bites her lip and nods slowly.

'Okay. I understand. I truly am sorry.' This time she seems sincere.

'Come here,' I say with a smile. She shuffles closer to me and I hold her tight.

'I love you, Eli,' Haila says into my shirt.

I hesitate and reply, 'I love you too.'

22

Ivy

At 3.47 p.m. on Friday, I utter the first words I've spoken in some time. 'M-mum … Where am I? Where's Eli?' I burst into tears. A whole array of emotions is coursing through me. I'm finally free. I've never felt so trapped in my life. My voice is weak and shaky. I try to sit up, but Mum gently lays me back down. My whole body feels heavy, as if a weight has been strapped to my chest.

'I-Ivy? Oh my lord, she's awake! Someone, come quick! Come quick!' A team of doctors come racing in and begin many procedures, such as removing needles from my hand. Trolly wheels screech against the floor, making scratch marks on the white yet ageing vinyl.

'It's okay, baby. You were stabbed, but you'll be fine. Everything will be okay.' Mum caresses my hand with her thumb. Worry is written all over her face. My eyes close, giving me a moment to process everything. All the memories come flooding back: Craig, the knife, the blood. Every gruesome detail haunts my mind.

Then I remember.

Eli. He saved me.

'Mum, I need to see Eli.' She nods and leaves the room, not uttering a word. I carry on crying, unable to stop. I hear one of the nurses say to let me cry it out. Eventually I calm down.

My eyes follow one of the nurses. She's too busy doing something with a syringe to notice me staring, but eventually she looks up, catching my eye. I read her name badge: 'Nurse Appleton'. For some strange reason, I can't take my eyes off her. The mesmerising smile stretched across her face hypnotises me. Wrinkles are patterned about her skin, though I can tell she is no older than forty-five.

'Are you okay, sweetie?' I try to nod, but it's difficult when there are so many tubes coming out of my skull. She smiles, trying to mask a giggle.

'Sucks, doesn't it? Going into a coma.'

'That's one way to put it,' I mumble.

Mum returns to the room, sliding her mobile phone into her pocket.

'I just got off the phone with him, darling. He's on his way as we speak. Now please rest until he gets here.' As much as I don't want to sleep, Mum's devastated expression pulls my heartstrings, so I close my eyes, pretending to rest. Why would I want to sleep when I've been 'asleep' for, like, eight days?

Seconds feel like minutes; minutes feel like hours.

The thought that Eli isn't coming crosses my mind, but I shake it out of my head, refusing to let my negativity get the better of me. He'll come. I know he will. Although I intended to pretend to sleep, within minutes I'm in a deep slumber.

Letting out a loud yawn, I crane my neck to look out of the window; it's pitch black outside. I've slept way longer than I intended. I turn to face the chair, which Mum had been using, and sitting there now is Eli. He looks so nervous, twiddling his thumbs and shifting about in the chair.

'Hi. I got here a while ago, but you were asleep, and I wasn't sure if I should wake you up, but your mum suggested that I let you sleep. Then I thought that …' Eli is speaking so fast I can barely make sense of what he is saying.

'Hey, calm down.'

'Sorry. I'm just nervous.' We sit there, not saying a single word. Eli hangs his head, staring down at his trainers. I can't help but laugh.

'What's so funny?' he asks, lifting his head to stare at me.

'Since when have we been too shy to say anything to each other?' Eli chuckles softly. I notice him relax slightly, his shoulders dropping and his default smirk reappearing.

'How long have I been in here?' Eli raises an eyebrow. My words are still slow, and my jaw feels stiff, so I try to limit my words.

'You don't remember?'

'My memory isn't too good at the moment.'

'Oh, okay. Well, it's a week and a day since you went into a coma.'

'Wow ... longer than I thought. Did I miss anything at school?'

'Nah, not really. I've nearly finished our project.'

'Sorry. I should've been there to help.'

'Don't worry. You just concentrate on getting better, okay?' I nod. It feels weird to have an actual conversation with Eli. Normally we are fighting or he is mocking me.

'The police haven't asked me about Craig ...' Eli begins. 'What do I tell them?'

Between the coma and my recovery, I've hardly thought about Craig. 'I don't know. I want to snitch, but it doesn't feel right. Something's stopping me ...'

'Like a stone's been rammed down your throat?' he finishes.

'Exactly. I don't want to tell them. They'll find out anyway, right?' *The police didn't work out what I did back in Leeds, so what if they can't put the pieces together in this puzzle?*

'No ... no, it doesn't feel right. If it comes to it, I'll tell them, ok? You shouldn't have to go through the pain. Leave it to me, all right?'

I nod. 'Thank you, Eli. You're the reason I'm here right now.' Tears prickle my eyes; the realisation that I could've been in my grave right now scares me.

Despite my best efforts to hold back my emotions, it all comes flooding out. Eli slides onto the bed next to me, holding me tight, gently stroking my hair. 'It's okay. Let it all out.'

Just as all my worries disappear, I become conscious of the situation. I pull away from him, gazing into his dark blue eyes. 'Eli. Why are you being so nice to me?'

He furrows his brow. 'Ivy, are you serious? You've been stabbed and then fell into a coma for a week. The least I can do is to let you cry into my shirt.'

'Awww, you're a sweetheart, aren't ya?' I whisper into his top.

'Don't push your luck. I can still be my normal devilish self if I want to,' he mutters, but there isn't a single menacing tone in his voice. We sit there for a while, completely still. My head moves up and down with the movements of Eli's chest.

'I brought the coffees you asked for ... *What the hell are you doing?*' a voice barks from the door. My eyes dart towards the voice, and standing there is Haila.

'Haila, I swear it isn't what it looks like …' Eli protests, but she completely dismisses him. Dropping the coffees on the floor, she turns and races off. Without hesitating, Eli darts after his girlfriend, calling her name down the corridor. Just like that, I was alone again. The overwhelming fear of being alone comes flooding over me. Alarming screams come flying out of my mouth before I can hold back. Nurse Appleton comes running in.

'Hey hey hey. Shhhh. It's okay, sweet pea,' she coos, holding my hand. 'Deep breaths, darling. It's okay.' My breathing begins to return to normal. 'Breathe with me. Inhale … and exhale. Inhale … and exhale. Good girl.' Within minutes I'm fully calm again.

'Thank you, Nurse Appleton.'

'Please, you're making me feel old. Call me Hannah.'

'Can I ask you something?'

'Sure.'

'How did it happen?'

She breathes a deep sigh. 'It's hard to explain, but the main cause was severe blood loss.'

'B-but I'm okay now, right?'

Nurse Appleton smiles. 'You'll have to stay here for a while, and it'll take a while to adjust to normal life, but you'll be up and about in no time.' She pauses and gazes at me, a pleased look coming across her face. 'You're really lucky, y'know.'

I giggle. 'I'm not sure "lucky" is the word that I'd use.'

'What I mean is you're recovering quickly. Some wake up from a coma unable to talk—eat, even. They have to start everything again, as if they are infants taking their first steps. Not you, though; you have been awake for a couple of hours, and already I can tell you'll be out of here in a week or so.'

We continue to chat for a couple of minutes, and I ask her everything except for how the police are dealing with this. I want to know, but at the same time I really don't. I guess I'm too scared to face the truth. What if they can't trace it back to Craig? I don't have the guts to turn him in and I'd feel guilty making Eli do it.

A rush of wind gushes into the room and Tyler charges in, flinging his arms round me. He starts bawling his eyes out. I don't think I've seen Tyler cry like this in years, and it feels strange.

'Oh, Petal. I've missed you so much!' He holds me so tightly I feel I'm in danger of suffocation. His phone chimes, so he gets it out and reads the text.

'The babysitter needs me at home. Sorry, Ivy. I'll be back tomorrow, okay?' He promises. I nod, a smile stretching from ear to ear.

'I'll look after her,' Nurse Appleton promises. Feeling reassured, my brother leaves, giving me a final wave.

After a while, Eli appears in the doorway.

'I couldn't catch Haila. She ran to her car, and boom, she's gone,' he mumbles. For some reason Eli doesn't seem at all that bothered that he has upset Haila. Mind you, if Haila were my girlfriend, I wouldn't care either, but that's beside the point.

'My mum is waiting outside for me, but I'll be back tomorrow, I swear.'

'You don't have to come visit me.'

'I know I don't. But I want to.' We smile at each other and hold our gaze for a couple of seconds while Hannah watches, smiling like a Cheshire cat.

'Awww, you two are adorable!' she coos.

'We aren't together, Hannah,' I say, smiling.

'I know,' she says. Eli waves me goodbye and leaves the room.

'Want me to go get your mum? I'm guessing she wants to spend some time with you,' Hannah suggests. She pours water into a glass and puts it on my bedside table.

'Actually, I'm pretty tired. Don't suppose you could get her in the morning, when I have more energy?'

She nods. 'Sure, doll.' She then wheels a trolley out of the room and down the corridor, making sure to keep the door open for me. I feel too enclosed when the door is shut, as though I'm all alone. Being alone brings back the haunting memories of Saturday night: the knife, the blood, and, most importantly, my helplessness. I was completely defenceless. I know it's mad, but I feel as though if the door is shut, Craig might pop out from behind the wall and attack me and no one will hear me scream. This time Eli won't be there to save me.

Did you know that the average person spends one third of their life sleeping? Considering I've spent the last week snoozing, I guess I'm no longer the average person. Mind you, Mum has always told me that I'm special, and I guess she's right. In just a year I've committed a spine-chilling yet completely secret crime, read over two hundred books, been bullied, been stabbed, and gone into a coma. Well, believe it or not, I like being different. I don't wanna be just another human who is born, goes to school, gets an average job, and dies; I want to make something of my life.

23

Eli

I don't think I've ever been so happy in my entire life as I am on this Saturday morning. Knowing that Ivy is awake and doing well has lifted a huge weight off my shoulders. Finally I feel like I can breathe again. Plus Grandma is making *samboosa* for the whole family, so it looks like my life is nearing perfection at the moment. I went to go and see Ivy yesterday, and she seems to be getting better. She is quite irritable, but according to the nurses, that is a side effect of a coma. I've decided to try to see her every day, just to check up on her. Mum insists on bringing Ivy some of her homemade brownies, but I doubt Ivy will be able to eat much.

Mum and I hop into her small Citroën four-by-four and drive to the hospital. She puts on *BBC Arabic Radio* and hums along to the music.

On a normal day, I'd be singing along with her, but I am just too focused on seeing Ivy.

Yes, I saw her yesterday, but a new wave of excitement is cruising through my body and making me feel nervous at the same time.

24

Ivy

'Ivy, have you had a glass of water yet?' Mum asks. She is staring right at me, her eyes riddled with fear.

'Mum, I've only just woken up! Give me a chance!' I protest. Her right eye twitches. 'Sorry. I'll have some now, okay?'

She nods, her normal smile returning to her face. 'It's important for you to keep hydrated,' she reminds me for the hundredth time.

I reach over to my table and take the cup. I down it in one go.

'Careful! You might choke yourself!' Mum squeals. She takes the cup and puts it back on the table. I roll my eyes. To take my mind off things, I pick up my *National Geographic* magazine and start flipping through the pages. Mum flops onto a sofa and starts scrolling through Facebook—or, as I like to call it, 'Instagram: Dinosaur Edition.'

Someone knocks on the door. I look up from my magazine and standing there, a pile of books in his hands, is Mr Kilt.

'Hi sir …? What are you doing here?' I say, masking a smile. It's not exactly normal to enjoy the company of a teacher, so I have to pretend I loathe him.

'What she means is, come on in!' Mum says, smiling at him and death-staring me. 'I'll leave you two to it.' She walks out, closing the door behind her. He chuckles and sits where Mum had sat.

'How're you doing, kiddo?' he says, leaning back in the couch. Mr Kilt is wearing a flannel check shirt and black jeans, completed with chunky boots. I'm not sure if he intended to but he looks like a lumberjack. I hate to say it, but his fashion sense isn't the worst I've ever seen, and I can't help but study it intently. He watches me with a confused expression.

'Ivy! Hello?' he waves his hand in front of my face.

'Huh? Oh yeah, I'm good.'

He smirks. 'I missed our arguments these past weeks,' he jokes. I smile and shift about awkwardly. I don't know what to do with my hands, so I just shove them under my sheets.

'I'm sure school was very quiet without me,' I say.

He nods. 'Sure was.'

We sit in silence.

'So did you come just to check on me or ...'

'Oh yes. I came to bring you some homework. Can't be having a bright spark like you missing out on schoolwork now, can we? Oi, don't you roll your eyes at me!' he warns.

'Don't you point your finger at me!' I argue back. He grins and puts a pile of books on my bedside table.

'I've been told by Mr Cabello that you need to read chapters one to twelve in the textbook and then write an essay on something called the demonisation of women in the media,' he say as he reads a crumpled piece of paper.

'Fantastic. I thought being in a coma would get me outta schoolwork,' I grumble. Kilt smiles.

'If you need to talk, just ring this number,' he says, passing me a card with a phone number on it. 'And I'll come here as soon as I can, okay? I can help with both schoolwork and emotional stuff.'

I bob my head in agreement. 'How can you help me with schoolwork? What would you know about Pythagoras' theorem?'

'Excuse you! I may not seem the brightest to you, but I'm a mean mathematician!' I chuckle and agree. 'Good. Want anything from the vending machine?' he offers.

'A Twix would be nice.'

'Coming right up!' he says, doing a weird air punch. As he goes to leave, Eli walks in.

'Oh hi, Mr Kilt,' Eli says, a dumbfounded look on his face.

'Hey Eli,' Mr Kilt says, continuing on his way out.

Eli's forehead crinkles—a classic way of Eli showing he is confused. 'What's he doin' here?' he asks, chucking me a box of brownies. I whip my hands out quickly enough to catch them before they whack me in the face.

'Ooo, thanks! He came to give me classwork.'

Eli laughs. 'Wow, what a jerk,' he mumbles. He perches on the end of my bed.

'Mr Kilt isn't actually that bad,' I argue.

Eli bugs out, and his mouth hangs open. 'You've got a crush on him! You like Mr Kilt!' he teases.

'I do not!' I lob the *National Geographic* magazine at him. He catches it and chuckles.

'How are you feeling today?' Eli asks. His voice lowers slightly.

'I'm feeling better. Still a bit tired though.' He nods, and I can tell he understands.

'Could you hear us … when you were in a coma?'

'Yeah. I could hear everything. I heard you and my brother …' My voice cracks.

'Hey, it's okay. We can talk about this another time, when you are feeling stronger.'

'Thanks.' I whisper. Eli pulls me into a gentle hug.

'Everything will be okay,' he murmurs. In the spur of the moment, he kisses my hair. We both freeze, and Eli pulls away from me.

'I'm sorry … I don't know why I did that …'

'No, it's okay,' I whisper.

His face softens. It's nice to have Eli here with me, as Tyler hasn't been with me much. I saw him for all of about ten seconds before he had to go back home. I do feel bad for him, as he is always having to play super dad. It must be so tiring. Eli slides under the covers next to me. I lay my head on his chest, and we watch *Gogglebox* on my medium-sized TV. Eli is very concentrated on the show, laughing and commenting along, but I can't help but glance at him every once in a while. I've never noticed his small dimples before, or the small slit in his left eyebrow.

Mr Kilt returns bearing a Twix.

'Here you go, kid.'

'Cheers, Mr Kilt,' I say before taking a bite out of the biscuity goodness.

'I'd best get home and take my daughter to ballet class,' he says with a sigh.

'You've got a kid?' Eli asks, clearly very shocked.

'Two, actually,' Kilt corrects. 'You got a problem with that, Mr Bishara?' Kilt says, knitting his brows.

'No, no. Just weird to imagine you with kids,' Eli replies.

'I work at a school, Eli. Kids are my middle name.'

'That's a weird middle name,' Eli jeers and he blocks the pillow that Mr Kilt throws at him with his hand. Mr Kilt walks out, and passing him is a tall man in a high-vis jacket. He wears a long black hat with a police symbol on the front.

'Mr Bishara?'

'Yes sir,' Eli says, hopping off the bed.

'I need you to come down to the station with a responsible adult,' the policeman says in an emotionless tone. 'We have some questions to ask you regarding the attack on Miss Ivy Towers on Saturday the fifteenth of September.'

'Sure thing. My mum's in the cafe.' Eli follows the constable towards the cafeteria, waving to me through the window as he leaves. We've talked about what to say to the police, but I'm still a nervous wreck. *What if he crumbles under pressure or says the wrong thing?* This could all go horribly wrong, and there's nothing I can do to stop it.

Several hours pass, but Eli doesn't return. Both hands on my cheap watch seem to be moving slower and slower as time goes by. Impatience has always been a bad trait of mine, and it's really showing now. Nurses come in and out to check on me, but I just nod and shake my head to all of their standardised questions. 'Are you feeling okay? Any pain in the stomach? Have you drunk enough water?' Blah blah blah! Would it kill them to leave me alone for a minute, or is that too much to ask? After two straight hours of fixating my eyes on the doorway, a text chime saves me from insanity. Martha has written,

> **Heya! I'm coming to see you. I should probably ask if you're feeling up for a visit, but who cares, I'm coming either way! See ya in a tick xxx**

A smile resembling that of a drunk old lady spreads across my scarred face. Martha couldn't have planned her visit for a better time. Within literally minutes of her notification, my friend comes bounding down the corridor like a lively Dalmatian. Her curly hair bounces around as she parades towards me.

She runs through the doorway and flings her arms around my shoulders. The pain this hug is presenting is unbearable, but I want to share this moment with my best friend. She pulls away from me and looks at me happily.

Velvet lipstick has been applied, quite untidily, on her lips, and her light brown hair has been heated into tight curls.

'Since when were you the bouncy, girly type?' I ask, beaming a helpless smile. Martha blows a curl out of her eyes.

'Never. I just thought I'd … y'know, dress up for ya! It's not every day you get to see your best friend for the first time since she went into a coma!' she replies smoothly, flopping onto the end of my bed and chucking her hot pink purse on the floor.

'Isn't it just freezing out there!' she moans, blowing warm air into her cupped hands.

I shrug. 'Dunno. I haven't been outside in … let's see here … a whole week,' I say, sarcastically but softly.

Martha sighs. 'Of course … yeah, uhm … sorry 'bout that. I forgot you hadn't—'

'Nah, don't sweat it. Now c'mon, gimme all the gossip. Have you got yourself a cute boy?' I ask, breaking the invisible ice. Martha sits up carefully. She gently shakes her head and stares at her shoes. *Oh great, now I've upset her.* I know she must've been feeling kind of lonely since I fell into my sleeping beauty slumber. This whole situation makes me realise just how many lives I've made ten times more difficult. If there was an award for most lives messed up, I'd get the gold award for sure. I mean there's my family, Martha, and the Wilson family. I have well and truly ruined everything for the latter.

'Sorry. Sore topic?' I suggest. Martha looks away, which confirms my guess to be correct.

'Aww, come 'ere, Martha,' I say with open arms. She slides over to me, and I try my best to wrap my arms around my friend. All the tubes and needles sorta get in the way, but it's the best I can do. We sit there for a while until Martha slides out of my grasp and fixes a look into my eyes.

'I love you, Martha,' I whisper. Her face softens, and her lips part slightly. Martha leans in and goes to kiss me. Instead of pulling away, which would've been the smart decision, I just freeze and let her peck my lips softly. *What the hell?* Gently, but firmly, I push her away from me.

'Martha ... what are you doin ... I ... I don't know what to ...'

Her eyes widen as she realises how wrongly she interpreted what I said. 'I thought you meant love like ... like *love*, not ...' Her voice trails off. *If only I were prepared for this situation, but I guess there's no book entitled* What to Do If Your Best Friend Tries to Snog You. Both of us wait for the other to say something but, neither of us knows exactly what to do. Martha's eyes watch me worriedly, waiting for my reaction.

'I'm so sorry ...' she eventually says, her voice shaking.

'Hey, don't be sorry. You can't help who you fall for ... So what are you?' *Did I seriously just say 'what are you?' If anyone can offer me tuition on social interaction, I'd be very grateful.*

'I'm bisexual, Ivy,' Martha says, completely avoiding eye contact, as if she's embarrassed.

'Why didn't you tell me?' I ask, a touch of hurt creeping into my voice. To be honest, I am in no place to judge Martha for keeping secrets from me. I have one massive secret that she will probably never know.

'I was scared you'd think I'm, I dunno, weird or somethin'. I'd hate for you to think of me differently,' she says defensively.

'What do you think I am, a dinosaur? Homophobia is soooo twentieth century,' I say in a mocking tone as I flick my wrist.

She giggles. 'If this was a book, you'd most definitely be the protagonist, and I'd end up ...'—she grimaces—'the gay best friend.'

I laugh. 'Ugh, that stereotype is also for the dinosaurs. You, my friend, are Martha Jones—the most beautiful, unique, and talented person I have ever come across.'

Martha beams a smile and goes to pick up her little handbag. 'I'd best head off. Kirk will be wondering where I am.' We both know that's a lie, considering Kirk doesn't give two hoots about what Martha is doing unless she's ruining his pristine reputation. I don't question her, though, because it's obvious how uncomfortable she feels. Before Martha leaves the room, she turns to me.

'Could you not tell Kirk—or anyone else, for that matter? You're kinda the first person ever that I have told, and I don't think Kirk accepts ... gayness.'

I nod, smiling sympathetically. She thanks me and makes her way to Reception. Poor kid. It must be so hard not having anyone for support. I'm so lucky to have my family and Eli by my side. Remind me to never take that privilege for granted.

— 25

Eli

This whole interrogation scenario seems quite phoney. These cops have obviously been watching too much *CSI*. A blindingly bright lamp has been shone on my face, and a female police officer sits opposite me, her elbows resting on the table. She has a stern look on her face, though I can tell she is enjoying the enforced melodrama.

The officer speaks into a small device. 'Interview with Mr Eli Bishara at 12.48 p.m. Present are PC Wickers, Constable Wynne, and mother of Eli, Mrs Deena Bishara. Now, Eli, do you understand that anything you do say may be given in evidence?'

'Why are you treating me like a criminal?'

Mum nudges me under the table and whispers, 'Just answer her, Eli.'

'All right, fine. I understand.'

'Good.' She scribbles down notes in her little notepad. 'We have only one question for you, and it is very simple. Please answer with either yes or no. Follow-up questions may proceed. Do you understand?'

'Yep,' I say.

She glares at me. 'You must respond with yes or no,' she says in such a robotic voice that I want to pour sand inside her to see if it causes a malfunction.

'Okay, okay. Yes.'

'Eli Bishara, do you know who stabbed Ivy Towers on Saturday fifteenth September 2018?' The whole journey in the police car had been leading up to this moment. I'd rehearsed the words over and over in my mind. No matter whether Craig tells the school I am a bully or drags me into the equation, I want to say, 'Yes. It was Craig Wilson.' I want to be the hero. But I can't. It really is like having a stone rammed down your throat. I choke upon my words and eventually spew out, 'No. No, I don't know.' PC Wickers looks over to her colleague, who appears to be resting against the wall in the corner. They exchange a look and face back to me. Neither of them is buying it.

'Eli, you do understand that keeping information from the police is perverting the course of justice and is, therefore, a criminal offence?' I nod. She glares at me again.

'Yes!' I yell. 'Shall I say it louder for the people at the back? I don't know, okay! Is that clear enough for you?' I stand up, but Mum holds on to my arm.

'Please, Habibi, calm down.' She turns to PC Wickers. 'Can't you see the poor boy is distressed?' Mum hisses. 'My baby has said he doesn't know anything, so why can't you just leave him alone? What is wrong with you people?' She rises from her chair.

'Mrs Bishara, you can't just—'

'I will do what I want when I want, thank you very much. We'll be leaving now.' By now I'm crying, but my tears are faint. I don't like to show emotion in public. We must be breaking a law by walking out on this interview, but the police can tell that Mum is having none of it. Mum holds me tight and walks me to the car park, where Dad meets us. We drive home in utter silence; Mum doesn't even put the radio on. Occasionally I let out an awkward sniff. All that crying has made me all clogged up, which is one of the most awful feelings ever.

When we arrive home, Mum ensures I'm straight to bed with a hot chocolate and a good series to watch. On a normal Saturday at 2.30 p.m., I'd be out playing basketball with Craig or making table decorations with Haila. But not today. Today is about mourning—not for the death of a living person, but for the life I used to have. For me and Craig's friendship. For Ivy's happiness. It's all dead now, and unless reincarnation really does exist, I'm never going to see them again.

Bzzzz bzzzz. My phone vibrates. There is a text from Ivy:

Hi. How'd it go?

I know leaving someone on 'read' is a really low blow, but how do I answer that? 'Oh yeh, it went fantastic! I promised I'd bring you justice but bottled it at the end! Gtg and dig myself a hole to live in for all eternity! Cya xxx.' Instead of straight-up lying to her face, I reply vaguely:

Wasn't too bad. I'll come visit you tomorrow to sort everything out, all right?

Technically speaking, it *wasn't* too bad. I had found it rather entertaining until PC Pigtails started getting all gobby.

I roll onto my side and pull out the picture from underneath my pillow. I clutch Khalid close to me, breathing in the musky scent of the old polaroid photograph. Some believe in destiny, and some believe in fate, but I don't. I think the world snatched my brother away from me way too early. He deserved better. Tears splatter on the photo, but luckily they run straight off it instead of ruining the image. It's kinda ironic, really; it represents Khalid. No threat or upset could ever get him down. Just as a raincoat is waterproof, my brother was negative-proof, no matter what life decided to throw at him. My brother was always smiling, and I'll forever love him for that. I'm sure he's still smiling now, watching me from heaven. It makes me sick to think of all the things I've done since he parted. He must be so ashamed. The only time that I'm fully at peace with myself is when I'm asleep, so, photo in hand, I press my eyes together.

I don't want to try too hard to sleep, because the harder I try, the more difficult it is. Memories of Khalid flood through my brain and fill me with warmth. I can almost feel his presence. It's as if he's right next to me, holding me.

❦

'But Eli, I don't like peas!' Archie whines. I don't know why I bother with these kids sometimes. They've started to feel like a second family to me, but that doesn't mean life is all fluffy bunny land. Every single one of these kids, particularly Archie, is pushing me to my limits. It's only a matter of time before I crack.

'You liked peas yesterday! Just eat 'em and you can have some cake after. Deal?' I am quite proud of my negotiating skills, but Archie doesn't seem to share my opinion. He shoves the plate off of the table and sends it crashing to the floor.

'For fudge's sake, Archie!' I yell, except I don't say 'fudge'. All of the kids let out a simultaneous gasp.

'Don't tell me Tyler, Ivy, and your mum have never sworn in front of you,' I moan.

'Actually they have. That's why we have this.' Milly climbs off her seat and walks over to the counter, picking up a container with the words 'swear jar' on the front. How niche can you get?

'All right, fine.' I take a pound from my pocket and drop it in the jar. 'Happy now?' I ask Milly. She smiles and puts the jar down.

Archie continues to have a hissy fit on the floor, thrashing his limbs in all directions and screaming profanities. I'm partially shocked at his language, but not completely, considering how worked up I've seen the kid get before. I make an attempt at picking him up, but the small child swings at me with his fist.

'Will you pack it in!' I shout. Deciding that I'm not going to be beaten by a two-year-old, I roll up my sleeves and dive into what is possibly one of the most dangerous fights in my life. Forget fighting druggies or year-twelves; an angry child is one of the most ferocious people you'll ever come across.

Despite Archie throwing himself around on the floor, I manage to grab his arms and pin them above his head. I then sit lightly on his legs so he can't move, without snapping the kid's limbs in half.

'I said pack it in.' My breathing is incredibly heavy from our combat. Archie tries to free himself, but I have him held tight. He launches a huge spit ball at me, which plants right between my eyes. Anger boils through me, but I push it away. I want to call Tyler, but I can't, seeing as he is visiting Ivy. I'd hate to ruin the small amount of quality time they get together. With six little kids watching our little episode, I haul Archie off the floor and carry him up the stairs. He kicks around, which, I have to admit, hurts like hell, but I just quicken my pace. I throw him gently onto his bed and say in a low tone, 'Just stay here and calm down please.' My legs carry me out of the room before the little monster can chase me down. I close the door behind me and hear the thrashing of fists against it.

When I return to the kitchen, all the kids are obediently munching on their peas, as if they are scared of me. Something tells me that I deserve a break, so after dinner I gather the kids into the living room to watch a show of my choice. Every single one of them seems unimpressed, but I couldn't care less. My favourite character starts screaming quite explicit words, but instead of grabbing their beloved swear jar, they all giggle along.

26

Ivy

Whoever invented circle theorems has some serious explaining to do. What possessed them to create something so incredibly boring? Lucky for me, Mr Conrow has ensured that I have enough circle theorem work to have the whole of England busy. If I were a teacher, I'd take pity on a girl who'd just come out of a coma, but not my teachers! No, they've ensured that my life continues to be a living hell. When I told my mum all this, she told me I was 'overreacting', which is probably true, but I take offence when it comes from my own mother's lips.

Mind you, Mr Kilt is the only teacher who knows why I went into a coma. None of the others are aware that I was attacked, mainly because they all have mahoosive gobs, and God knows I don't need that kind of attention when I return to school. That's another thing about being a default; they all want attention and fame. I don't want soppy 'get well soon' cards and special treatment from teachers. I just want to immerse myself back into my school life and continue as normal. My GCSEs won't pass themselves.

Just as my mind finally starts to settle itself into the wonderful world of circumferences, I hear a bunch of giggling and squealing approaching my room. *It can't be!*

'Ivy!' Cole squeals as he runs over to me. I swivel round in my chair and let him run into my open arms. Tears of joy and sheer emotion spill out of my eyes. All of my siblings come running in and fling themselves on me.

'Careful, guys! She's still delicate!' Tyler says behind them. My streams of tears turn into rivers. My heart has never felt so warm. Since I've woken up, I've felt slightly empty, as if a part of me is missing. But now my brothers and sisters are here, I've never felt so alive.

All seven of them bound around the room like puppies and occasionally come over to me to give me another heartfelt hug. I wince when Coco hugs me too tightly and presses against one of my stab wounds, but I hold back my cries. This moment is too delicate to ruin. Tyler sits on the bed, Eva in his arms. She's fast asleep despite all the racket.

'This kid could sleep through a hurricane,' Tyler says quietly, smiling down at our baby sister. She's wearing a pink onesie and a little lilac floral headband. She has her minuscule thumb planted in her mouth and is sniffling quietly in her sleep. I wish I could be as sweet as Eva. It's hard to believe that I was like her once. Now, I'm just a dodgy teenager with overwhelming hormones and enough issues to distribute them equally between every person on the earth.

'How you feelin' then, my little Petal?' Tyler coos playfully. I beam a cheesy smile and reply, 'I'm feeling better, and Nurse Appleton thinks I'll be out in a couple days. I mean, thank God! This place stinks to high heavens of disinfectant and hospital food.' He chuckles. 'Nice to see you can stand up now.' He points to me sitting at my desk on the opposite side of the room to my hospital bed.

'Yeah, I'm getting there. It still feels a bit painful. It's like when you sit on your legs for an hour then try to walk.'

Tyler shudders. 'I hate that feeling.' Something doesn't feel quite right. The atmosphere is slightly off, but I can't work out why that is. My eyes scan the room until I realise what's unsettling me.

'Tyler, where's Mum?' He moves his eyes to look away from me. My brother always does this when he's about to lie to me, as if he can't bear to not tell me the truth. He goes to open his mouth, but I interrupt, 'Please. I don't want a lie. Where is she?'

'Ivy, I ...'

'Tyler ... where is Mum?' I start to shake again. My body can sense the bad news that is coming my way. After taking a deep breath, Tyler turns to me and says, 'While you've been away, she's been drinking ... a lot. When you woke up, her drinking became less frequent but ... but last night she came home heavily drunk, and this morning she still wasn't in a fit state to see you, so I told her not to bother. I was really angry, Ivy ... I may have said things I didn't mean.' A single tear falls from his right eye and lands on Eva's onesie. 'I'm sorry,' he whispers. I pull myself up out of the chair and slowly hobble over to him using my royal blue Zimmer frame.

'Tyler, you have nothing to be sorry for. If anything, Mum is the one who should be here to apologise. You shouldn't be picking up the pieces for her.' I smooth down his dark brown hair and pull him into me. He rests his head in the cup of my shoulder. We sit like this for a long time until the little ones grow restless. By the time they decide to leave, May and Milly have used my homework as their own canvas. Instead of being angry, I simply smile because they've drawn a picture of our whole family in front of our old house. I hug them all, and we say our goodbyes. Tyler escorts them out of the hospital, and I wave to them until they are no longer in view.

I lie in bed, looking over the picture and caressing it with my thumb. A sinking feeling lies in the pit of my stomach when I study the picture closer. We all have big, cheesy grins, and we are all holding flowers. But on closer inspection, I realise that Mum isn't holding a bunch of bright red roses; she's holding a beer bottle. Aggression overtakes me; I shred the picture until it is impossible to piece it back together. A ginormous scream flies out of my mouth as I fling the confetti into the air. I cry wails of emotion until my throat hurts. Mr Kilt comes running into my room.

'Hey hey hey! What's up, Ivy?' He slides onto the bed and holds me close. I sniffle into his black blazer. I whisper to him that I just feel angry about life. There's no way in hell I'm opening up to him—not yet. I don't let people into my life that easily, because it's easy for them to walk into my life, but it's just as easy to walk out. Mr Kilt tells me everything will be okay and that I'll be out soon, but it isn't true. I will be out of hospital soon, but I'll never escape this life. The only way to get out is death.

I eventually manage to regain enough composure to speak properly. He continues to hold me in his lanky arms. My eyes look up to him, and I mutter between sniffles, 'I thought teachers weren't allowed to make physical contact with students unless it was necessary.' Mr Kilt smiles to himself and replies, 'Well, this is pretty necessary, don't ya think?' I don't have the brain power to form a sarky comment, so I simply sigh and close my eyes. His cologne smells of fresh ocean breeze and makes the hairs on my arms stand up. *Finally, an aftershave that doesn't stink of warm, cheap shower gel and toothpaste mixed together.*

'Why are you here so late?' I ask, lifting my head to stare up at him. When he smiles, it ever defines the weird wrinkles that adults always have on their foreheads.

'I came to say goodnight to you. Must be pretty lonely around here.' I nod. 'Now, are you sure there is nothing else going on? Nothing I can help with?'

A small chuckle escapes my lips. 'Well, if you could do my English essay, that would be fabulous, but apart from that, no, nothing really,' I lie profusely.

'Well, in that case, goodnight, Ivy.' He rises from the bed and makes his way out.

'Night, sir,' I call after him.

⁂

'Do you want the good news or the bad news?' Nurse Appleton asks me two days later, sitting beside me. Optimism has always seemed to be a great flaw to me, so I reply, 'The bad news, please.'

Hannah shakes her head at me and laughs. 'Well, I'm afraid you won't be able to see me anymore.' She frowns and looks at her feet.

Why does my life have to keep getting worse by the minute? Hannah is one of the best things that happened to me since I awoke, and now she's being taken away from me!

'You're leaving? Did they sack you? You don't deserve this! You're the best nurse ever! How could they do this—'

She holds her hand out for me to stop before I become even more irate. 'Ivy, dear, you won't be able to see me anymore because you are being discharged!' she squeals. My eyes temporarily bug out, and I fling my arms around Hannah, enveloping her in a hug. I attempt to contain my excitement, but muffled screams fly out of my mouth as my head nestles in her T-shirt. Hannah tells me that I can leave any time today and goes off to get my discharge papers prepared. A whole congregation of people come into the room, including Tyler, to prepare for my departure. I spring out of bed and hobble over to my big brother, my wounds giving me a painful reminder that I'm still as fragile as a baby. Various staff members strip my plain white bed and straighten up the room, readying it for the next unlucky victim to stay here. We collect my few possessions and put them in my suitcase.

Tyler takes my suitcase for me, and I slowly pace behind him. Despite my physiotherapy, I'm still incredibly slow at walking. Anyway, I'm exempt from tedious PE lessons for at least a couple of months. I give Hannah one last hug, and she whispers to me, 'Good luck, darling. I'm proud of you.' Tyler thanks Hannah and helps me to the car. When we are safely in the vehicle, Tyler starts the engine and says to me, 'Are you ready, Petal?'

'Ready as I'll ever be!' I say, beaming. We zoom out of the car park and drive away from my nightmare. *Goodbye hospital, hello future.*

27

Eli

As soon as I learned of Ivy's homecoming, Mum drove me straight over to her house. I am carrying a warm dish of samosas, my life flashing before my eyes. Though Mum and Dad have showed acceptance towards my new-found friendship with Ivy, I think they may feel slight resentment towards her. My parents don't want anything to get in the way of my wedding, and I guess they see Ivy as a potential marriage barrier. But they are wrong. Ivy doesn't attract me in the slightest, so they have absolutely nothing to worry about. Haila is the only one for me.

Mum doesn't even get out of the car but waves me off as I make my way to Ivy's front door. When I knock, I hear a shout from a child telling Tyler that someone is at the door. Tyler answers and, with a warm smile stretched on his lips, welcomes me inside. As I walk in, I place the dish on the kitchen table.

Ivy is lying across the couch, watching some animated kids' film with a toddler, but she flies off the sofa when she sees me. We exchange a hug, and she invites me to go to her room, where there are fewer people. I help her get up the stairs, which takes a while, but I don't mind.

'Glad to be home then?'

Ivy nods happily. 'You bet I am. Being in hospital was so boring I thought I was gonna lose my marbles!' she exclaims. In all honesty, I don't know if I could've faced being in that hospital for so long. There isn't much to do there, and keeping someone as intelligent as Ivy cooped up in there seems rather torturous. She nervously bites at her lip and stares through the murky window.

'You wanna ask something, don't you?' I deduce. I hold hands with

Ivy, which takes her by surprise. She freezes, turns to face me, and releases a sigh.

'Yeah … I just want to know what you told the police. I'm sure you were really brave.' She couldn't be more wrong if she tried. I was the polar opposite of brave. In fact, I was so cowardly that even a baby would've been bolder than me. Ivy put her trust in me, and I failed her. Ivy is looking at me worriedly.

'I'm sorry … I just couldn't do it.' She tries her best not to look disappointed by plastering on a sympathetic smile, but I can see past her expression. 'I've really messed this up, haven't I?' I murmur.

'No, you haven't. I shouldn't have put all that pressure on you. The police will work it out in the end.' She pulls me into a tight hug that makes me feel safe and secure. Luckily I remembered to bring my laptop so we can continue with our project. As we complete our slide show, I can't help but steal furtive glances at Ivy. She's casually bobbing her head along to her playlist and singing quietly to herself. For the first time in a while, Ivy is wearing bold makeup, complete with winged eyeliner and bright red lipstick. A particularly upbeat song starts playing through her speakers. Ivy jumps up and uses an aerosol deodorant container as a microphone. The song has her up on her feet, dancing around the small, dark purple room. All I can do is laugh, as I'm feeling too awkward to join in.

'C'mon! Dance with me!' she giggles, taking my hands and making me stand up. Ivy eventually gets me to loosen up and start dancing and by the time the song has ended, I feel free from all my worries. I've never felt so stress-free in my life. Whilst manically dancing, we trip on each other's feet and crash to the ground, cackling with laughter. The door creaks open, and a little girl stares down at us.

She has her hair in two French plaits, and she is sporting an autumn-themed floral dress.

'Dinner's ready!' Coco chimes. I help Ivy to her feet, and we make our way downstairs.

'This is really nice, Miss Towers. Secret recipe?' I say in an attempt at making conversation. Yes, I know I'm rubbish at it. Miss Towers doesn't even look up at me. She simply grumbles something along the lines of 'Thanks, kid, but they are fish fingers. It ain't rocket science' under her breath and continues to stab at her fish with a fork. Ivy stares daggers at her mother, clearly very embarrassed.

'Mum, don't be so rude,' she hisses. No response. We eat in an uncomfortable silence until Ivy's mum abruptly rises from her chair.

'I'm off out,' she mumbles. Mrs Towers grabs her coat and a vodka bottle and makes for the door.

'Where are you going?' Tyler asks, watching her worriedly.

'None of your business,' she says before slamming the door closed behind her. All the kids watch the door with fear in their eyes. I can only imagine how heartbreaking it must be to watch one's own mother drink herself to death.

'Bedtime story anyone?' I ask to break the tension. The kids' faces lighten up, and they all rush upstairs to Tyler's room, leaving their rather disgusting fish fingers at the table.

'You're like an angel sent from heaven, Eli. They'd never get that excited about my bedtime stories,' Tyler laughs, clearing the table and dumping the plates in the sink. Ivy tries to help him tidy up, but her brother insists that she rest. My cheeks go warm from both pride and awkwardness because I don't know how to react to compliments. Being closer to Ivy has made me lose my arrogant tendencies, and they've been replaced by a serious loss in social skills. I shut myself away from the outside world whilst Ivy was in hospital, so socialising feels new to me. Ivy lets out a deep sigh as she cradles Eva in her arms. Tears start welling up in her eyes, but I notice her blink them away before they have a chance to escape her eye sockets. I walk over and put my arm around her.

'It's okay, Ivy. She'll sort herself out in the end, all right?' She nods and presses herself to me, squashing Eva between us.

'I'd better go upstairs. Can't keep the little treasures waiting!' I say with a sigh and a smile.

When I reach Tyler's room, all the kids are snuggled up together, waiting for me. I take *The Crazy Parrot* from Coco and begin reading the strange story of a, probably stoned, parrot. They all giggle with delight at the right moments and make 'awwww' noises when something sweet happens. By the time I have finished reading, they are all yawning, so without hesitation, they make their way to bed.

My footsteps are light down the stairs to prevent the meltdown of seven kids at once. Tyler and Ivy are watching a romcom, so I slide on the couch to join them.

'Romance is dumb,' Ivy says after a rather passionate French kiss. Tyler and I give each other a look, and Tyler says, 'How is it dumb? Surely having someone you truly love is the best thing in the world.'

Ivy shakes her head and grimaces at yet another intimate love scene. 'Think about it. If you've had, like, four different relationships, you haven't truly loved a single one of them, because you break up. Once you break up, you move on to the next person like some game of touchy-feely leapfrog. It's all a waste of time,' she explains.

Tyler clenches his jaw. 'Ivy, my dear sister, it's all about trial and error. You should try it sometime,' he says in a posh voice. Ivy lobs the remote at Tyler and laughs. My laughter is faint and slightly fake because Tyler's point has made me come to a realisation. Haila is my first girlfriend ever, so what if she isn't the right one for me? This whole marriage could be a grave mistake.

Tyler chuckles to himself and says, 'If you're so against lovers, then what about you two? I haven't seen a boy–girl friendship this close before.' He motions to me and Ivy.

Ivy narrows her eyes and smoothly responds, 'Our friendship is strictly platonic. My attack made us realise just how important we are to each another, but that is all. You won't see me smooching him anytime soon.' Her comment makes me blush profusely.

'Plus there was you and Si—' Tyler says, but Ivy stops him with a stern glare. I wander whom he was referring to.

Another even more extended kissing scene appears on the screen. The man bites aggressively on his partner's neck whilst she makes rather disturbing noises.

'Oh my gawd, that's gotta be cannibalism!' Ivy says, blocking the screen with her hand. 'That's it! I'm off to bed!' She hoists herself up from the cream faux leather couch. 'Ty Ty, can you help me up the stairs?' she pleads, doing puppy-dog eyes.

'Your wish is my command,' he says, holding out his arm for his sister to take. I rise from the couch.

'I'd best get going anyways. See ya soon.' They both give me a wave as I leave via the front door.

When I leave the house, a cool evening breeze passes through my lungs and gives me a calming sensation.

Bzzzz Bzzzzz.

Mum has sent me a text:

Home time, darling. Early start tomorrow! Wedding rehearsals all day! xxx

Fabulous. Goodbye lay-ins, hello stress.

— 28 —

Ivy

Wednesday. It's time. From the moment I regained consciousness, a sickening feeling of worry has been lying inside of me. I knew I couldn't put it off forever, but now that the moment has come, I don't even know if I can face it. Today is the day I tell the police my recount of my attack.

Tyler decided—well, demanded—that he escort me to my interview. Holding a half-finished bottle of spirit, Mum offered to take me, but Tyler obviously wasn't going to let that happen. Mum looked quite upset when Tyler spouted off about how she's unfit to care for us, let alone drive a car with a fragile girl in it. His little outburst really dampened her spirit, no pun intended, and I was momentarily angry with Tyler—that is, until I realised that he is doing it to protect me.

Everything Tyler does is to protect our family.

Eli has volunteered himself for babysitting duty whilst Tyler and I go to the police station and Mum gets a taxi to another pub. Even though Mum couldn't come to the interview, she made sure I had a banana 'in case I was hungry'. With trembling fingers, Mum pressed the fruit into my hand and whispered, 'If the police hack you off, just lob this at their face. That'll shut 'em up,' which, I have to admit, did earn a smile from me. I didn't have the heart to tell her that I despise bananas and would prefer an apple, because I guess it's the thought that counts. Tyler gently bobs his head to the song playing through our retro radio, while I agonise in silence. *Who knows how this interview is going to go? Most likely I'll mess it up and spout out a load of rubbish.* Tyler's grip on the steering wheel tightens tremendously when he looks over to me and sees my face racked with worry.

'Ivy, please don't stress. Everything's fine …' He trails off when my expression goes from worry to pure anger.

'Fine? How is everything fine, Tyler? I've been stabbed, gone into a coma, and barely escaped death! I've got a huge secret that I'm desperate to tell someone, but you and Mum won't let me, 'cause it will "ruin my reputation" or something!' I use air quotes for effect. Tyler opens his mouth to talk, but I'm not finished yet. In fact, I'm only just getting started. 'And now I'm about to go into an interview that I will most likely screw up! What if I give them false information by accident? That's perverting the course of justice! I could go to jail!' My grip tightens around the banana so hard that its skin finally gives way and it splats pulp all over Tyler's car.

My brother bites at his lip to stop himself from exploding like the banana and says in almost a whisper, 'No one is going to jail.' I know what he means, but I hope Craig is going to jail. The rest of the journey consists of a cold silence and the small voice of Taylor Swift playing through the radio.

My eyes take in every detail of my surroundings. We are sitting in a waiting room with whitewashed grey walls, and there are supposedly reassuring posters strung up all over the place. It is evident that I am ten times more nervous than Tyler. My brother is slumped in his chair, scrolling aimlessly through social media, while I sit there twiddling my thumbs and fidgeting about in my chair like a five-year-old. A door slams in the distance, causing me to jump up, and my eyes dart towards the noise. Tyler sighs. 'Petal, calm down. Soon enough this will be over.' I hate my brother with a burning passion right now. You may say 'hate is a strong word', but that is exactly how I feel.

I hate him.

Why can't he see how much stress I'm under? I've spent lots of time preparing myself for this dreaded interview, and he has the guts to tell *me* to calm down? I'm sorry, but did he get stabbed and nearly die? I don't think so. My anger is swirling inside me, so I hiss, 'Don't you dare tell me to calm down, Tyler Alex Towers.'

My brother wrinkles his forehead and glares at me. 'Gawd, you're being so dramatic.' My pupils shoot fireballs at him, but before I can tear his head off his body, a woman in an all-black dress suit comes into the waiting room and says, 'Ivy Towers? We are ready for you.' Tyler mumbles something about how she is talking as if we're in a GP surgery, but I just elbow him and attempt a confident strut ahead of him. I don't know what's got into my brother, but it ends now—well, right after the interview.

We follow the lady into a back room, and she appoints us our seats. In all fairness, she looks pretty sweet, but I'm not gonna let looks fool me. Another officer is already is seated opposite us. He looks slightly less welcoming. The nice woman, Zoe Lyons—I read her name badge—explains the process of the interview and stresses the importance of telling the truth and all that malarky, but I already know this stuff. I've been googling everything there is to know about police interviews since the minute my eyes opened again. My head nods to show I understand, because I don't wanna seem rude by blurting out that I know all this already.

I am not surprised when another lady, dressed smartly, enters the room and sits by me. We are introduced: 'This is the duty solicitor that will protect your interests today.' She half bows to me and shakes my hand, and she then prepares to take notes.

'Are you ready to begin?' Zoe asks formally.

I nod, and she insists that I speak up out loud. I comply. 'Yes.' There is a small recording device at the end of the table. 'What's that for?' I ask, looking over at the gadget. There was nothing on the internet about this small piece of technology before me. She reads the exasperated expression on my face.

'Don't worry, dear; it's just so we can replay what you say and make sure we get every detail right.' I'm satisfied with her answer, so I duly shrink back into my chair. Zoe presses the button on the gadget and announces, 'Interview commences at 0945 hours.'

The officer, Officer Stevens, is the one asking the questions, while Zoe writes down all the notes. He leans his left elbow on the desk and begins to question me.

'Ivy, please would you explain how you came to be attacked?' he begins in a clear and very deep voice. My eyes dart over to Tyler. His angry, mopey face has disappeared and has been replaced by a reassuring smile. I take a deep breath before speaking.

'Well … I was at my friend's house doing homework—'

The officer interjects, asking, 'What was the homework about?'

I give him a confused look and hastily reply, 'Why does that matter?'

'We just need to know, Ivy,' the solicitor explains, a warm tone to her voice.

'All right ... well, it was about teen pregnancy.' Zoe scribbles notes down. Why does it matter what the homework was about? That has zilch to do with it!

'Eli and I had an argument, so I stormed out of the house—'

Again the infuriating Officer Stevens cuts me off. 'What were you arguing about?' Even Tyler scoffs at that question. The officer glares at my brother and says in an authoritative voice, 'Matey, I can have you escorted out of the building if you don't keep your trap shut, a'ight? Now pipe down.' The solicitor shakes her head at his bluntness but dismisses it all the same.

'We were arguing 'cause Eli criticised the issue of teen pregnancy but my parents had my brother as teens.' Tyler flinches at this, and Zoe has a face of pure sympathy. Mr Hard Man, on the other hand, keeps a completely straight face.

'After this argument, you felt angry at Eli Bishara, I assume?'

I reply with a blunt 'Yes.' Simple question. Simple answer.

'And I assume Eli Bishara felt angry at you too? So angry that he might've wanted to hurt you?'

I'm about to agree when I come to a realisation. 'Hold on a second! Are you counting Eli as a suspect?' I enquire, fury overtaking me.

'Miss Towers, it is simple procedure. He was with you on the night of the attack. We must treat everyone the same,' Officer Stevens replies in a single-toned voice. My impression of the cops had always been that they are smart and incredible people, but this interview is seriously impairing my judgement.

'It wasn't Eli. I know it wasn't.' Zoe and Officer Stevens share a look.

Stevens leans towards me. 'Well, if you don't know who did it, how can you be so sure that your beloved Eli didn't literally stab you in the back?'

That hurt. How dare he make puns like that in such a serious situation. I'd like to stab him in the back. I keep that thought in my head to avoid spending time in jail.

'Listen, PC Plum; if my sister says she thinks he didn't do it, why can't you just take her word for it?' Tyler asks, shooting bullets from his eyes and straight through Officer Stevens' robust face. Stevens is about to bite off my brother's head, but right at this moment I find myself doing something I never thought I'd do.

'I … I do know who did it …' I say firmly to break them up. Both Zoe's and Stevens' eyes dart to face me. Tyler looks equally as bemused. I hadn't told Tyler that I know who attacked me, because I knew he'd only go and beat Craig up, and Lord knows we don't need that added palaver on our hands.

Zoe has her pen on standby to write down the culprit's name. Officer Stevens is staring at me intensely, which only serves to increase my discomfort.

'Craig Wilson attacked me,' I say in a weak and heavily emotional squeak. Neither Stevens nor Zoe reacts in any way to my confession, presumably because they don't know who Craig is. Tyler, on the other hand, blows his top, ignoring the solicitor. We need to take a break, and Zoe calls a halt, stating, 'Interview suspended at 1038 hours.' She switches the recorder off.

Tyler leaps out of his chair and flies out of the room, slamming the door so hard that I'm surprised it's still on its hinges. I ask to go after my brother. Zoe and the solicitor give a sympathetic nod, whilst Officer Stevens huffs and puffs like a disorientated locomotive.

After hobbling out of the door, I search everywhere for Tyler, but he is nowhere in sight, so I opt for checking outside.

Eventually I spot him in the driver's seat of our car.

'I'm sorry I didn't tell you sooner … I just couldn't …' I say in a low tone, sliding into the front passenger seat and closing the door behind me.

'Scumbag,' Tyler snarls. 'Absolute scumbag.' I don't know if he's talking about me, or Craig, but I opt for the latter. Tyler's eyes look wild as he bows his head to contemplate in anger. I hold on to his arm, and he doesn't shrug me off. *Good, I now know he's not angry at me.*

'Are you angry at me, 'cause I would completely understand if you are.' My voice trails off as he pulls me into a tight hug. Warm tears fall from his eyes and land on my hair.

'Of course I'm not angry at you,' he quickly reassures me. 'But why didn't you tell me?' My brother lifts his head up to look at me. His eyes are full of hurt, which only makes me feel more guilty.

'I didn't know how you'd react ... I couldn't bear it if you hurt him and went to jail. I need you, Tyler. We all need you.' By now we are both bawling our eyes out and hugging tightly. We sit there for a while in a warm cuddle.

'Let's go home, Petal. I'm sure if the police need any more stupid questions answered from you, they can come over,' Tyler states in a sarcastic but sweet voice. I put my seatbelt on, hugging my knees up to my body in a compact ball for the duration of the journey.

When we arrive home, Tyler helps me straight upstairs, ignoring the glances from the kids and Eli. With a kiss to my forehead, he leaves me to drown my sorrows away in bed with a double espresso and a tonne of trashy romance movies. I did jokily ask my big brother for a bottle of liquor, but he didn't find that so funny.

Knock knock.

'Come in!' I yell. Eli comes in and slides onto the bed beside me, taking the remote out of my hand and turning off the TV. 'Do you mind? I was watching that!' I protest, trying to grab the controller from him. Eli just smiles and chucks the remote on the floor.

'You must be distressed if you're willingly watching a romantic film by yourself,' he chuckles, and his face droops into a frown.

'How was it? The interview ...' my friend asks. He's trying to appear composed, but I notice him nervously picking at a hanging piece of skin on his left thumb until it bleeds.

'It was okay, I guess. I told them ... I told them that it was Craig,' I say in a small voice. I don't actually look up, but I can feel the happiness beaming off of him. Taking me by surprise, he pulls me into him and whispers, 'I'm so proud of you.' The door creaks open, and a small but heavy body flops on top of us.

'Owwww!' we yell simultaneously. All my stab wounds crease together, creating an unbearable pain. If this hurts less than giving birth, I'm in for a bumpy ride if I ever want brats of my own.

'Cuddle time!' giggles the sweet voice of my little sister, Coco. Eli wriggles out from my hug and picks Coco up, swinging her onto his back and pretending to be a plane.

'Weeeee!' she squeals as Eli runs around my teeny room, dodging removal boxes full of novels and encyclopaedias.

'Prepare for landing!' Eli says, holding his nose to mimic the voice of an airline pilot. He gently throws Coco onto my bed and starts tickling her as I sit there, watching and laughing.

Bzzzz bzzzz.

Eli takes out his phone and reads the message before breathing a deep sigh. 'My mum wants me home,' he grumbles. I try to hide my disappointment by giving a simple nod. Before Eli leaves the room, he turns to me.

'When are you comin' back to school?' he asks before quickly adding, 'No pressure to come back now or anything. You come when you're ready.' His pure sweetness makes me grin like a Cheshire cat.

'I'll hopefully be able to go back on Monday. Mr Kilt is gonna sort out a wheelchair for me in case my legs get too tired. They've been giving way quite a lot, and Lord knows that doesn't need to happen in the school corridor.' We both chuckle at that thought.

'See ya Monday, or sooner.' He smiles and waves me and Coco goodbye. I agree to let Coco stay in my room and watch a film, despite it being two hours past her bedtime. Sometimes the poor kid gets left out by the others, so I kinda have a soft spot for her. We watch a documentary about polar bears whilst being snuggled up in my single bed. Did you know that polar bears have black skin under their white fur for insulation? I wish humans were like that. I'd love to be all warm and fuzzy

Bam!

The front door closes heavily, and I hear Tyler fussing over someone. Mum. I look out of my murky window and watch the silhouette of a tall man stride down the driveway and into his rather expensive-looking car. *I wonder who that was.* Leaving Coco to squeal at the baby polar bears, I tiptoe across the hall and wince at every painful step down the stairs. Sure enough, Mum is sitting on the couch, completely wasted, whilst Tyler soothes her. She doesn't deserve Tyler's care—not when she acts like this.

'Mum, who brought you home?' I ask, my feet pattering against the shiny wooden floor. She gives me a sideways glance and a creepy, nearly demonic smile.

'A nice young man helped—hiccup!—me home. You gotta pwobwem with dat, sonny Jim?' Even I can't help but laugh at that. My mum is such a character when she's off her head on vodka shots. Tyler doesn't smile.

He simply stops wiping the sick from around her mouth, drops the tissue, and walks upstairs.

'I've got coursework to do,' he says, answering our unspoken questions.

'C'mon, Ma, you'd best get to bed.' Even though I'm struggling to walk myself, I suck it up and help Mum get to her bed. When we finally make it to her box room, she flops onto her creaking bed and falls asleep soon after, mumbling, 'You're a good girl, Ivy Towers.' Mum can call me a good girl all she likes, but we both know that isn't true. We both know what I did in Leeds, and I'll never forgive myself for that. This is a weight that I'll always carry around with me no matter where I go.

— 29

Eli

'Where have you been?' Mum asks me as I hang my coat up. She knows my whereabouts. I informed her fully this morning.

'Uhm, I was at the Towers' house, babysitting …' My mum shakes her head in disapproval before tucking a stray hair back into her perfected bun and striding off up the stairs. Women are so hard to read sometimes. Mum would normally love for me to be doing stuff for others and showing my 'love for the community' or whatever. Next thing I know, she's acting as if I just killed someone. I try to run after her, but my mother's footsteps are quick and careful. I make it into her bedroom just before she slams the door.

Everything about my parents' bedroom is pristine. Every speck of dust has been swept away, and every item has its own specific place where it must stay at all times. I guess Mum is so precise about her room because it's the only place she can really be in control. I and—well, my brother—trash the place like it's nobody's business. Well, at least we did, before he passed and all. It's still hard for me to talk of his death. How he died is a story for another time.

Mum starts folding the ironed clothes on her bed. She has her back to me, presenting me with her beautifully patterned and very exotic dress.

'Mum, why do you have such a problem with me hanging out with Ivy? She needs a friend right now! Mum, it's hard for her—'

'But why does it have to be you?' she cuts in, spinning round to face me, hurt swimming in her pupils.

'It doesn't have to be me, but I want to—'

'Why? Do you want to marry her or something? You know, habibi, I am so sick and tired of "Ivy" this, "Ivy" that! Why don't you talk about Haila once in a while? *Is that too much to ask?*' Tears start to build up in the rims of her eyes, but she wipes them away with the back of her hand. It all makes sense now.

'Ma, I don't wanna marry Ivy. Haila is my number-one priority!'

'It certainly doesn't feel like that! What do you do as soon as you come home, huh? You run straight to Ivy to check she's okay!'

'Yeah, 'cause I'm worried about her!' Tears of my own are streaming down my face, but I just let them fall. My mother needs to see how ridiculous she is being.

'Why can't you worry about Haila? The poor girl doesn't see you for days! But not Ivy. No, Ivy gets everything!'

She picks up a pile of laundry and starts making her way across the dark landing. I chase after her, determined to get my point across. She's always telling me to be more caring for others, and now that I'm finally doing it, she has a hissy fit! Women really do make no sense. She carries on storming across the landing until she pauses outside Khalid's room. We haven't emptied out his room. Mum and Dad wanted to clear it out so we could use it as a guest room, but I wouldn't let them. My brother may be dead, but I'll always feel like he's there with me as long as his room stays exactly as he'd left it.

Without even turning to face me, Mum says in a small voice, 'I bet Khalid would put his fiancée first if he had the chance to have one.' It's as if Mum has turned round and stuck a huge dagger straight through my heart. How could she say something like that! I push past her, purposely knocking into her shoulder, and race to my room. Before I open the door, I turn to her. My eyes are brimming with more tears.

'I hate you,' I say through clenched teeth. 'I really hate you.' The shock and upset in her eyes make me feel better. I turn and storm into my room, slamming the door behind me, while my mum watches on, laundry in hand. Her footsteps fade down the hallway until I hear the sound of her bedroom door closing lightly behind her. Instead of punching things and unleashing my anger, I sit against the door and cry into my hands for hours.

I already unleashed my anger on Mum, and now all that is left inside of me is sheer emotion. I don't understand why it matters if I spend more time with Ivy than Haila. Either way, I'm marrying Haila. None of this changes that. My body is so feeble and fragile from my wailing that I can't even muster the body strength to haul myself off the floor and up to bed, so I just lie gently on my side and fall asleep on my cold, hard wood floor. The chilly sensation from the floor cools down my burning cheeks. Tonight is gonna be one uncomfortable night, but I can't move. I'm just too weak.

❦

Mum doesn't even talk to me on Monday morning. I tried my best to start up a conversation at breakfast, but she just glared at me and stared into her corn flakes. Dad has been quite cold to me too over the weekend. I guess Mum told him all the gory details about our little dispute. I bet she didn't tell him the whole story, or he wouldn't be acting as if I'd just shot a baby. There isn't much point in me trying to set my alibi straight with Dad though. Anything my mum says, he'll believe her like some gullible little toddler.

Every day when I leave for school, I always shout, 'Bye, Mum! Bye, Dad! I love you!' and they always call back in unison, 'Love you, darling!' I know it's really cringeworthy, but since my brother's death, we've learnt to appreciate that every day could be our last. I could leave for school and never come back. That's what happened to Khalid.

No, Eli, don't let these negative thoughts get to you! I remonstrate silently as I drive over to Haila's house. I did offer to give Ivy a lift, but Tyler is making sure to escort her himself. The poor guy has had his life turned upside down by all this. At least now that the police know who stabbed Ivy, we might get them the justice they deserve.

I pull up to Haila's home and honk my horn. My girlfriend strides out from the door, looking as flawless as ever. Her tanned skin is glowing like a summer's sun, and her hair is pulled into a dark purple hijab with pretty white roses patterned about it. For some strange reason, she has sunglasses perched on her head even though it's nearly minus five degrees outside.

Haila slides into the passenger seat and leans over the gear lever, her face almost touching mine. We share a passionate kiss, and she draws back into her seat. My girlfriend clings onto herself and gives an exaggerated shiver.

'Gawd almighty, it's freezing out here! Can you close the roof over please,' she directs, batting her eyelashes. I love to have the rooftop down so I can feel the wind on my face as we drive, but I guess it is kinda nippy. I hold the tiny lever and watch as the roof unfolds on top of us.

'Happy now?' I say with a seductive smirk. Haila pecks me on the lips once more.

'Yep,' she replies simply, and she starts texting one of her many girlfriends.

We make it to school just in time for the bell. Haila decided she wanted a pain au chocolat from the bakery just as we were about to pull into school, so I had to race off to get it. That girl drives me nuts sometimes.

School knows about my involvement with Ivy's incident, so they've decided to move me and Martha into most of Ivy's lessons to help her ease into things. Luckily, Haila is in Ivy's classes too, so I get to be with all my favourite people at once. I have to admit I don't completely hate Martha anymore. She's kinda okay when you get to know her. I've hung around with Ivy's best friend quite a lot recently, as my group has sort of rejected me. Somehow, they all seem to believe Craig's lame sob story that I threatened him or whatever.

Mr Batch scribbles the name 'Winston Churchill' across the board and starts his draining lecture on the late prime minister. Ivy hasn't arrived yet, and I'm beginning to worry. Haila sits at the desk next to me, but I make sure the desk on the other side is free, for Ivy. With Haila to my left, her hand in mine, and Martha two seats across from me, I slowly try to take in the information that Batch is telling us. He's like some sort of factual water fountain; fountains spew out water, and you get something good from them only if you throw money—or, in our case, homework—at them.

Just as the lesson reaches its halfway point—thank God—the door opens and Ivy walks slowly into the room with Tyler loosely holding her right arm.

— 30 —

Ivy

It's like my ultimate nightmare is coming true. The two things I hate most are attention and vulnerability, and it looks as if I'm getting both at the same time. Lucky me! I wanted to walk in by myself, but Tyler just wouldn't let that happen. Mr Kilt was gonna come with me, but who knows what rumours would spread if I came in with him by my side. Eli and Martha motion to the spare seat between them, which warms me up inside. Haila leans back in her chair and mumbles to herself.

Mr Batch offers me a welcoming grin as Tyler helps me lower myself into the chair. I decided to keep the wheelchair in Kilt's office because I won't need it constantly.

Tyler goes to leave, but before he does, he turns to me.

'If anyone gives you any hassle, just tell me. I'll sort 'em out, all right?' he whispers. I nod and smile. He winks at me and gives a soft wave to Batch as he leaves. Every single eye in the room is directed straight at me. Mr Batch notices the ever-increasing awkward silence.

'As I was saying ... Winston Churchill.' This teacher really does understand me. None of the other teachers seem to have the capability of realising that not all students want to be the centre of attention all the time.

I take down masses of notes because, despite my revision at the hospital, I feel really left behind on everything, even maths—and I'm quite good at maths, if I do say so myself.

After what seems like years of studying World War II, the bell goes and the whole class files out. I ask Martha and Eli to wait for me outside while I chat to Mr Batch.

'How are you feelin', Ivy?' he asks as he wipes off the tonnes of notes from the whiteboard. My fingers fiddle about with a hangnail until I wince in pain and notice the blood trickling down my finger. The sight of blood still makes me feel squeamish, but I don't let the psychological pain get to me.

'Not bad. I didn't really appreciate the death stares from everyone, though.'

He sighs and spins on his heel to face me. 'Yeah, sorry about that. This lot are a nosy bunch, I must say.' The teacher sighs and clenches his jaw. He looks over at the standard school clock.

'You don't wanna be late for your next lesson.'

'Sir, I've just been stabbed and fell into a life-threatening coma. I'm sure all the teachers will excuse my tardiness for at least … thirty-two point seven days.'

He laughs quietly to himself. 'You are something special, Ivy Towers.'

'Yep I've been told that one before.' I go to leave the room, but before I do, Batch stops me.

'Oh, Ivy! Before you go, I have something for you.' He ruffles his dark curls and goes over to his desk, picking up a folded piece of paper. My history teacher walks over to me and hands to me my drawing I drew in detention. A smile stretches across my lips before I can hide it away.

'You didn't give it to Mr Kimberley?' I ask in pure shock.

'You kept your end of the deal, so … If I were you, I'd make sure that picture stays well and truly hidden. Wouldn't want it ending up in the wrong hands, now would we?' He smiles at me and walks over to the window. Without even saying goodbye, he just stands there, staring into the plain PE field.

'Okay then …' I whisper under my breath as I leave the room.

Instead of getting annoyed at me for taking so long, Martha and Eli are overly happy to see me. Haila has disappeared somewhere, probably in a huff because Eli isn't treating her like the sun of his solar system.

The rest of our lessons are long and tedious, but I'm kinda enjoying it. It's nice to be back in the swing of things.

I haven't felt normal in ages.

'Is it just me or was Rory Thompson totally eyeing you up in history?' I say to Martha, giggling, at lunchtime. Eli nods and Martha pushes me playfully. It's nice to be under our oak tree again, laughing and sharing secrets, despite the freezing weather. Never in my life did I think Eli Bishara would be here too. How things have changed. We decided to get my wheelchair from Kilt because my legs were aching like hell.

'So Eli, why aren't you hanging out with your normal group of basketball freaks?' Martha says between mouthfuls of a tuna sandwich.

'Craig told them that we had a tiny fight but I escalated it and threatened to beat him up or something. It's beyond me why those idiots believed him. It doesn't matter, though, 'cause I've got you two now.' Eli blushes as soon as the words leave his mouth. We all sit there, not knowing what to say. How I hate silence; it's so scary.

'We have maths next,' I say, pretending to read my timetable even though I studied it rigorously the entire weekend. Let's just say I was nervous about my first day. My best friends groan in unison.

'Kill me now,' Eli mumbles, with his head in his hands. I flinch at his choice of words. Death is kind of a sore subject for me right now.

'Eli …' Martha whispers from the corner of her mouth. Eli looks up from his hands and frowns.

'Oh, I'm so sorry, Ivy. I forgot …'

'No, don't sweat it. It's … it's fine.'

Eli smiles for a split second but returns to an instant frown when he notices someone approaching us—Haila.

'Baby, I've been looking everywhere for you!' she says in a sweet yet menacing tone. Eli's girlfriend takes his arm and tries to hoist him up, but he tugs away.

'I'm not going anywhere, Haila. I wanna sit with these guys.' Martha gives Haila a victorious look and makes a shooing motion with her hand.

Haila scoffs. 'Fine! Be with these freaks! Why should I care?' she says before spinning around and storming over to her bunch of fellow defaults.

'Good riddance,' Martha murmurs. I nod along, but Eli just sits there, staring after his girlfriend. The bell rings for next lesson.

'C'mon, Romeo. Trigonometry awaits us,' I giggle. Martha wheels me to maths with Eli walking beside us.

Our laughing and chatting comes to an abrupt halt when we enter the classroom and discover Craig is sitting at the back. What in God's name is he doing here? I told the police what he did! This must be illegal.

'Let's go sit in front,' Eli mutters. The period passes by so slowly that I begin to question whether life has just come to an all-time halt. Just as Miss Foley starts to explain loci, a man in a high-vis jacket appears in the doorway. He has a proud stance with a stern look on his face, though I can tell he is enjoying his job way too much. The wrinkles on his head are strongly defined and stretch across the whole of his temples. I could recognise that aggravating face from a mile away—Officer Stevens.

The officer removes his tall black hat from his head and holds it to his side as if he is in the military. Pfft. In his dreams.

'Sorry to interrupt your lesson, ma'am, but I don't s'pose you have a Craig Wilson in your class?' Stevens asks, scanning the room with his dark, beady pupils. My attacker's cheeks flare into two bright red patches, and he starts fiddling about with his hands nervously. You have no idea how much pleasure it gives me to see him suffer so much. Jeez, when did I become the devil's daughter?

Miss Foley instantly assumes that Craig could be in some sort of trouble, and this shows on her youthful but aged face as she stares at Craig. 'Yep he's right here!' she answers, motioning to Craig to stand up. Her hand seems to be trembling. Eli, Martha, and I can barely hide our concern either.

Officer Stevens waits for Craig to join him reluctantly. Everyone starts whispering and oohing. Miss Foley looks so shocked it seems she can barely hold herself up. *Poor old soul.*

'I think you'd better do this outside,' she suggests sensibly.

Officer Stevens grabs Craig firmly by an upper arm and leads him into the corridor, closing the door after them. I watch through the small window as Craig tries to wriggle from his grasp, but the officer pushes him against the wall with ease. He grabs the handcuffs from his tool belt and starts tightening them around Craig's wrists. Inside, the whole class burst into conversation.

'Craig Wilson, I am arresting you on suspicion of attempted murder.'

We can hear the arrest from inside. Gasps fly out of the mouths of everyone in the room, me included. Forgive me for not doing my research, but I didn't know that was attempted murder! I thought it would be a battery charge or something like that. Gosh, I can be so dumb sometimes.

Officer Stevens speaks in a loud and authoritative voice whilst pinning Craig to the wall. 'You do not have to say anything, but it may harm your defence if you do not mention, when questioned, something you later rely on in court. Anything you do or say may be given in evidence. Do you understand?'

'Yes sir,' Craig whispers.

The whole class falls deadly silent. I look over and see that Miss Foley has her head between her knees and Zoe Teal has her hand on the teacher's back, offering breathing instructions.

Without warning, Eli grabs my hand under the desk, catching me by surprise. Instead of wriggling my hand free, I squeeze his hand tighter. The door opens halfway, briefly, as the officer pops his head through.

'Good day, miss,' Officer Stevens says to a rather shaken Miss Foley.

As soon as the door closes, the entire class bursts into an excited buzz of conversation. God forbid that any of them should work out the reason I went into a coma. Attention is a nightmare. It's almost as bad as sympathy. Yuck, sympathy! People use that weird tone of voice that shouts, 'I'm just using this voice so it looks like I care!' Thankfully, Miss Foley is so distressed that she is told to go home. We gossip and chat until the cover teacher walks in—Mr Kilt. Wow, the odds really aren't in my favour.

'Right, year eleven, shut up!' he yells at the top of his voice. Nobody acknowledges him in the slightest, so he grabs a gigantic thesaurus and slams it on the desk. That gets everyone's attention. Every pair of eyes shoots across in the direction of the huge bang.

'That's better!' he exhales. 'Now, since I don't know a single thing about trigonometry, you're all gonna do textbook work.' There is literally no point in having a cover teacher if he isn't gonna, y'know, teach! The teacher drops himself into the plush chair and starts scrolling through the internet. What a douche. Come to think of it, I dunno how he qualifies as a cover teacher when he doesn't even teach. He's involved in all the emotional malarky.

The majority of my classmates use this lesson as a chance to slack off, but I, on the other hand, take this as an opportunity to catch up. Believe it or not, I'm working at a grade-seven average, which is utterly devastating.

Hospitals are supposed to make you feel better, but I honestly feel ten times worse since leaving that place. Life feels so new to me. This would never normally bother me, but I'm out of the loop on all the gossip. Not that I care who's dating whom, but I like to have this sort of information so I have one up on certain people. Leverage, if you will. In all honesty, school is a bit like a small civil war: everyone has allies and secrets about others they are holding for ransom. Call me a drama queen, but it's true. No one is safe around here, socially speaking.

<hr>

To my surprise, when I got home last night, Mum was actually there. That is, she was in the house, not out drinking or partying. It kind of took me aback to see my own mother curled up on the sofa watching *Take Me Out*. Maybe that bloke that took her home knocked some sense into her. I really hope so. My brothers and sisters are starting to notice that something is wrong with Mum, and I don't fancy taking a crack at explaining why she stinks of stale booze.

School sucked slightly less than yesterday, if I'm honest. We made stir fry in food technology, and Martha exploded a whole bag of bean sprouts all over the oven! I don't think I've laughed that much in years. Everyone found it funny,—including Miss Fallon—except Haila, who just stood there scowling. Who knows what her problem is, but I don't really care. There's no chance I'm gonna go out of my way to impress a default.

'I'm home!' I yell, chucking my bag by the door. Archie and Poppy come running and toddling down the hallway and throw themselves into my open arms. Tyler appears from the living room with Eva in one hand and the landline phone in the other. A deep frown is set on his face. I've seen that expression before; something is wrong.

Without even questioning my brother, I take the phone out of his hand.

'Hello?'

'Ivy? Hi, I'm afraid we have some bad news.' My stomach plunges as if I'm cascading from one of those mega-drop towers at a theme park. The voice on the other end of the phone is Zoe's. *Thank goodness.* I couldn't deal with Officer Stevens giving me devastating news in a monotone grumble. Zoe continues before I have a chance to speak. 'We are no longer considering Craig Wilson as a suspect. Mr Wilson has provided us with an alibi which has been confirmed to be true by his mother and father, Maya and Kevin Wilson.' The corridor surrounding me blurs as tears block my vision. I try not to cry, because I need to hear everything she has to say. I need concrete information before I can be at peace with myself.

'But it was Craig! I know it was! His parents are lying! Please, you have to believe me!' My voice is loud yet croaky and feeble. I can't help but start crying. Archie and Poppy cling to Tyler's legs in fear, and my brother watches me.

Zoe waits for my sniffling to die down slightly.

'And as everyone else anywhere near the crime scene has a secure alibi, we will be closing the investigation.' Both my legs collapse beneath me, and I sob in a crumpled heap on the floor. Zoe carries on explaining everything through the phone, but her voice is small and distant. Tyler starts to wrap his arms around my shoulders, but I push him off, drop the phone and run up the stairs, pulling my door closed behind me. I can just about hear Tyler soothing my little siblings as they cry in distress. Poor things must be so confused.

Slam!

The whole house shakes a little as someone enters the house. I know it isn't Mum, because I remember passing her whilst she watched a film on the sofa. It can't be any of my siblings, because they are all home.

Eli.

The normal me would come bounding down the stairs to greet him, but today I just stay curled up on my bed, bawling into my duvet. Craig's alibi is wrong, no matter what he tries to tell them. I suppose lying to the police is his parents' way of getting revenge on me for what I did to Simon. I guess I deserve it after all I put them through, but that's beside the point. They could've handled it differently. Lucky for me, we are smack bang in the middle of winter and darkness is already upon us. The vague amber lampposts beam down their spotlights on potholes filled with brown-tinted rain. Nobody will notice my small body on top of our roof.

I haul myself through the slanted window in my bedroom ceiling and onto the peach-coloured rooftop. I wipe the smeared mascara from my face and stare up at the stars. Isn't it cool how no two stars are the same? I suppose it's the same with humans, except humans all wanna be like each other, nowadays. Originality is old news. It's sad, really. As long as you follow the latest social media trends, no one will hassle you. Silence soothes me, and even though the air is very nippy, I find comfort in being alone up here. Privacy has been non-existent in this house since my siblings were born. A faint pattering of feet echoes around me as someone climbs the metal ladder. Every footstep comes with a loud *creakkkkk*. I'm just about to tell them to get lost when a head pops through the hole in the roof: Eli's.

'It's nice up here. I wish I had a ladder to my attic,' Eli says in an attempt at conversation, but I just stare into space and keep my lips pursed shut. Eli sighs. 'Tyler told me about Craig … I'm so sorry, Ivy. You don't deserve any of this—'

'How is he? Tyler, I mean?' I find myself interrupting. My voice is quiet and weak. Eli's eyes shoot over to me, and he bites the inside of his lip.

'He went out as soon as I got here. He's really upset, Ivy …' Eli's voice trails off as he notices tears start to prickle my eyes. He shuffles towards me as slowly as possible so he doesn't go plunging from the roof at full speed, and he holds me close to him.

'The kids are kinda worried about you, but I soothed them with a tonne of jelly beans.' My head bounces up and down on his chest as he laughs to himself. Using all the strength I can muster, I lift my head to look into his eyes.

Eli's lips curl into a sweet grin. We stay like that for a while, just gazing into each other's eyes.

'I don't know what I'd do without you, Eli Bishara,' I whisper. Before I can even make sense of what's happening, Eli squeezes his eyes shut and leans in towards me. His lips press gently onto mine, sending sparks through my body. As though a bolt of lightning has just zapped between us, we both move away from each other.

'I'm so sorry! I don't know what I was …' Eli grabs his jumper and starts climbing down the ladder before I can even cram in any words.

From this moment on, I know that things between us will never be the same again.

31

Eli

What have I done?! Ivy's probably gonna hate me forever now. *You're so stupid!* I think, slamming my left palm against my forehead. As soon as I left Ivy's house, I just started walking. I didn't know where I was headed, but I knew one thing: I certainly wasn't going home. Me and my parents aren't exactly best buds at the moment, and the last thing I need is them nagging at me.

I eventually find a destination where I feel safe from any nagging or social interaction: the kids' park. It must be a weird sight to see a sixteen-year-old sitting alone on a kids' swing at night in the middle of winter, but I couldn't care less. Alone time is the perfect way for me to comprehend what I just did. My feet push gently against the ground so I swing back and forth a little bit. By now it's so late at night that even the herds of teens have deserted the park and given up terrorising small children. Despite me replaying the event over and over in my head, I still can't understand why I just kissed Ivy. For one, I'm engaged. Haila would skin me alive if she found out about this, or even worse, she could break up with me.

Just when I start to believe that things couldn't get any worse, I notice the silhouette of a small girl coming towards me: Ivy.

She plonks herself down on the swing next to me and stares up at the stars.

'Pretty, aren't they? The stars. Like little rays of sunshine that sparkle up the darkest nights,' she mumbles. I'm not entirely sure if she's talking to me or herself, so I keep quiet. Ivy's mysterious tawny eyes meet mine, and instead of looking upset, she smiles what seems to be an actual happy smile.

'I don't know what came over me, Ivy, I truly don't. One minute we were staring into each other's eyes, and the next …'

'You kissed me,' she says, completing my sentence. 'Honestly, don't sweat it. It was … nice.' *Nice? Wow, that makes me feel special.* 'If I'm completely honest … I kinda liked it.'

My eyes widen so much I'm surprised the balls don't fall out of their sockets. 'Ivy, we can't do this! I'm engaged! Like, *engaged*!' My voice rises before I can stop it. Ivy looks a little hurt by the anger in my voice, but I don't feel angry. I feel alarmed—scared, even.

'Imagine what Haila will do to me if she finds out!' My head falls into my hands, and I groan. My brain literally hurts right now.

'What if … what if she didn't find out?' Ivy says in a quiet voice. I lift my head from my hands, and Ivy gives me a mischievous grin.

'You mean like a secret relationship?'

She nods. Ivy leans in and I don't draw back. We share a magnificent and prolonged kiss. A cool breeze swirls around us and hurls brown leaves in the air. The unused swings sway beside us as if someone is watching us. Ivy has always said that kissing is extremely unhygienic, so it's beyond me why her morals are suddenly out of the window. Ivy pulls back and starts shivering and clutching her arms. It slowly occurs to me that she is only wearing a skirt and a T-shirt.

'Gosh, you must be freezing! Here, take my jumper.' I pull my hoodie over my head and help her put it on. We rise from the swings and share one last quick kiss before deciding to part ways.

'Remember. This is a secret and has to stay that way,' I order.

Ivy smiles and turns to leave, still wearing my hoodie. It almost looks like a dress on her, as she's so small. As I make my way to the park exit, I realise something. We can't keep this a secret forever. I'm getting married soon. It's only a matter of time till the rubber meets the road.

Lucky for me, the alleyway in which Ivy was attacked is now open to the public. I shouldn't be rejoicing at this, because it's a sore reminder of that dreadful night, but it does mean that I don't have to walk an extra ten minutes, so I'm happy to use it. My fingers trace along the walls of the dark passage as I amble down the street. Various potholes are dotted down the path, so I watch my footsteps very carefully. Rough clay rubs against my fingers until it goes from hard to smooth. I stop dead in my tracks and look over at the wall. In the place of one of the bricks of the wall is a small screen. Oh … my … gosh. It can't be … my GoPro! My fingers prise the camera out of the compact hole in the wall, and I start sprinting down the street. If this has on it what I think it does, everything could change for the better.

32

Ivy

I'd hoped to Facetime with Eli on Wednesday for a little while after our kiss, but I guess I'm getting my hopes up. He is engaged, after all. Four unanswered calls were enough to tell me that he just didn't want to talk. It's okay, though, because I'm gonna see him at school today and we can talk properly. Last night's conversation was a little bit thin on the ground. There was more smooching than talking, if I'm being honest. But it still hasn't sunk in. From the minute I met that guy, I never thought I'd end up sucking face with him. In fact, that is the last thing I thought we'd do. Luckily, I snap out of my little daydream just as we come to the school's bus stop. I practically skip and hop off the bus, which must look ludicrous, but I really couldn't care less. Nothing anyone can say or do will dampen my spirits.

☙❧

'Have you read the last chapter?' Martha babbles to me at lunchtime. 'Oh, I totally cried my eyes out when Pablo risked everything for Cloe!' I'll never get tired of our daily *Angel's Curse* gossip. That book is worth a thousand words. We are leaning against some random lockers and chatting away, completely ignoring the fact that we are having the geekiest conversation in the middle of the school corridors. This sort of thing drops one down at least 6.4 rungs on the social ladder, but that doesn't bother me in the slightest. Smart should be the new trendy. A hand comes from behind me and plants on my shoulder, causing me to almost jump out of my acne-covered skin. I spin around to find Eli standing there, practically hopping with excitement.

'Ivy, I need to tell you something, like now!' Eli can barely keep still and starts hopping from side to side. Martha gives me a sideways glance.

'Go on then, Tigger,' I giggle.

Rrrrrinnnngggg!

'Oh, we gotta get to last class. Do you mind telling me later, after school maybe?' Eli's face drops like a kid finding out his birthday is cancelled. He nods and turns to walk to his next lesson. Martha and I give each other a confused look and make our way to PE. Normally PE would be my worst nightmare, but owing to my mass of injuries, all I have to do is sit on a bench and read. Martha has a box full of cleverly written notes to excuse her from PE, so we have a fantastic hour ahead of us.

Lying on my single bed on Thursday evening, I do my 'homework' as I message Martha and listen to old rock songs. I find a strange comfort in listening to the hugely outdated music. I dare call it music in front of Tyler. He says the correct word for this type of melody is a 'racket'. My brother prefers modern pop. I can't say that surprises me though. Standard songs about soppy break-ups are right up his street.

A small banner appears in the corner of my laptop screen. An email? Who on earth still emails? My eyes read the name of the sender over and over again: 'City of Dover Police Department'. The message reads as follows:

> Subject: Your Case.
> Miss Ivy Towers,
>
> We are delighted to inform you that we have a new piece of evidence, provided by Mr Eli Bishara, which confirms that Craig Wilson is, in fact, your attacker. We sincerely apologise for any distress caused by our mistake. Further information on your court date will be emailed to you shortly.
>
> Yours faithfully,
> City of Dover Police Department

After pinching myself to make sure this isn't a dream, I fly down the stairs and into the kitchen, where Tyler is helping the kids with their homework. I thrust my laptop at him and start bouncing up and down.

'Look! Look! Look!' I scream.

Tyler arches his left brow and takes the laptop. 'Ivy will you calm d … oh my gosh!' My brother places the computer on the table so he can join me in leaping in the air. The kids look extremely confused, and their eyes follow us as we dance around the room like party animals. Even Mum hauls herself off the sofa to come and see what all the commotion is about. She doesn't seem as excited as I'd hoped, but what can you expect from a woman who's experiencing the hangover of a lifetime?

Tyler orders pizza to celebrate. None of my little siblings understand what's going on, but they gladly accept the masses of pepperoni pizza that Tyler brings back to the kitchen. As we all sit around the kitchen table and everyone munches on fatty food, I can barely bring myself to take a bite. A whirlpool of nausea churns inside of me. Whilst everyone sees the optimistic side of things, I can't help but notice that this is just the beginning of a long and tedious journey. Who knows what sentence Craig will get. There's even the possibility that he only gets a couple of months. Then he'd be out in the world, ready to get blood-curdling revenge on me.

❦

On Friday, A humid breeze combs through my hair and swooshes it around my head. Aesthetically autumn-coloured leaves make mini tornado spirals around me as I make my way up the long flight of stairs to my school. For once, the hundreds of people bustling about don't cause me to panic. Today I feel like a lion freed from its cage. My pessimistic views from last night were quickly squashed by my brother, who claimed I was being ridiculous. I suppose he is right. I was worrying too much.

It takes all my willpower not to hop and skip to sociology. On an average day, even the thought of doing a presentation would make me want to hurl, but not today. I want to do this in front of my class—the whole world, even. No presentation is going to get the best of me.

Twirling around in a circle and dropping my bag by my side, I practically fall into my chair. Martha shakes her head, smiling discreetly, while Eli beams along with me.

Without warning, I reach over and give him an excitable hug. After a small hesitation, Eli puts his arm around me.

'Thank you so much, Eli. You're a lifesaver,' I whisper into his ear. Martha stares at us in confusion, her head cocked to the right. I look over at her and realise how touchy-feely I'm being. *Act cool, Ivy!* I shout silently, and I draw back into my seat.

'Are you ready, Eli? 'Cause I sure am!' I say, resting my left arm on the back of my chair in an attempt to look casual.

'Mmm-hmm,' Eli mumbles, taking out his laptop and gearing up our presentation.

My eyes scan the classroom, and every time I make eye contact with someone, I smile and wave at the person as if we are best friends. My pupils continue to look across the room until they lock with someone else's: Craig's.

My smile drops like a clay bird that's been shot out of the sky. He should be in a prison cell, not sitting two metres from me! Despite him being a couple of rows across from me, I manage to grill him from my seat.

'What on earth are you doing here? They found the evidence!' I shout in a hushed tone because the class is starting to settle down.

Craig gives a toothy smile and leans back in his seat, stretching out his arms like giraffes' necks. 'You see, Ivy, I could afford bail, 'cause I'm not poor like you,' Craig replies in a smooth voice. As much as I want to strangle him with my bare hands, Mr Cabello starts class before I get the chance. Oh, that boy is so lucky.

'Good morning, year eleven. Now, you all know what's happening today, don't you? Presentation time!' He almost yells his words in excitement. Cheap thrills much? Every soul in the class, except me and Cabello, groans and moans like a stereotypical teenager would. Cabello slaps his hands together. 'Which lucky pair would like to go first …?' His wide eyes look over the sea of sixteen-year-olds and land on Martha and Tilly. Both of them look exasperated and tired. For some reason, I find myself doing something that the normal Ivy would never do.

'Sir, Eli and I will go first!' I chime in before he has a chance to pick on Martha and her partner. Cabello allows it and welcomes us to set up our laptop.

Eli gives me the ultimate death stare as he connects his computer to the projector, but it doesn't faze me; for some reason I feel like helping people today, so that's exactly what I'm gonna do. Martha mouths 'thank you' to me, but Cabello notices.

'You'll be going up next, Martha and Tilly.' Instead of arguing, they just accept their inevitable fate and shrink back into their seats.

'Although teen pregnancy has affected thousands over the course of this year, the rate is much lower than when our parents were kids, so, uh … well done!' Eli says nervously. A low rumble of laughter fills the room and helps him to relax. He beams a smile and continues talking.

By the end of our presentation, our classmates are clapping so wildly that I start to feel like a popular boy band being applauded in the Wembley Arena. Okay, so maybe I'm exaggerating a bit, but the whole class seemed to enjoy it. A couple of them were even wiping tears away, but they are the sort to cry at a school play; you know the type.

The majority of the other presentations are okay, I guess, but ours was the best. Craig and Mike's was … what's a nice way to put it? Pants. It was pants. Cabello didn't praise any other group as much as ours. You may think I'm showing off, but this lot have had their time under the spotlight, whilst I was cooped up in a hospital bed. Now is my time to shine.

Just as the lesson comes to a close, Mr Kilt knocks on the door and asks to take me. For once Mr Kilt is an absolute lifesaver. This class is really starting to drag on.

I flop into my usual armchair, the navy blue one, and make myself comfortable. I've sat in this chair so many times that the seat has moulded to mimic the exact shape of my body. I sit on the chair sideways, my legs swinging softly because I'm too giddy to sit like a normal person.

'Who are you, and what have you done with Ivy?' Mr Kilt jokes.

I poke my tongue out at him. 'They've got evidence of Craig hurting me, Kilt! Everything's changing!' I almost scream my words, my voice shaky because I can't help myself from bouncing up and down in my seat. My giddiness comes to an abrupt stop.

'What's up?'

'Why is Craig still in school if they know what he did?' My voice is almost a whisper. *Wow, mood swings on point.* Mr Kilt breathes a deep sigh and taps his pen against his temple. Rows of wrinkles line up on his forehead. I fight the urge to offer him some of the anti-ageing cream my mother so helpfully bought me for Christmas. The poor woman doesn't understand that teens don't want to look ten years younger, but I put it in my bag just to please her.

'It's hard to explain, but basically Craig has been granted bail, so they are allowing him to continue on at school until the trial. It's stupid, I know. Oh Ivy, please don't cry …' It didn't even occur to me that I am crying, but when I wipe my hand below my eyes, warm tears smear across my finger.

'It's not fair,' I whisper.

'One thing you need to understand is'—Mr Kilt rests his elbows on the desk and plants his chin in between them—'that life is unfair.'

'That doesn't make this right, Mr Kilt. Please, can you do something? I can't be in this school with him every day; I just can't …' Tear after tear starts falling down my face.

'I'll request to have him moved out of your lessons, but that's the best I can do for now. I'm sorry.' I accept his offer and start fanning my eyes with my hands.

I sit there for a while, just blinking over and over again.

'You can go to next lesson now, Ivy—'

'I know,' I interrupt. 'I just don't want my eyes to look puffy and red when I'm in English.'

Kilt releases a deep belly chuckle and lets me wait it out in his beloved office.

Every other lesson today drags on like nobody's business. Instead of interesting facts and information, all I hear coming from the teacher's mouths is 'Blah, blah, blah, blah, blah.' I think every teacher notices my lack of concentration but dismisses it because of my current affairs at home. I'm probably ignoring my morals completely by doing this, but I'm kinda using my situation as an advantage.

Even Mr Batch's lesson is a complete drag, and I normally quite enjoy history.

Chucking my unused PE bag by the shoe rack, I amble towards the living room. The squeaky voice of a little pig sounds through the wall, so I assume Tyler is watching TV with the little ones. I swing the door open, and sitting there on my sofa is a tall man. The man's hands are pressed tightly together and are resting in the crook of his lap whilst he looks down at the floor. He is wearing a pair of neatly pressed trousers, a well-ironed shirt, and a light grey waistcoat. His eyebrows are slim and close to his dark green eyes. His identical cheekbones are strong and square. A huge mop of dark curls is planted on top of his stout structure. *It can't be ...*

'Mr Batch?' The man looks up at me, and sure enough, sitting in my living room is my history teacher.

'Ivy?' He practically leaps off of the chair as though a bolt of lightning has just shot down his spine.

'Why on earth are you in *myyyy* house?' I stretch out the pronoun just to emphasise how much he has no right to be here.

'Your house?!' he nearly shouts, his voice trembling at every painful syllable.

'Yes, my house!'

His eyes grow wide. 'Towers. Ivy Towers. Like ... like Camilla Towers,' he stutters. Why is he saying my mum's name? My mother comes down the stairs in a pink leopard print bathrobe and her hair tied up in a white towel. She struts over to my teacher and pecks him on the lips, though he doesn't return the gesture.

Wait, no. He can't be. 'You and ... and him? *Him?!*' I scream in my mum's face. I've never seen her look so confused.

'What's wrong with Leo?' she says in a quiet murmur. I can feel the veins in my face popping out and showing on my forehead.

'He's my history teacher, Mum! My freakin' history teacher!' I yell.

'Hey, don't take it out on your mother! How was she supposed to know?' Batch scolds.

'Oh, you can shut your mouth and all!' I bellow, tears brimming in my eyes. It's a good thing Tyler is out with the other kids, or there'd be more than just me crying.

'You know, Mum, even with your standards, that really takes the mick!' She doesn't even argue back but stares at her bare feet. Mr Batch starts to walk over to me, but I hold my hand out.

'No! No, don't come anywhere near me!' I warn. He stops in his tracks and takes a step back, holding his hands up in defence. I turn and bolt for the stairs, with Batch right on my heels.

'Ivy, wait!' he calls.

Just before he can grab my left arm, I shut the door in his face. I slide down against the door and hold my head in my hands.

'Ivy, please …'

'Just leave me alone, Batch. I don't wanna talk to you!' I command. I hear a light thud as he sits against the door on the other side.

'I'm sorry it has to be this way, but … I love your mum. Cam means the world to me.'

'It's Camilla, not Cam! She hates being called that, and you'd know that if you knew anything about her, but you clearly don't, so don't you dare claim to love her!' My voice is croaky.

I haven't experienced anger this intense since her last lover walked out on us. Footsteps creak up the stairs, and I hear the low murmuring of voices. I don't catch much of the conversation, but I hear one thing which makes me feel sick to my stomach: 'She's just being ridiculous, Leo. We'll be together forever, and there's nothing my silly daughter can do to change that.'

Together forever? Together forever! I can't live with Batch! Out of all the horrific things that have happened to me, this comes into the top five.

Their footsteps die away until I hear my mum's door close. I grab my phone out of my pocket and text the first person that comes to mind.

Me:

Hey, Eli. I need to rant to someone, and you're the first person I thought of xxx

Eli:

Lucky for you I'm a good listener. Wassup Xxx

Me:

You're never gonna believe this, but Mr Batch is dating my mum :(

Eli:

BAHAHAHA

Me:

Excuse me, this isn't funny! You said you're a good listener :/

Eli:

Mateeee Batch could be your stepdad soon

Me:

Can you be serious for a second please!!!!

Eli:

Ivy, don't sweat it. If anything this is good news cause you can get extra homework help and all that. If I were you, I'd milk this like a cow's udder.

Me:

Hmmm I guess you're right, but either way I don't wanna be living with my history teacher! If word gets out I'll die. I DON'T WANT A SOCIAL DEATH SENTENCE!!!

Eli:

Yo chill. I bet they won't even get as far as moving in together. Before you know it they'll be splitting up and you will be an expert historian! It's a win-win xxx

Me:

Thanks for helping me look at the bright side of things <3 this is just what I needed Xxx

Eli:

Nah it's cool. Just make sure you text me if there's any more drama. Now I gotta go. I'm at some poncy restaurant with Haila and the fam byeeeeee Xxx

Me:

Okay thx. cya at school Xxx

Did you know that snakes can't bite food so they have to swallow it whole? I think Mr Batch must be a snake, seeing as he has basically swallowed up my chances of a social life all in one go. Once word gets out, I'll be the joke of the school, and before you know it, I'll be getting shoved into bins and poked at all over again. Okay, so maybe calling him a snake is a bit far, but I'm beyond mad at him.

As I'm lying in bed Saturday morning, my phone goes.
Ping!
I snatch it up and read the text.

Eli:

Yo look outside! It's proper snowingggg :D

I prise myself from my bed, and after rubbing the gunk out of my eyes, I look out my mucky window. Sure enough, the street is coated in a thick, white quilt of glimmering snow.

Me:

Omg! It hasn't snowed in FOREVER!

Eli:

Ikr! Bring the kids to the park and meet me in ten. I challenge you to an epic snowball fight ;)

Me:

Challenge accepted. Get ready to loseee :p

Eli:

Haha! You wish, Cotton xx

I'm about to reply with a sarky insult because he called me 'Cotton', but the kisses he added to the end of the text earn him some brownie points. I chuck on some black jeans and a blue hoodie and practically leap downstairs. All my siblings are strewn about the living room and kitchen. The smaller ones are glued to the TV, whilst the others eat breakfast and chat excitedly about the snow.

I plonk myself down next to Tyler and pinch a grape from his plate. He rolls his eyes at me but grins all the same.

'I heard you weren't too happy about Mum's new lover,' he teases, nudging me.

'Excuse you! I have every right to be angry. Her little relationships always mess us up, not to mention the fact that he is my teacher. I think she should avoid all attempts at a relationship from here on out to prevent any further tragedy—'

Tyler cuts me off by widening his eyes and nodding his head towards the stairs. I swivel round like a vintage spinning top to see that, standing behind me, wearing one of Dad's old PJ sets, is Mr Batch.

'What is *he* doing here?' I ask the room. No one dares reply. He simply walks past me and starts helping a struggling May put jam on her toast.

'Here, sweet pea, I'll help you,' he coos as if she's a baby. I shoot off my chair and explode like a ticking time bomb. May is smiling from ear to ear as though he's just announced that he's taking her to Disneyland or something!

'Sweet pea? May hates being treated like a baby. Don't you, May?' She shifts awkwardly in her chair and doesn't reply. *Fabulous, nice to know I have someone on my side.*

'Ivy, I know this isn't ideal, but your mum and I—'

'Yeah yeah, you love each other; I got it! You don't have to keep reminding me, Batch.' He bites at the corner of his lips and avoids eye contact. Good to know I've made him uncomfortable. Now he knows exactly how I feel.

'You know you can call me Leo. "Mr Batch" seems a bit ... formal.'

'No, "Mr Batch" seems pretty good to me. I will never call you Leo, because you are my teacher, and that's all you'll ever be!' I scream. My voice is irritatingly hoarse, so I can't yell to my full potential. His left eye twitches a bit, but he stays silent. Mum ambles downstairs, rubbing her eyes. She kisses Batch on the lips and starts making coffee.

'What's all the shouting about?' Mum grumbles even though she knows perfectly well what is going on. Her eyes catch mine, but she quickly diverts them to him. I stalk over to the utility room and start gathering all the kids' wellies and raincoats. Whilst Batch, Mum, and Tyler all watch me, I help the kids with their shoes and prepare myself to leave.

'What are you doing?' Mum groans. Pulling my woolly hat tight over my messy curls, I turn to give her a 'what do you think I'm doing' look. I herd the kids out of the room and to the front door.

'Don't expect us home until he's gone!' I call down the corridor. I hustle them out of the house before Mum can come racing after me.

The toddlers insisted we bring the ginormous five-seater buggy, so I am forced to push it through the deep, icy fluff. Clumps of snow crunch beneath my navy-blue wellies as we practically dance down the street. A biting wind nips at my skin, but I just pull my scarf up closer to my face. Isn't it magical how the snow appears to have glitter in it? When Tyler and I used to play in the snow, I called it 'fairy dust'. It sounds silly now, but I really thought the sparkle made it magical. How I miss those days. Innocence is such a privilege. Being grown up isn't all it's cracked up to be. You know things that you wish you didn't—things that can kill you, both physically and mentally.

When we eventually make it to the park, the kids run straight to a massive pile of snow and start a snowball fight. Eli is already on the swings, rocking gently back and forth. I smile and sit beside him, Eva in my arms. Despite the freezing weather, my baby sister is sleeping like an angel. Shame she can't sleep this soundly when it's two in the morning.

'Still alive then?' Eli jeers. I give him a 'don't even go there' look and stare at my Doc Martins. 'Not coping then?' he asks. I look up, and our eyes meet and interlock like the key to a forbidden dungeon.

'I hate it, but it's not that bad,' I lie. Eli almost bursts out laughing at my attempt to mask the truth. 'Okay fine, it is that bad. I just … we really clicked in lessons, y'know? Not in a weird way, obviously, but he just seems to understand me. I could tell him how I felt, and Mum would never know 'cause my school and home life were separate. But not anymore. Now I'm sure he'll report anything I say straight back to my dreaded mother.' Eli attempts to suck his teeth, but it comes out as a strange gurgle. We both giggle a little but instantly fall back in silence.

From out of nowhere, a huge compacted white ball catapults towards Eli and plants smack in the middle of his face.

I can barely hold myself up I'm laughing so much, though Eli doesn't find it so funny.

Then everyone goes as still as stones.

'Whoever just threw that better go hide behind a tree or something, 'cause I'm coming to get ya!' Eli shouts, leaping off the swing and roaring like a provoked lion.

The kids scatter in all directions, shrieking and laughing. A full-blown snowball fight breaks out, but I just sit on the swing, holding my baby sister in her lilac blanket. I watch as Eli picks up Archie and starts spinning around, making my brother cry with laughter. How I love him. Wait … did I just say 'love'? It feels weird to say that, whether it's in my head or not. Maybe it feels weird because we've only been in this secret relationship for, like, five minutes. Or maybe it hurts because I know I can never truly have him. Haila will always be there as a painful reminder of what I'm missing out on.

As we burst through the door like a pack of wolves, I hope to God that Batch isn't there, but my wish doesn't come true. He and my mum are cuddled up on the sofa like a newlywed couple. Ugh, it makes me sick to my stomach. The kids all run upstairs to get out of their wet clothes with Tyler, but I just stand there staring at them, Eli by my side. I scoff and flop onto the small armchair whilst Eli awkwardly steps from side to side. Mum is all smiles and giggles until she looks up and sees me glaring intensely at her.

'Darling, please not now. I'm really not in the mood for this,' she whines. Batch holds her closer, and she snuggles into his chest. What a sight for sore eyes.

'Well I'm not in the mood to have him curled up on my sofa, but here we are!' I argue in a theatrical tone.

Mum doesn't fight back but looks over to Eli. 'Eli, sweetheart, can you go upstairs and check on the kids?' she asks in such a sickly sweet voice that I'm surprised honey doesn't trickle out of her mouth. He nods and quietly shuffles up the stairs.

Mum sits up and gently shrugs Batch's arm off her shoulder. She leans in closer to me, and to my surprise, there isn't a hint of alcohol on her breath.

'Listen. Leo is helping me to stop drinking. Since we got together, I haven't touched a drop of alcohol. Isn't that what you wanted?'

Oh, so now she's trying to guilt trip me! 'Don't try to sugar-coat it. The point is you are dating my teacher, and I want it to end *now!*' I stretch out the last word, and I scoff. 'Jeez, your taste in men is seriously worrying. Apart from dad, all of your little relationships have been utter disasters. I don't know why you even bother anymore—'

'That is enough! Don't you dare speak to your own mother like that!' Batch chimes in, leaping off the sofa.

Excuse me, but who asked for his opinion? 'Oh, get a hold of yourself, Batch! You're no one special!' I screech. Mum has shrunk into the chair and is in a ball like the one Archie curls into when Tyler and I fight.

'You know what, Ivy—just got out of here and stop being so dramatic!' Batch yells, pointing towards the door.

Tyler comes bounding down the stairs with a murderous look stretched across his face.

'Who do you think you are, telling my sister what to do?!' He asks, pointing in his face. Batch takes a step back.

'Look. I know this is hard for us all—'

'Oh, don't give me that!' Tyler yells, spit flying out of his mouth. 'You have no idea what this family has been through! The last thing we need is another man to come in and ruin everything again!' I look over to

Mum, who has mascara-tinted tears running down her face and staining her white top. We all fall silent. All this mention of Mum's old boyfriends hits a place in my heart that I didn't even know existed. I don't wanna go into too much detail, but let's just say some of Mum's exes were quite violent—especially to us kids.

Tyler grabs my wrist, and we race up the stairs, leaving Batch to calm my mum down. When we reach the top of the stairs, he pulls me into a tight hug. I'm not even crying, but Tyler seems to think I need the moral support. 'Don't worry,' he whispers into my hair. 'Everything will be okay.' My brother releases me and disappears into his room.

When I open my bedroom door, Eli isn't in there. But the ladder to the roof is pulled down.

'Hey,' Eli greets me in a hushed tone as I climb through the gap in the ceiling. Since our first kiss up here, I've invested in two big bean bags in case it ever is to happen again. The plastic cover I stole from the buggy seems to have kept them protected from the snow. I fall onto the beanbag next to Eli, and he puts his huge arm around me.

'I have to say, I never thought I'd see Mr Batch curled up on your sofa,' he admits, chuckling quietly.

'Yeh, me neither. What if he moves in, Eli?' I ask, worry creeping into my voice.

'Then you can come stay with me,' he offers.

'Oh yeah, because that totally won't look suspicious to your mum and dad. Nobody can know, Eli. Well, except Martha. I kinda told her last night …' I wait for him to explode and have a go at me, but instead he just looks down at me and smiles.

'How'd she react?' he asks, looking back up at the stars.

'She was super excited. I think she wants us to be official and open. Her exact words were "You need to be more exciting, Ivy. Explore your wild side." Whatever that means.'

Eli smirks and stares into my eyes. 'You really are beautiful, Ivy Towers,' he coos in a low voice that makes my nerves tingle.

'You're not too bad yourself, Eli Bishara.' He leans in and presses his lips gently onto mine. Even though I know the horrifying statistics about French kisses, I honestly can't hold myself back. Sparks are flying like New Year's Eve fireworks.

'C'mon, let's go inside,' Eli whispers, close to my ear. Hand in hand, Eli leads me through the hatch and back into my room.

※

Last night was magical. Imagine everything you've ever wanted compacted into a couple of hours. We went further than I ever thought I would in a lifetime. Eli is too cute for words.

Sometimes I realise just how much I don't deserve him.

'Darling, you look perfect tonight,' Eli sings softly along to the radio as he drives through the village. As he sings the last words, he looks over to me and smiles. I can't stop blushing, and when I look in the mirror, I look like a burnt cherry tomato. My hair streams around my head, as Eli insisted on winding down the car roof. I'm still getting used to the fact that people drive underage here and don't get arrested. I'm used to driving sneakily and owning a fake driving licence, but that's not a problem here.

We park at the far end of the car park, under a weary old tree.

'Aren't you just the cutest thing on this planet,' he says in a low voice. He leans in and pecks me on the lips. I gently push him off and giggle like the little flirt that I am becoming.

'Stop! Someone might see us!' I squal, but the last thing I want is for this moment to end. Life always has those moments that you just want to pause and live through over and over again. This is one of those moments. In the corner of my eye, I see someone in a loose-fitting black dress practically running towards us. Eli rests his arm on the car door.

'Hey, Martha!' It feels as if I haven't seen her in forever, but it's been only two days. She gives me a discreet 'we need to talk' glance and can hardly wipe the grin off her face. Eli seems oblivious to her quite obvious gestures.

'Eli, we are gonna go to the girls' room before maths. Mind meeting us in class?' Martha asks.

'Sure.'

'Thanks, baby.' I kiss him softly on the forehead and climb out of the car.

As soon as we are out of sight, we start squealing and jumping up and down like fangirls at a boy band concert. We don't even make it to the bathroom before Martha starts asking for details.

'Tell me everything!' she squeaks.

'Well, it was … fun. Eli is really sweet—'

'How far did you go?' she interrupts. I smile at her but instantly look away. Her eyes bug out. 'All the way?'

'All the way,' I confirm. Martha prepares to let out another scream, but I cover her mouth before she has the chance to. I give her every juicy detail as we chat in the corridor. We're about to pass my locker when I notice a piece of scrap paper stuck to it. I tug it off and read it. It's a death threat.

> You'd better watch it, nerd, or prepare to say your very last words.

Martha reads over my shoulder and presses her hand to her mouth. 'Who would do such a thing!' Her voice is as shaky as it would be in an earthquake.

I crumple the note up and shove it deep into my bag. 'It's just a death threat. People do it all the time. Now, I dunno about you, but I'm starving! Let's go get pancakes from the cafeteria!' Before Martha can even answer, I start racing down the corridor. My stomach feels all funny, as if someone's just socked me straight in the ribs. I brace myself and continue walking. I can feel Martha's eyes on me, but I ignore it.

33

Eli

Ivy has been full of smiles during the entire day. In every lesson, she is asking questions and putting her hand up like a teacher's pet. This is strange. Ivy never puts her hand up. Don't get me wrong, the kid is smart, but she isn't the type to contribute in lessons.

During break, Martha warned me about the note that they found. I can't believe someone would do that after all she's been through. Whoever it is had better hide, because when I find them, they'll be the one saying their last words. Call me dramatic, but no one, and I mean no one, hurts my Ivy.

Ivy's excitable mood seems to have dulled down, because throughout the whole of history class, she doesn't even pick up a pen. She just glares directly at Mr Batch.

I do feel bad for the guy, to be completely honest. He just fell for the wrong person and is now caught up in the downward spiral of the Towers family. When it comes to us doing silent work, Batch and Ivy have the ultimate stare-off. I have to say, she does have a very intense glare. I'm gonna make a mental note to never get on the wrong side of Ivy Towers.

After an hour of awkward stares, the bell finally goes. Ivy doesn't even hang around waiting for me and Martha. She tries to run out of the room, but Batch stops her.

'Ivy, can we have a chat please?'

34

Ivy

'I understand how difficult this situation must be for you, but there's nothing we can do about it. Me and your mum … we really are in love.' The word 'love' sends my stomach into unbearable knots. 'If you just give me a chance, I could be a really great stepdad to you … oh, Ivy, please don't cry.'

My face has crumpled into a grotesque expression, and tears fly out of my eyes. I wail like a baby and hold my head in my hands. Batch walks over and puts his hand on my shoulder.

'I know it's hard, but we'll get through this together.' The poor guy thinks I'm crying about him dating my mother. Rather, I'm crying because of that note found on my locker. He lets me cry it out and when my sobs die down, he stands back.

'Go get something to eat. It'll make you feel better.' My stomach is churning, and the last thing I need is food, but I nod all the same.

As I trudge towards our tree, I realise that Martha and Eli have noticed that the hop and skip in my step have completely disappeared. They give me pitying looks, which I really don't appreciate, as I lower myself into the wheelchair beside Eli. I don't know why they went and got my wheelchair from Kilt, but more importantly, I don't know why he gave it to them. Surely I should be the only one who is able to retrieve it, seeming as it is—you know—mine.

'Can you quit with the sorrowful looks? I'm fine.' There's that look again—the sort with the half frown and raised left eyebrow. Martha opens her mouth, but Eli glares at her before she can speak. We all know that Martha isn't exactly an all-star when it comes to sympathetic small talk.

'Your eyes are pretty red—'

'Well I never!' I snap. Eli twiddles his thumbs and shifts about on the PE bag that is his temporary seat. His kit must be drenched, considering there is still slushy snow all over the place. But he and Martha insisted we sit here because it's my favourite place.

Before I can apologise, Eli takes hold of my freezing left palm and squeezes it gently. 'It's okay, babe. Now just … just tell us what happened in there. Was it about the note?' Martha instantly elbows Eli so hard that he winces a little.

She told him?

'Does privacy mean nothing to you, Martha Jones?' Her face drops like a bunch of out-of-season flowers. Eli lets go of my hand as if it's just spewed out black ink all over him.

A small part of me demands that I unleash all my anger on her, but the angel inside me won't allow it.

'Okay, so maybe I didn't completely hold it together in there, but I'm fine now. I just cried a little and got the hell outta there, that's all.'

Eli tells me he understands, but Martha stays stone-cold silent and picks at the orangey-grey pepperoni on her pizza. I nearly do a happy leap when the bell finally goes.

Instead of going to last lesson, I have a meeting with Kilt. The man goes as pale as Casper the ghost when I show him the note. Goodness knows why. It is hardly a disturbing note. Defaults do this sort of stuff all the time, and I'd think he'd be used to it. Snatching the paper out of my hand, my mentor insists that he'll get to the bottom of it. I doubt he will, unless he can hire a handwriting expert to scope out the culprit, but we all know that his budget doesn't stretch that far.

At the end of the day, I don't manage to find Martha or Eli, so I'm left to catch the bus alone. The worst possible thing happens as I amble through the busy corridors. I see the bus in front of school through a far window. It is about to leave, which means I am forced to do something I haven't done in months—run.

My legs can barely keep up with the pace I'm trying to run at. Before exercise, I always kid myself into thinking that this time will be different and this time I won't trip over my own laces during a damn egg race (true story.)

Every time, I'm grossly disappointed.

As I publicly embarrass myself by waddling down the corridor like an injured penguin, I collide with the one person that I hoped to avoid—Haila Adil.

A tornado of rose-gold notebooks with cheesy statements like 'Chase your dreams' and orange foundation bottles whirl above us and come crashing to the floor. Seriously, though, why would you wanna chase your dreams? Chasing involves running, and who likes to run? No one.

'Seriously, Cotton?' she shrieks, scrambling to pick up all her frilly pink accessories off of the bacteria-infested floor. Her foundation is history, but I think I did her a favour on that one.

'It was an accident, Haila, jeez,' I mumble, startling both me and my enemy. I rarely stand up for myself when it comes to Haila, mainly because I'm secretly dating her boyfriend and I don't want to give her anymore reasons to murder me in my sleep. Her beady little pupils shoot up to meet mine, and I instantly know my life is over. As she returns to a standing position, she gets right up close to my face.

'You'd better watch it, nerd, or prepare to say your last words,' Haila growls in my ear. She slides her designer sunglasses over her silky hijab and stalks off towards the main entrance.

When I finally reach home, I practically fall through the front door. Our home is strangely quiet, but the judgemental glances of Mr Batch meet me at the doorway.

'Hey,' I grumble as I stumble through the house and into the kitchen. Besides Haila threatening to slaughter me, one of my main focuses today has been orange juice. I can't be the only one that gets serious cravings for random things. To my horror, when I whip open the fridge door and brace myself to lift a heavy bottle of orange, it isn't nearly as heavy as I expect it to be. In fact, it is so light that I exert too much force and slam my hand into the top of the fridge.

'Leo, why is the carton *empty?*' My voice rises on the last word without any warning. My mum's boyfriend seems rather taken aback by my choice of name for him. His mouth flutters as he tries to form words.

'So … we … we're on first-name terms now, are we?' he stutters. A victorious smirk tugs at the corner of his lips.

'Don't flatter yourself. Anyways, that's beside the point. What I want to know is why this carton has zilch left in it! Nought! None! Nil pois!'

He holds his left hand out for me to stop. 'Yes, yes, I get it. I had the orange juice this morning. Is that a problem?' Leo replies in such a smug tone that I want to shove the carton right down his throat.

'Yes … yes, it is a massive problem! I was gonna have this after school, but you had to go and drink it, didn't you!' Who knows why I'm getting so irate over this, but I'm really not going to hold back. I throw the carton to the floor and start screaming into the palms of my hands. The front door flies open, and all of my family burst down the hallway. I look up from my hands but continue to screech, despite my huge audience. Tyler drops a bunch of shopping bags on the kitchen table and gives Leo a puzzled look.

'I drank the rest of the orange juice,' he answers to the unspoken question.

Tyler gives a strange nasal cackle and shakes his head. 'Rookie mistake. Rule number one of living with a teenage girl: never get between her and her comfort foods, or it's bound to get messy.' I give Tyler a rude gesture whilst his back is turned and he's putting rich tea biscuits in the cupboard. Tyler reaches into one of the other shopping bags and pulls out a carton.

'Don't worry, Petal. I gotcha.' He hands me the juice, and I swear I almost do a happy leap.

'Thank you, thank you, thank you!' I squeal, jumping up and down. I don't even bother grabbing a cup. I just unscrew the cap and pour it straight down my neck. Leo watches on with an utterly baffled look fixed on his face. *Poor man.*

'Looks like I've got a lot to learn,' Leo says, attempting a cheery voice, though I can't help but notice the deflation in his tone. This feels like the perfect time for me to make a speedy escape to my room. As everyone tidies the kitchen and packs away the shopping, I slip out.

My body relaxes into my faux memory foam mattress. I'd always dreamt of sleeping on a real memory foam mattress, but we've never been able to afford one. Isn't it just so stupid how money limits our life experiences? If only money didn't exist—but we all know that would end in a bloodbath. With my full orange juice carton in hand, I settle myself down to release the stresses of today. This relaxation time has become sort of a ritual for me. Life piles on the pressure ten times quicker than I can load it off, so I figure that some alone time will be beneficial for both my physical and mental health. My fingers tap lightly on the right arrow on the remote control until I come across a documentary on tropical birds. *Exciting!*

Just as I immerse myself into the wonderful world of keel-billed toucans and Moluccan cockatoo parrots, my entertainment is rudely disturbed by the creaking of my door. Leo's head peeks round the door, and a goofy grin spreads across his cheeks when he sees me.

'Ever heard of knocking?' I growl. My anger disintegrates as his smile disappears and is replaced by a sorrowful frown.

I sigh. 'Don't worry about it,' I reassure him. The goofy grin reappears, and he perches at the end of my bed. His eyes pan across my duvet.

'Nice bedsheets you've got there.' When I was younger and we lived in a bigger house with Dad, I had a double bed all to myself. I was only three, but Dad thought I was mature enough to have one. On my birthday, he got me a duvet with a beautiful pattern. Different books are dotted all around the baby-pink quilt. Some of my favourites are on it. For instance, *Charlotte's Web* and *Little Women*. Even if it overhangs my single bed now, I've refused to ever get rid of it. It smells of Dad—a mixture of a warm, musky cologne and the faint scent of Merlot. Dad always told me that we were too classy to have even a bottle of beer in sight. How I wish he were here now.

My fingers caress the cover, and my skin tingles at the soft texture.

'My dad got it for me,' I say so quietly that I'm surprised he even understands me. Leo puts his hand on top of mine. I don't pull away.

'You know I'm not trying to replace your dad, right? I'd never do that.' His voice is sincere, but I can't help but not believe him. His Adam's apple bulges as he takes a deep gulp.

'Yeah, I know,' I murmur. A pause that seems to last forever settles between us. 'I just miss him. He always knew how to cheer me up.' I laugh gently. 'One summer we went to Barbados, and every night, he took me to the beach. Just me and him. Father and daughter. We'd watch the clear night sky and give the constellations funny names. He'd buy me an ice-cold bottle of cloudy lemonade and himself a Jäger bomb. We'd lie under the moonlight and occasionally take a sip of our drinks. The delicate sand would seep between my toes, and he'd hold me close ... ' I snap out of my little journey down memory lane and look up. *Oops, I kinda zoned out a little bit.* I mumble that I'm sorry, but he just tells me that Dad seems like an amazing person. He was. I mean he is. I don't know anymore. My father could be dead for all I know. Happy families.

'Looks like I'll never be as good as your dad, but I'll try. But first, you're gonna have to let me in a bit because right now I feel like a stranger in this house. Tell me everything, good and bad. I wanna be a part of it all.'

So I explain our entire existence from start to finish. I tell him how Coco hates any food that is orange and how the twins do kickboxing twice a week. He tells me that his name is short for Leonardo and expects me to laugh, but I tell him that I have no right to laugh, since my real name is Ivanna. I tell him about the time Archie peed in a water fountain and how Tyler refuses to watch fantasy movies because they are 'unrealistic and far-fetched,' which is the whole point of them. I tell him everything except what happened on the night of 26 June 2017. That story can never be retold. Not by anyone. Ever.

When we eventually finish our conversation, it is pitch black outside. Mum calls us for dinner, but I tell him that I'm not feeling too well, so Leo goes downstairs alone. My stomach feels like wet mashed potatoes, and the last thing I want to do is add more to the gooey mess churning inside of me.

Ping!

I'll make you regret everything—Simon.

If my stomach felt like mashed potatoes before, now it feels like pure porridge—cheese porridge. Who'd be so sick as to sign off messages to me with 'Simon'? Whoever it is knows what happened, and that shakes me. It shakes me to my core.

35

Eli

My original plan for tonight was to lock myself up in the security of my room and FaceTime Ivy for as long as possible. Ivy has this way of masking her emotions whilst they kill her inside, and it's really dangerous. You can only imagine what could happen to her if she has no shoulder to cry on. I barely have to imagine. When my brother died, no one was there for me. The river of sympathy was as dry as the Sahara Desert for both me and Khalid.

However, my plans were foiled as quickly as they came about by my mum's announcement that we're going to an Indian restaurant with Haila's family. *Fabulous.* I hate pretending to love her. Pretending was never necessary before Ivy came along, but now I really don't care for Haila anymore. Ivy made me realise that I can do better.

Compared to the other girls at our school, Haila is an angel. But now that Ivy has rocked up, my standards have skyrocketed.

I guess it's all about perspective.

Now, I'm sitting at a table surrounded by family and people I could almost consider a second set of relatives. Haila is practically sitting on top of me, with her body pressed right up next to me. Normally I'm all for a plush double chair at a restaurant, but right now all I want is a single chair so Haila will back off a bit. I must sound like such a douchebag. Haila's soft left hand is clasping mine like an electric blanket, which makes it almost impossible to eat my chicken korma.

'How're you kids doing with your GCSEs? They must be very tricky.' Brownie points to Haila's mum for trying to start up a conversation, but it goes down like a lead balloon. Mum and Dad are still giving me the silent treatment after our argument, and the tension between Haila and me could barely be cut with a heavy-duty butcher's knife.

'I'm doing well. Maths is particularly difficult, but I'm working with it. I dunno about Eli though. We haven't talked much recently.' I can almost feel Haila's cold, hard stare boring through my cheeks, but my eyes stare straight forward. I tell the adults what they want to hear—that school is going great and my grades are skyrocketing—so they all beam proud smiles and congratulate me. Haila's grandma even offers me a toffee, as if I'm some sort of Victorian child singing a hymn at the side of the street to earn the odd tuppence or peppermint. I pocket the sweet and give Haila a victorious wink. She huffs and puffs, but I couldn't care less. The rest of the evening is spent exchanging polite conversation, with me pretending that I give a toss, while Haila's Aunt Gloria drones on about her sister who's travelling around Europe and gawping at pointless landmarks.

By the end of the evening, I can barely keep myself upright and am glad to finally lay eyes on my bed. The screen of my laptop releases a blinding light that brightens up my room like a lone star in a haunting night sky.

Eli:

Hey Ivy :) you up? xx

Ivy:

I am now. I can't sleep cos my stomach is all jiggly :'(

Eli:

Aww, that sucks. At least you're awake to talk to me ;)

Ivy:

Yeh, I guess so. I kinda worked out who sent me that note. It was Haila. I've also been getting eerie texts, and it's clearly her.

My fingers hover over the keyboard, but I have no idea what to say. My stomach feels just as bad as Ivy's, and I feel the chicken korma as it rises up my throat. I should feel upset by this, but I don't. In fact, I feel happy—excited even.

Eli:

Ivy, this is fantastic!!!

Ivy:

I wouldn't say fantastic is the best choice of word …?

Eli:

Noooo, don't you see?!

Ivy:

You're gonna have to spell this out for me cause I'm really not understanding you.

Eli:

This is the perfect way for me to split with Haila! I can say that I don't wanna be with someone who threatens other people and it would be unethical for me to marry her! Oh this is perfect!

Ivy:

It might just work! You know Eli, for a jock ur actually pretty smart.

Eli:

I hate you.

Ivy:

Hahaha. You know you love me really.

Ivy:

Typing …

Ivy:

I gtg. I think someone heard me typing and I'm supposed to be asleep -_-

Eli:

lol alright bye <3

It must be urgent, because she doesn't reply after that. Oh, how I love that girl. After repeatedly typing out a message and deleting it, I manage to create the perfect message to send to Haila. It's five words:

We don't belong together. Sorry.

Sending that text feels like the biggest weight off my shoulders, and for the first time in months, I can breathe. I've recently felt as if there's been a clamp closing in on my lungs, but it's gone now. I'm free. A wave of fatigue floods over me, so I put my laptop on the bedside table, and within seconds I'm fast asleep.

36

Ivy

The court date creeps ever closer over the next month. Meetings with lawyers have been paramount. I have to make sure that everything I say helps keep Craig behind bars for as long as possible. He's hurt me worse than I could've ever imagined, and we can't risk that happening to anyone else. No one deserves that. With every passing day, the threats have gotten worse. They've even escalated to the point of graphic death threats. It must be someone I know. Who else could it be? This is all I can think about as I lie here in the comfort of my bed. Well, it used to provide me with such invaluable comfort. Now nowhere feels safe. Everywhere I turn, I feel watched. Whoever is messaging me wants to scare me off. It's working. As much as I want to sleep, I can't. They don't want me to, so I won't. A furious dictator is ruling my life, and I can't get rid of them.

No. No, no, no, no, no, this can't be. My eyes are staring down at the stick, and they won't stop no matter how hard I try to prise them away.

I try to convince myself that maybe if I glare at it long enough, the word will just wash away. Tears run down my burning cheeks and drop onto the small window in the middle of the stick. For a split second the word disappears, but as soon as my thumb wipes away the murky liquid, there it is again, in big bold letters, as clear as day: 'pregnant'.

I crumple to the ground, screaming and chucking the stick across the room. How could this happen? A whole array of anger-induced questions buzz about my head, but then I come to realise something. I need to stop blaming the world for our mistake. We should have been more careful, but it's more easily said than done. It happened in the moment and made me just so happy.

Nothing was going to ruin that moment for me, and no way would I have chosen that beautiful moment to run down to the local pharmacy and buy protection. It may have been stupid, I admit, but now I have an actual human being growing inside my body.

A sudden feeling of dizziness overcomes me, so I lower myself to the bathroom floor, blubbering like a child and gazing at the crusty ceiling. For a minute I just lie there, wondering what on earth I'm going to do with myself. After a while, I manage to clutch the edge of the sink and pull myself up. I am not prepared for the monstrosity that meets me in the mirror. My face is a bubble of snot, tears, and blotchy red skin. God forbid the baby adopts most of my genes. It'll look like an ogre. I try to imagine what a cross between me and Eli would look like, but I just can't picture it.

Knock knock knock.

'Ivy? You all right? We heard a scream.' The voice on the other side of the door is Leo's.

'Uh, yeh, I'm … I'm fine. Just a spider, but I chucked it out of the window.' My voice is croaky and my excuse is atrocious, but thankfully Leo is too inexperienced to know otherwise.

'Okay, all right then. Breakfast is ready when you want to come down.'

'I'll be down in a tick!' I say in the cheeriest voice I can muster. Just as I begin to calm myself down, my phone pings.

Be careful. You have no idea what I'm capable of.- Simon

Great. Another creepy message, presumably from Haila. How did she even get my phone number … unless Craig gave it to her? No, Ivy, don't let this freak you out. It's easy to get a phone number, so it could be anyone. Besides, Craig is in deep enough water with the police; I doubt he'd want to make his situation worse. Anyway, I have bigger problems on my hands, the main one being the minuscule human living inside of me.

I splash some cold water on my face and practise smiling in the mirror, before taking a deep breath and releasing myself from the security of my bathroom. With a deep-set grin implanted on my face, I stride into the kitchen and plonk myself down beside Tyler. Everyone glances at each other, but no one has the decency to ask me why I look as though I've just met my lifelong idol. After making everyone's lunches and adding a chocolate to Tyler's, just in case he finds out, I tug on my shoes and make for the door.

'I can give you a ride, Ivy. Not like it's out of my way or anything,' Leo offers. I grin and take his offer graciously. He gives my mum a look as we leave the house, but I dismiss it.

We approach the school gates, where a mixed group of kids and stressed-looking teachers are streaming into the car park.

'Actually, can you just … stop here?' It takes Leo a while to understand why I wanna be dropped off so far from the building, but he eventually laughs and stops the car.

'Too cool to be seen with your teacher, huh?' he teases, elbowing me gently.

'You got it!' I say cheerily.

Before I open the door, Leo puts his hand on my shoulder. 'Are you sure you're okay? You seem overly … jolly today.'

I let my happy facade slip for only a split second, but Leo spots it instantly. I don't want to give him a chance to quiz me, so I clamber out of the car and say, 'Can't a girl be happy for once?' and I slam the door shut. I practically dance into school to let everyone know that everything is okay. I'm okay.

— 37

Eli

Today, Friday, marks a week since I parted with Haila, and I feel strangely free. It's like a show that I watched on Netflix. These girls were living within a violent cult, and they didn't know the rest of the world existed until they were freed. I didn't know I was being held captive until I was released from the prison of my relationship. Okay, so maybe I'm being a tad dramatic, but you get what I'm trying to say. Mum and Dad both hate me—like, *really* hate me. And as for Haila's mum, I don't think she could physically despise me more if she tried. Ivy practically comes bounding towards me with a huge grin stretched across her small face. It's almost comical watching my poor girlfriend trying to act happy. I mean, she probably is full of joy, but I've never seen it get to this extreme before. Something seriously good must've happened.

'Hi Ivy, what's up … Hey, hey, hey, what's going on?' I ask as my girlfriend frantically tugs me down the corridor. She eventually finds a crevice in the corridor that we can both manage to squeeze into. Even when we are stationary, she doesn't let go of my sleeve, as if she needs support. As soon as we are out of view, her face drops like a penny from the top of the Eiffel Tower. I assumed when Ivy came dancing through the front entrance of school everything was okay, but I'm guessing everything isn't as happy as Larry. She takes a few deep breaths and says two words I never thought she'd say.

'I'm pregnant.'

It's as if my whole life has been snatched from under my feet within a second. The corridor becomes a blur and starts to whirl around. My vision is a blur of my girlfriend's worried face and walls of lockers and oblivious teenagers. My eyes start to settle, and I let the news soak in like a warm bath. Except this bath is anything but warm. In fact, it's ice-cold.

Ivy's face crumples, but she covers it before the tears start flowing. I pull her in to my chest and caress her hair with my hand. I reassure my newly pregnant girlfriend that everything will be okay, but I know it will be anything but. We can't be parents! We are too young, and who knows what my parents will have to say about this. *Oh my gosh, my parents. We are doomed. Okay, Eli, think logically. What is the best thing we can do in this situation?*

'Ivy, come with me.' I wipe her tears away and lead her outside. We go to a far corner of the field and sit on a bench.

'What are we doing?' she asks, still wiping tears from her face.

'Get out your phone. Just ... just trust me on this one, okay?' She looks incredibly confused but gets it out all the same. I take it and type in the number of our local GP. 'You gotta call them and ask for an emergency appointment, okay? Can you do that?' She nods to my plea, without making eye contact. I put my arm around her whilst the phone rings.

'Hello? Yes, I'd like to make an appointment, please. An ... an emergency one. Will I be alone?' She looks up at me with small bloodshot eyes.

I mime, 'I'm coming.'

'No, my ... uhm ... my boyfriend is gonna come with me. 12.45 today? That's fine. Thanks. Bye ...' She hangs up and buries her face into my shirt.

'We'll just make our excuses and leave. Everything will be fine; I'm sure of it.' I feel like I'm trying to reassure myself more than Ivy.

I've always wanted to be a father, but at sixteen? Well, at least it's legal. If I were underage, I don't even know what we would've done.

❦

'So how can I help you today?' the GP asks in a soft and caring tone. Ivy hasn't let go of my hand since we left school. Her warm, small palm pressed in mine presents a small comfort in this difficult time.

'I'm pregnant. I took a test this morning, and it was positive.' I squeeze her hand tighter, and she squeezes mine back.

The GP presses us further. 'So I assume you're the father?' she says, looking over to me. I nod. 'Lovely. And might I ask how old you both are?' Ivy tenses slightly at the question, so I answer without hesitation.

'We both turned sixteen in early September before the school term started, actually.'

I only added that little snippet of information at the end in the hope of her starting up a conversation so we don't have to go into the nitty-gritty details.

Instead she simply nods and enters these facts on her computer. When she's finished updating her notes, the doctor turns to look at us in a calm, professional way.

'Now, I'm sure this must be very scary for you, but I'm here to help. I can't force you to do anything, but if your parents or guardians don't know about the pregnancy, I suggest you tell them. They may not react the way you want them to, but it's better they should know soon.' We both fidget uneasily at the prospects.

'Now, are you planning to keep the baby or to have it aborted?' She cracks this question as if we've had time to think about it. Ivy looks up at me with a half-smile on her lips. Without discussion, Ivy looks over to the doctor.

'We want to keep it,' she affirms.

It feels like a punch to the gut, but I guess it's her decision. Whether I'm a part of the baby's life, it's Ivy's choice whether she wants to keep it or not. I can't force her to abort it. The doctor looks over to me with a pitiful look in her eyes, but I refuse to meet her gaze. She proceeds to ask several other questions, and by the end of the session we begin to appreciate our new circumstances.

On the way home, we decide to take a pit stop at the *McDonald's* drive-thru. Even now Ivy doesn't let go of my hand, allowing me only to change gear. Ivy keeps looking down at her phone to read the occasional text. Whoever is texting her mustn't be very nice, because her nose wrinkles every time. I wouldn't say the car is silent; I'd merely say it's peaceful. Though neither of us is talking, the distant buzz of customers and McDonald's workers drifts into the car, and the quiet hum of birdsong dances through the air. As we wait for our food, Ivy looks up at me.

'I'm sorry. Keeping the baby should've been your decision too,' she almost whispers. The pure shame in her voice sends a surge of guilt through my body. I stare into her eyes intensely, but with a soft smile.

'Baby, it's okay. I want this baby, and I want to be the best father and boyfriend I can be.' At my words, my girlfriend relaxes into her seat and lets go of my hand.

I skilfully munch on fries whilst driving cautiously towards Ivy's house. We decide not to go back to school because we have only one lesson left: PE—one of the most pointless lessons on this planet. Lucky for us, no one is home, so we cuddle up on the sofa and watch some trashy American reality show. Ivy lies in the crook of my arm with an unsettled look on her face.

'What's up, Cotton?' She's started to let me call her that, even though the original use wasn't so kind.

Ivy twirls her dark brown hair around her index finger and purses her lips slightly. 'How are we going to tell everyone, Eli? Between Martha, the kids, and Tyler … oh my gosh, Tyler. He'll kill me, Eli, and I wish I was exaggerating! What if Mum doesn't want to be a grandma yet? What if everyone at school finds out? I'll be a laughingstock! Not to mention the teachers! The judging looks will kill me, Eli! Before we know it, I'll be one of those young mums in pink tracksuits on the bus with a cheap stroller and—'

'Okay, okay, calm down. Take a deep breath, baby.' Her head bobs up and down on my chest as she inhales and exhales.

Slam!

We both sit bolt upright at the sound of the front door. *Who's home so early? They're all supposed to be at school or at work!* Tyler and two other guys join us in the front room. One of them has a man bun perched on top of his bulky figure. *Kirk.* The other has glowing dark skin and a curly brown afro, which I really envy. He has a black-and-white bandana tied round his hairline, which I wish I could pull off.

Tyler's arms are folded so tight I'd be surprised if he can unfold them again.

38

Ivy

'Bunking off school now, are we? Not a good look, sis,' Tyler says, dropping a six-pack of beers on the coffee table. I fold my arms, both to show how much I don't care and to try to keep the sickly feeling inside my stomach at bay.

'I could say the same thing to you.'

Tyler gives me a sideways look. 'I don't have lessons in the afternoon today; sixth-form perks, remember?' he says in a high-pitched and extremely patronising voice. Kirk and the other guy, whom I've never met before, chuckle and fall into the other chairs. *Rude.*

My stomach is really starting to play games with me, and I think Eli has noticed. After one look at my green face, he runs off to get a bucket from the kitchen. Tyler notices, sits beside me and holds me whilst I gag like a mad lady.

'Kirk, paracetamol's in the left cabinet in the bathroom. Could you get it please— quickly!' Kirk rushes upstairs to fetch the medicine.

What on earth is paracetamol gonna do for me in this situation? Poor guy isn't the sharpest tool in the toolbox. Then it hits me. I scream and scream and scream in the hope that Kirk will come back downstairs before he realises.

It doesn't help; it only alarms the three clueless guys downstairs.

'Shhh, it's okay, Petal. Just a bit of nausea.' The stranger guy almost bursts out laughing at my nickname. My stomach twists into a double knot—no, a triple knot—and I chuck up all over the guy's shoes. *Karma.* He curses under his breath and goes to the kitchen to wipe it off. Eli runs back into the room bearing a bucket, but it is too late.

'Yo, Eli, look what I found!' Kirk shouts as he stalks down the stairs. *Please, I pray, let it be something else. Anything else!* But it isn't. Kirk bursts into the room holding the pregnancy test. I forgot to pick it up when I hastily discarded it this morning. *Ugh, Ivy, you're so dumb sometimes.* Tyler's eyes dart from the stick to me a thousand times over before he can even begin to comprehend what's happening. The other guy walks back into the room and is about to talk when he notices the tense atmosphere hanging in the room.

Tyler looks me deep in the eyes. 'Ivanna Melanie Towers, Tell me the truth. Is that pregnancy test yours?' Full name. He hasn't called me that since I was nine, when I accidentally on purpose put his Match Attack cards through the shredder. All eight eyes are on me, watching, waiting for an answer.

'I-I …' *C'mon Ivy; say something!* I may be silent, but my mind is screaming a billion words. 'I'm gonna be sick.' I leap out of the chair and sprint to my room before any of them have a chance to grab me. I hurry to the safety of our rooftop.

Ping!

It'll happen, Ivy. I always know where you are, and soon I'll make sure you're somewhere you deserve—in your grave. -Simon

I simply shut my phone off and stare into the distance. My peace is soon disturbed by Tyler's mate climbing through to the roof. I shift away from him as he sits beside me. He shakes his head and smiles.

'What's so funny?' I practically growl. This just makes his smile grow even more crazy. How I want to punch that smug little face.

'You just remind me of Tyler; that's all—so feisty yet so small. And thanks for asking, my name is Chris.' Chris puts his long left arm around me. My body tenses in the same way as it does when coming to a sudden drop on a roller coaster.

'Chill out, Lil T. Your bro isn't that mad. Well, he kinda is, but he'll simmer down eventually.' I lift his arm off my shoulder and shift away even more, until I'm in danger of dropping off the side of the house.

'I'm not a little Tyler; I am me—Ivy Towers. Now, if you'll excuse me, I wanna cry by myself for a bit.' Instead of leaving as I hoped he would, he just lies back and stares at the clouds.

'By "Ivy Towers" do you mean "Ivanna Melanie Towers"?' he teases, and he almost bursts out laughing. I shoot him a deadly look that would send shivers down the spine of even the most hardened criminal.

'Call me that again and your life ends, got it, Chris?'

'All right, all right, lil T. Lawd, I can only imagine how your baby gonna act. It'll be a right little vicious one.'

Now I feel selfish. In all this drama, all I've thought about is myself. I almost forgot about the innocent child growing inside me. It needs me to care for it, but I don't know if I'm capable of that.

Just as I'm seriously starting to consider chucking Chris off the roof, Eli pops his head through the hatch and saves his life.

'Yo ... Chris, is it?' Chris nods. 'Can I talk to Ivy for a bit ... in private?'

'Sure. In a bit, Lil T.' Chris salutes me as he leaves the roof. Eli's eyes follow Chris as he goes.

'He's very ... charismatic.'

'Mmm-hmm.'

Eli sighs. A soft, warm breeze glides around us. A strong beam of sunshine rains down on us and gleams on my boyfriend's clear blue irises. His hair is perfectly slicked back, and so are his thick eyebrows. Clouds obscure the sunlight, and for a moment, all goes dark. A shiver creeps up on me, and the hairs on my arm stand up. Eli notices and slips his navy-blue jumper over my head.

I look up at him and smile. 'You're gonna make a great dad, baby.'

'Nah,' he denies modestly, but I see the glimmer of a smirk pull at the corner of his lips.

'I've seen you with my siblings. You're a natural. Me not so much.' I stare off into the distance. Instead of green fields or the soft waves of the Pacific Ocean, rows and rows of bleak grey houses meet my gaze. Eli takes hold of me and swivels my body to face him.

'You, Ivy Towers, are going to be the best mother any baby could ask for. You may not believe it now, but I know you will. Understand me?'

I nod and stare up at the sky. On the horizon, the sun starts to set, casting a radiant flame of scarlet and opal over the normally black-and-white estate.

'We're gonna buy a little cottage, far away from everyone,' Eli says. 'Our child will dance between the flower beds, picking up a rose to smell it. We'll play tag in our own little woodland area at the end of our four-hundred-foot garden. When we're all worn out, we'll go inside and have a homemade meal. First, a freshly made soup garnished with coriander and lime. Then a full roast of beef and potatoes, and as many Yorkshire puddings as one can muster.' He is lost in his imagination and is talking to himself more than to me. I don't dare interrupt; I just lie there smiling and imagining along with him. 'Afterwards, we'll have strawberries that we grew ourselves with fresh clotted cream. We'll walk to a nearby field and watch the stars at night. I'll tell our child all the different names of constellations, and you'll make them a daisy chain. We'll call our child our little prince or princess, and we'll lie under the night sky. Our lives will be perfect.' And just for a minute I believe it. I really start to think that maybe my life could change.

Maybe I'll no longer be in this mental prison. Maybe I might want to get up in the morning and face this big, wide world head on. But after that small glimmer of hope comes the pessimism. After all, every rainbow comes with rainfall. None of this is going to happen to me. We won't be happy. Since Simon, I've learnt not to hold on to hope. When I was standing by his bed, I realised something. Nothing good lasts forever. At some point, something will go wrong. It just has to. At least it does for me. That's just how my luck goes.

— 39

Eli

Home isn't home anymore. Legally it is, but that's it. Never had it occurred to me just how much you can make a person hate you. Each morning I get out of bed praying, hoping Mum will forgive me and that all I've done will be cleaned from the slate. In my opinion, I don't think I've done a single thing wrong. The whole point of marriage is that you profess your love for a particular individual and vow to spend the rest of your lives together. I want to do neither of these with Haila. She doesn't make my heart flutter anymore. She doesn't make me realise just how lucky I am. Ivy does.

Dad seemed to fully understand my position when I told them. He nodded in the right places and offered a sympathetic smile. Mum's reaction is a whole other story. She did the one thing worse than getting angry and punching me. She cried.

No one wants to see their mum cry. It makes your stomach do funny things, and the fleshy red muscle inside of you feels as if it's single-handedly being torn apart. The wedding is off, and everyone hates me, but I haven't told them about the pregnancy. That would tip Mum over the edge.

Yesterday was difficult. We hadn't expected Tyler to find out in quite the way that he did. His friends weren't much of a help either. After we sat on the roof, I decided to go home before the emotions really started flowing. There's only one person that I hate to see cry more than my own mother—Ivy.

It may make me seem ungrateful to my parents, but Ivy really is my rock. After all she's been through, I quite literally can't comprehend how she is still pushing on. I certainly couldn't do it myself. Now it's morning, the most dreadful part of the day. I've been awake for quite a while already, but I haven't moved—not a single muscle. Why? Because as soon as I do, this new day starts, and with it there will come new challenges and more hatred from the woman herself—my mother. Craig's trial is coming up, and it literally couldn't come sooner. Every day I see his face in my head with his smug grin is another day when Ivy isn't receiving the justice she deserves. At least he's in a cell. They're holding him until his trial, which honestly feels like an age away, even though it's next week. With great reluctance, I pull myself from the comfort of my bed, get dressed, and brace myself for the day. After a deep breath, I make my way to the kitchen. Mum and Dad are having one of those grown-up chats where they use those stupid low voices. I'm not stupid. I know when something is wrong. Mum notices my presence but doesn't acknowledge me. Instead she murmurs some final words to Dad and leaves the room.

'Nice to see you, too,' I call after her.

Dad grabs my arm, taking me by surprise. 'Do you have any idea what your mother is going through?' he asks sternly, glaring at me with wide eyes.

I snatch my arm from his grip. 'What she's going through? Oh, that's rich! Everyone hates me, Dad. Everyone.' My voice breaks unexpectedly, and a single tear falls down my face. Dad's expression makes no change.

'Ever wondered why they hate you, huh? Maybe because you broke the heart of the most beautiful girl in this city!—'

'Is she the most beautiful though? You might think so, but I don't, Dad.' Now I'm completely bawling my eyes out. 'I love Ivy. As for Haila … she doesn't make me happy. Isn't that what's most important? My happiness? Or is it all about you guys?' My voice is beginning to rise. 'I want to spend the rest of my life with Ivy, so that's exactly what I'm going to do!' Mum's frame is now in the doorway, her eyes watching me carefully. I need to pick my words with caution, but I don't want to. It just isn't fair anymore.

'Oh, and for your information, Ivy is pregnant, so there!' I yell. I instantly cut myself off, holding my hand to my lips as if I'm trying to cram the words back into my mouth. Tears start to build up in Mum's eyes, but I show no sign of sympathy. She can't win me over with the waterworks—not this time. Mum gives Dad a look, and he nods, agreeing silently.

'W-what?' I ask, looking back and forth between them. Dad inhales a sharp breath.

'Eli, we love you. We really do, but … we don't think it's best for you to continue to live here.' I look over to Mum and see a pile of bags by her feet, which I hadn't noticed during my rant.

'But you can't just … This is my home! Where am I supposed to go?' I demand, throwing my hands in the air. Mum flinches, but her eyes continue to stare at the floor. It's obvious she can barely comprehend this any more than I can.

'Well, we've put some money in an envelope for you. There's cheap accommodation all over the—'

'Wait, are you serious?' I whisper, my body recoiling slightly. Dad walks over to Mum and puts his arm around her. Shouldn't I be the one he is comforting? On impulse, I say something I never thought I'd say to my parents.

'Fine. I know where I'm not wanted.' With that I am gone. Struggling with my five duffel bags, I stumble out of the front door, dropping my keys as I leave. I won't be needing them anymore. Once I'm a safe distance from my home—well, I can't really call it that anymore—I crumple to the ground. I throw my head back and scream into the sky, hoping for some kind of answer from God.

How could they do this to me—their only son? Well, I suppose I'm not their only son. I'm sure Khalid wouldn't do this, because he's big, strong Khalid—almighty Khalid. But he's gone now. Instead they're stuck with me, the other one—small, weak Eli. the disappointment of the century.

40

Ivy

Even though the house is full to the brim of kids, I feel so alone. Mum has gained the strength to go to work, and Tyler has gone out with his mates, leaving me with the seven little devils that are my siblings. I'm glad Mum is starting to get her act together, because she was in danger of becoming an alcoholic. She may have turned to alcohol, but I know she got out of it before it was too late. Tyler hasn't talked to me since Kirk revealed my pregnancy. Every time I try to start up a conversation, he just walks away or blatantly ignores me. Mum is okay with it, surprisingly, though she's hardly in a good place to be giving a fair judgement. I'll give her the benefit of the doubt and say she's off the alcohol, but she tends to just sit there as if she's waiting for something to happen. Today is her first day of work since I went into hospital, and I'm proud—and slightly relieved. We need that money. I offered to get a job when we first moved here, but life hasn't really given me the chance to get one.

It's almost as if my heart has a space in it that needs to be filled. The space is growing and growing, but I can't find the correct-sized silica mould to fill it. I suppose I shouldn't feel so empty if I have another human inside of me. Poor child. Who'd want me as a mother? The trial is due tomorrow, and it's literally all I can think about. What if I say the wrong thing? Craig could find a loophole and hey presto, he will be out! I can only imagine what would happen thereafter. At least the kids are keeping me nice and busy. They've all insisted that we start our own little vegetable patch, so I'm now covered in what I hope is soil.

'Archie, chuck mud at Coco again and I swear to you I'll—Archie!' I drop the trowel on the floor, cupping my face in my dirty hands. My brothers and sisters all seem to find my meltdown utterly hilarious, stifling their fake little giggles.

'That's it. I'm done. Grow your own damn vegetable patch,' I mutter, tearing the itchy gloves off of my hands and chucking them to the floor. I spin on my heel and go to walk inside when I collide with a tall and incredibly sturdy body. I look up, and Leo's oddly sculptured face looks down at me.

'Are you playing nice, Ivy?' he teases, smiling at me. I try to walk past him, but he sidesteps with me.

'Do you mind getting outta my way, Leo? I don't have time for this,' I grumble. Leo doesn't know about the baby, because I've yet to tell him. We've grown close recently, and with that relationship he's brought an incredibly overprotective guard over me.

Every time I take a step, so does he. Sick of this awkward morris dance, I barge straight past him and into the house. I can hear the tapping of his shoes as he follows me, but I just continue to walk in the hope that he'll go away.

'Will you just leave me alone?' I almost yell, twisting to face him. Leo looks slightly taken aback by my outburst. The poor guy isn't used to living with a teenage girl—especially not a pregnant one.

'Can you quit acting like a heavily pregnant hormonal woman?' It feels like he's just kicked me straight in the stomach. How I wish I could stop acting like this, but newsflash sunshine: I'm pregnant. That's exactly what I want to bawl out, but I end up shouting an extended chain of expletives. My sort-of-stepdad's mouth drops open like that of a baby waiting to be spoon-fed puree. He runs his lanky fingers through his large, curly mop, which I've noticed is a coping mechanism for when he's feeling either extremely happy or the polar opposite. Needless to say, the poor man has done this particular action many a time during a conversation with yours truly.

Leo takes a sharp and lengthy breath. 'Ivanna Melanie Towers, go to your room now,' he breathes out.

My eyes squint unintentionally as I try to figure this man out. Is he for real? 'If you think I'm going to my room, you've got another think coming to you,' I snarl, folding my arms and giving him my hardest glare. He's completely unfazed by it. 'You're not my dad, and you never will be,' I snap.

Leo's eyes flinch momentarily, but he doesn't let it weaken him. 'You really need to quit the childish attitude, Ivy.'

'Likewise,' I retaliate. I watch as Leo mentally facepalms.

'This is getting ridiculous, Ivy.' I hear the doorbell ring. Tyler must've forgotten his key.

'Tyler, if that's you, you can turn right back around. I've had enough lectures for today.' I say, storming towards the door. I throw it open, and the face that greets me isn't my brother's. Clutching five enormous duffel bags is Eli. The bags fall off his shoulders and onto the doorstep.

'Eli, I—' His face crumples. I throw my arms around him, and he returns the gesture, holding me so tightly that I worry he might squeeze my internal organs out of my mouth.

'Shhh. It's okay,' I reassure him. I set his bags down by the door and help him into the living room. In all my years, not once have I seen someone looking so distraught—and I've seen some pretty horrific circumstances in my time. Once Eli's most dreadful wailing subsides, he catches his breath and tries to explain.

'They don't want me, Ivy ... I'm nothing to them.'

'Who's "they"?' Leo chimes in from the doorway. I give him a glare that could rattle even the most hardened criminals.

'My parents. They know everything.'

'Know what? I'm sorry; you've lost me.'

No! Please, please, please don't say it.

With bloodshot eyes, Eli looks up at Leo. 'Mum and Dad ... they know about me and Ivy's baby.'

Great.

Leo totally outdoes me in the glaring contest. I don't even dare to look up at him, but I can feel his glance burning holes through my body.

'Ivy, why don't we go and make Eli a hot chocolate?' Leo suggests. Congratulations to the man for staying calm for this long. I certainly couldn't if I were as angry as he is.

'It only takes one to make a hot chocolate,' I retort. After accidentally catching eyes with Leo, I decide that it's in my best interest to just do as he says.

'A baby? Are you serious!' Leo screams as soon as the kitchen door is closed. I'm pretty sure the kids hear us from outside but are too scared to investigate.

'As serious as it gets. You don't think we'd be sick enough to joke about a baby?' I say. If looks could kill, Leo would be a mass murderer. I know I need to play this well or things could get messy. *Bring on the sob story.* 'Listen. I'm as surprised as you are. I just didn't know what to say,' I explain.

'"Hey, Leo! One little thing—I'm pregnant!" That'd be a good start!' he spits. Ha, if only it was that simple. I don't see how he can pretend it's an easy conversation to have. Pregnancy is no joke. I thought that with him being a fully grown adult, he'd understand it's no walk in the park. 'Listen. I'm just having a tough time coming to terms with it all. What do I tell people? That I'm about to be a grandad at thirty?'

'You're not going to be a grandad! Read my lips, Leo. You are *not* my dad!' The words escape my mouth before I can cram them back in. Over the weeks, I guess Leo has got the impression that he's like a dad to me. Don't get me wrong, Leo has become a major part of my life. Role model? Yes. Friend? Yes. Dad? No. The idea of Leo replacing my own father makes me sick to my stomach, even if my father did walk out on us. We all make mistakes, right? The only problem is, sometimes we are too stubborn to admit it. I want to see Dad, and I'm sure he wants to see me, but he can't. Coming to terms with the fact that he was wrong to leave us would be hard. One day, though, I'm sure of it, he will walk through that door and he'll hold me tighter than ever. He'll tell me that I'll never see the back of him again.

Leo's face falls like the water plunging from the peak of the Niagara Falls.

'Ivy, I know the pressure of the court trial has been hard on you lately—'

'You have no idea,' I mutter.

'And I know that the attack turned your life upside down—'

'That's putting it nicely.'

'But this is the tip of the iceberg. Babies are a big deal.' Leo places his hand on my shoulder as if indicating affection. 'You may think you are ready, but you're not. Babies need full-time care, and you're just not ready to provide that,' he says. My body starts to feel as numb as ever, and the heart that beats inside me starts to slow down. Why does nobody understand me? I am fully aware that I'm not prepared for a baby. The last thing I want is to care for another innocent human at the age of sixteen.

But I can't help this.

This baby needs a mother. Even if I can't guarantee five-star care, at least I'm trying. That has to count for something, right?

In all this melodrama, it has only just occurred to me that Eli is waiting alone in the living room. Just as I think about making my excuses and joining him, the front door slams shut. The footsteps pause in the living room and then quickly approach us. Tyler storms in and looks at me with an incinerating glare.

'What's going on?' he asks.

Leo puts his arm around me but I shrug it straight off. 'It's okay. He knows,' I explain. I try to ignore the upset on Leo's face as he realises that he was the only person out of the loop.

'Eli's been kicked out of his home,' I say. 'Can he stay?' Obviously I mean this as a strictly rhetorical question. There's no doubt as to whether Eli is staying or not. No one is getting in the way of this. No one. Tyler wrinkles his nose as if a surfeit of skunks have just released their unbearable gases right here in the kitchen.

'First he knocks you up, and now he wants to kip on our sofa? As if,' he chuckles. Not even a second thought? I knew my brother could be cold, but I never realised it could get to this extent. The back door swings open, revealing seven mud-covered kids. They sprint inside and cause what can only be described as an instant headache. If the kids hadn't come in, I would've knocked Tyler clean.

'I knew you were a heartless idiot, but this ... this really takes the mick,' I whisper, tears streaming from my bloodshot eyes. Again the front door slams closed, and in walks Mum. Leo greets her with a warm embrace and a kiss that makes my insides feel all funny.

'Mum, tell Ivy that her scumbag of a boyfriend can't stay here,' Tyler says. A surge of anger rushes through me, and I throw myself at him. Soon enough, a chunk of his precious locks is no longer attached to his head. By the time Leo can jump into action, Tyler has a broken nose and his head is dented at the side. *What have I done?* Every one of the kids screams and hides behind Leo, all of them crying their eyes out.

'P-please don't hurt me, Ivy,' Archie whispers.

'No. I would never—' I reach out to him, but Leo pushes me back.

'Don't touch him!' he cries. My lips quiver as I try to form words. In all the time that I've known my little brother, never have I ever seen him so scared. But now I have.

And it's all because of me.

Mum kneels beside Tyler and tries to mop up the stream of velvet that's flowing out of my brothers' head. It's as if I've time-travelled back to that dreadful night. Each painful second drags by. *One. Two. Three.* My eyes blur with tears, momentarily masking the devastating truth before me. Last time it was me on the floor, my life slipping away by the minute. Now it's my brother. The blood—it won't stop coming. *I can't breathe. I can't...*

'Someone call an ambulance!' Mum cries. Tyler doesn't utter a single syllable. *Unconscious. Just like I was.* Eli sprints into the room, having heard the commotion. On instinct, Eli ushers the kids upstairs and tells them to play. I can hear Eva crying from her cot upstairs. *That piercing shriek. How I wish Tyler would shriek. Cry out in pain. Then at least I'd know he's alive.* Leo hurries to the landline and calls the ambulance. I can't move my feet. They're cemented to the marble floor.

'Cam, you need to put pressure on the wound.' Leo repeats instructions from the operator. The crying from upstairs hammers through my head. Mum's desperate reassurance to Tyler twists my stomach. Leo is trying to calm Mum down, but her hysteria is inevitable. Eli—he's just standing there watching. Waiting. I can't move.

Mum pauses her mix of soothing words and crying to stare up at me. The emotion in her eyes has an aspect of ambiguity. She looks hurt that I'd do such an awful thing to my brother, angry at how much of an awful person I've shaped into, and frightened that this could be the end of all of us as a family.

This is what kills me. Even seeing Tyler with a smashed in head can't cause as much pain as the look Mum gives me. I'm a disappointment.

Run.

That's all I think to do. My legs carry me out the door and down the street until I reach the woods. Outstretching trees tear at the skin on my leg, causing immense pain. But I don't care. I need this.

I keep running until I come to the clearing. The ledge. I sit on the edge of the cliff, staring down at the rocky beach beneath me. A hundred feet, maybe? If I were to fall, accidentally or not, it would kill me, most certainly. A golden glow gleams from the sky and rains down on my burning skin. Each ray of sunshine picks a different place on my skin to burn. They all connect to make the fuse to my heart. In the distance, I notice a surfer dancing across the undulating waves. His body reacts to every movement of the sea, ready for any occasion. Eventually he is swept from his feet and is sent plunging into the icy depths of the water. I hold my breath as I wait for him to come up from the waves. A few painstaking seconds later, he emerges from the waves and shakes the water from his hair.

'Ivy,' a worn-out voice calls from behind me. I don't dare check to see who it is, I just let him sit behind me. He puts his hand in mine. I'd know that warm palm anywhere.

'Eli. I'm so sorry …' I whisper. A tear escapes my eye, but I don't show any sign of a meltdown. He pulls me into a hug, and I feel warm tears dropping onto my scalp.

'Sorry? Ivy, none of this is your fault. We should've been more careful. This baby, its—'

'No. Not the baby. I … I haven't been honest with you. I'm an awful person,' I cry. Uncontrollable wails fly from my mouth, and I cry the ugliest I have in years. I need to do this.

'Nothing you can say will make me think of you as an awful person. Nothing.'

'You don't understand. I did it. It was me,' I scream. My lungs tighten to the point where I no longer feel able to breathe.

'What did you do? Please, Ivy …'

'Simon!' I cry. 'He's gone. He's never coming back!' I crumple into his arms and scream till my throat can't take any more. Eli tells me to breathe regularly, and after a few minutes, I feel stable—to an extent.

'Now please, explain. From the beginning.'

So I do. I didn't want to tell him this, and I know that after he knows what I did, he'll wish he didn't. He'll wish he had nothing to do with someone like me—a monster.

'I was never a good person. Each school day was just a new challenge for me to hurt people. I was a bully. Me and my friends were the ones to be afraid of. Of course, Mum and Tyler knew about this, but they were too scared to tell me to stop. I really was a brutal person. I'd hurt people. Badly. Knives were no stranger to my hands. Many lives were changed at the hands of three people: me and the Wilson brothers, Craig and Simon. At first we were just three friends against the world. One day something changed. Simon and I were no longer friends. We became soul mates, so to speak. I loved him. He loved me. Everyone in the village knew that if you hurt me, you'd have hell to pay at the hands of Simon Wilson. We were untouchable. Teachers didn't dare contradict me. Up until then, I was just scary. Then I became something completely new—an alcoholic. My two reliances were Simon and vodka. The booze—it gave a certain numbness in my heart that helped me to forget how much of an awful person I had become. Every swig, every drop, helped. For just a few minutes a day, I felt numb to the world. That's all I wanted: numbness.

'Simon was the only thing better than the booze. The dark eyes, the fawn hair placed carefully on his head, that glimmering smile … He made me feel safe. Mum was far from fond of me. Tyler always loved me, though. He hated how I'd turned out, but he was always trying to protect me. Even though I was at my wildest, I kept things under control. I was safe. Until one night.

'We'd come from a party, Simon and I—a rather wild one. Let's just say that by the end of the night, neither of us was in a fit state to drive or make any rational decisions. However, I foolishly decided to drive. The wind gushed through my hair as I sped down the country road. We sang along to the radio. Our intoxicated laughs almost drowned out the upbeat music playing through the car. I didn't have a driving licence due to my young age, but I'd learnt to drive nonetheless. Let's just say I often engaged in stealing vehicles. Out of nowhere, a deer jumped into the road. I'd never hesitated when hurting a human, but I just couldn't hurt an innocent animal. They don't deserve it. Not like humans do. I swerved. Falling. Falling. Falling. Crash.

'I woke up to the rain pounding down on my limp body. My right leg … It wouldn't move. Broken, I thought. Smashed in from the impact of the fall. I put my hand to my head, only for it to be smothered by blood. Then it dawned on me. Simon.

'Using all the strength left in my arms, I army-crawled over to my boyfriend. I cried his name till my throat gave in. No answer. He was lying in the passenger seat, his head completely battered. I whispered to him, and his finger twitched slightly. Still alive? I knew he had a slim chance of survival, but I couldn't risk it. If he survived, there was a witness for me breaking numerous laws, and before you know it, I'd be in jail. That's when I found myself picking up a rock. I didn't want to do it; I really didn't. But I had to. With a cry, I slammed the rock on his head. I took his wrist and pressed two fingers to his veins. No pulse. My body felt weaker than ever. My pulse—I could feel it in my head. *Da dum. Da dum. Da dum.*

'My pulse was there, but Simon's wasn't. I'd killed him. My soulmate. My best friend. I knew exactly what would happen next. The police would arrive. They'd arrest me for murder, and my family would fall apart. So I did what anyone would've done. I swapped our positions.

'I didn't know that dragging a dead body would be so difficult. But I did it. With each painful grunt, I pulled Simon into the driver's seat. I placed myself in the upturned car, in the passenger seat. I'd seen many unconscious people over the years, so I knew how to position myself. I looked up, and I could see a figure up by the road. Craig.

'He'd seen it all, including the swap. He must've followed us from the party. He climbed carefully into the ditch and took me in his arms. He told me he'd keep everything quiet. I felt safe for a minute, knowing that my secret would never get out. What I didn't know was that Craig was just pretending. He caught every moment, filmed on his mobile. He made me feel safe so I wouldn't suspect what he was capable of doing to me. Simon's death was the hard bit. The rest was easy.

'I played dead, and Craig called the ambulance. For the next few weeks, I was the poor little girlfriend who had suffered injury at the hands of my maniac boyfriend. Simon was a year older than me, so everyone in the city assumed that he had influenced me to drink. The people in my village knew what I was really like, and they knew it wasn't Simon's fault. Not that the police listened to them. I mustered up the courage to tell Tyler and Mum. Mum couldn't stand the bad reputation she'd obtain, so she kept quiet. We grew closer over those weeks. That little secret we shared. Except it wasn't little. It was colossal, and it was chilling.

'Together, we acted innocent. The general public took my side of the story. They shunned my dead boyfriend for his sins and congratulated me for my bravery. People in my village started to react. They'd vandalise our home and send me death threats. They knew me better than anyone, and they wanted me to pay. That's why we moved. My siblings—they weren't safe there. People would hurl insults at us in the streets. The police refused to prosecute me because they believed it was Simon's fault, but all the village wanted was for me to be behind bars for good.

'Luckily for me, I've always been a reasonably smart kid. That's where Queen's came in. I took the entry test and passed easily. Mum found a job at some nail bar in Dover, and we moved within the week. From then on, I was forced to change everything about me: name, appearance—everything. I used to be called Leonora, and my hair was a strawberry-blonde colour. Mum made sure I changed my identity, because she still didn't trust Craig. She could see through his lies when I was too much in denial to see it.'

When I finish talking and look over, Eli is over two metres away from me. He's staring into the distance as if he can't bear to look at me.

'Please, Eli, say something,' I whisper. Nothing. 'Say something!' I cry. I lean over to take his hand, but he scrambles up and stands away from the cliff.

'A murderer,' he whispers.

'N-no'

'… A murderer.'

'No, please. Eli …'

'You're a murderer, Ivy,' he repeats out loud.

'No, please. *Stop saying that!*' I scream, blocking my ears with my sweat-covered palms.

'He's right.' Before I can look at the source of the voice, I feel a push. As soon as I fall off the cliff, the person grabs both my wrists, suspending me off the edge. The icy palms. I'd know them anywhere. Craig's.

'Craig, no!' Eli shouts. Even after I tell him all that, he still tries to save me? I don't deserve this. I look up, and the evil smirk of Craig meets my eye. He's enjoying this—watching me suffer.

'I've waited for this day for months,' he growls. 'The chance to finally bring you to justice.' I don't dare struggle, lest he drop me. How did he get out of that holding cell?

'How did I escape?' he asks, reading my mind somehow. 'My dad has a few contacts.'

'Police, please. Quickly! He's gonna hurt her!' Eli cries down the phone. He then shrieks, 'Craig, please! She has a baby inside her. Are you really going to kill it too?'

'Hmm. Kill two birds with one stone? Seems pretty good to me,' he chuckles. I can feel my heart in my head again. It feels just like that night.

Ba dum. Ba dum. Ba dum.

'Simon … he didn't deserve it, did he?' Craig hisses. I don't utter a word. '*Did he?*' he yells, shaking me.

'No!' I cry. My whole body trembles as if I've been put in a blender.

'But you …' He laughs an evil laugh. 'Oh, you deserve to feel every bone in your scrawny little body crack against those rocks.' I make the mistake of looking down to see that the tide has come in. Not only will I be crushed, but my body will also be washed away to sea.

'Armed police!'

Oh thank you, God. Thank you. Thank you. Thank you.

'Craig Wilson, do not move.' A marksman aims a tiny laser dot on the back of his head, ready to shoot at any moment.

'That night, when I stuck that beautiful blade into your stomach, I felt a wave of glee. I really enjoyed that, Ivy,' Craig boasts. 'Now I'm going to enjoy this.' He drops one of my arms so it dangles by my side. I hear the familiar voice of Eli scream from behind him.

'Craig Wilson,' a deep voice shouts, 'if you make any sudden movements, we will shoot!'

'You thought you'd get revenge on me. Well, guess what? You'll never see the day of that trial. In fact, the last thing you'll see is my face as I drop you from this cliff.'

Eli crumples to his knees as he watches the scene unfold.

'Any last words?'

I look over. 'Eli …'

'Quickly!' Craig spits.

'Craig Wilson. Pull her back onto the cliff and put your hands up!'

'Noooooo!' Mum screams from behind the police. 'That's my daughter! He's going to kill her!'

'I'm …'

'Quicker!' Craig roars.

'I'm sorry, Eli. I'm just sorry.' And with that I was falling again. Down. Down. Down.

To hell.

I look up to see Craig's joyful face watching me plunge from the sky. A blend of shrieking and crying echoes from the cliff. Another face appears beside him. *Haila.* Her grin matches Craig's exactly as they watch me fall to my death.

Bang! One. Bang! Two. Bang! Three. There goes another life. Maybe it is for the best that I should die. Now I can stop hurting the people around me that I love. They never deserved it, not one of them. Not the girls I bullied or the people I attacked. None of them did. This needs to happen. I'm a burden.

Goodbye, world. Maybe now you can all stop hurting.

41

Eli

'Ivy. Oh, Ivy ...' I laugh through each painful sob. 'You sure had me fooled. Who knew, eh? Who knew that someone as kind and ... and as inspirational as you could be a ... murderer? You hurt people, baby. You really did. And now the three people that I loved with all my heart are dead. I guess I'll never get to know what my own baby looked like. We were so happy, Ivy. Through all this pain and suffering we somehow managed to survive. Because we had each other, and that's all we needed. Not anymore, though. I guess I'll just have to endure this heart-wrenching pain ... alone.' My hands tremble around the clasp of the flowers. I'd chosen these especially at the nursery in town. One hour I'd spent pondering between chrysanthemums and roses. I settled for a bunch of velvet roses because I felt the deep red represented my late girlfriend: bold and strong. I guess her bolshiness was her downfall in the end. Maybe if she wasn't so opinionated, I wouldn't be standing here throwing flowers over her casket. Martha comes forward and stands beside me. She gives me a smile even though her eyes are sad and red. She opens her mouth to speak but bursts into tears before she can start.

'Sorry, sorry I'm ...' Martha pauses and takes a deep breath. 'When I thought about what I'd be doing today at this time last week, it was geometry and reading *Macbeth* and ... well it most certainly wasn't this.' She laughs nervously. 'Ivy was my right-hand man. No matter what I was going through, whether it be troubles with my parents or physics homework, she was there for me. Always. In fact, she's the first person I came out to.' She looks over to a girl in the crowd and motions her over. The girl takes Martha's hand.

'Ivy, I'd like you to meet Freya, my girlfriend.' For a moment, everyone in the crowd smiles and some clap.

'I hope you're proud of me, Ivy. I know what you did was wrong, but I love you, and I know that the Ivy I came to rely on … was a fighter.' Martha's face crumples, and Freya takes her back into the crowd, rubbing her back gently.

Miss Towers comes forward and holds my hand so tightly that I begin to worry she'll pop a blood vessel. I've always believed in karma, but no one deserves the pain that she is going through. Each day since Ivy's death has gone by more and more slowly. The devastating realisation that Ivy will never come back has started to take its toll. Mind you, The Towers' and I have helped each other through it. Despite the trauma I've been through, Mum and Dad still won't take me back. They want me to suffer, and I guess their wish is coming true, because I don't know how much longer I can do this. Leo offered Ivy's room to me, but I refused. I just couldn't face going into that room. Seeing her science posters and familiar duvet would be too much for me.

As they start to lower the casket into the hole, Miss Towers bursts into a fit of hysterical crying. Leo pulls her into a hug, and I find it hard to hold back my emotions too. Tyler sits in his wheelchair with the kids crying beside him. He tries to soothe them, but he struggles, as he can barely control himself. Even though Ivy is the reason that he'll never walk again, I can tell he still loves her to pieces. Ivy told me that Tyler was struggling with school when they first arrived. The day after she passed, he got his exam results back. He got straight As. I guess she'll never get to feel the pride for him that I do. He's kinda like a brother to me after all we've been through.

Mr Kilt stares at the coffin with tears flowing from his eyes. His face reveals no emotion, but he loosens his black tie, as if it's suffocating him.

'This day commemorates the life of Leanora Melanie Towers and the baby girl she would've given birth to in a few months' time,' The pastor says. He looks at me and gives me the motion that it's time.

'We love you, Ivy. You'll never be forgotten!' Miss Towers screams. I throw the roses on top of the casket before they start shovelling dirt over the coffin.

Goodbye, Ivy Towers. You really were an amazing human being; murderer or not.

☙❧

Everyone is in bed now, though not one of them is asleep. Even Eva can sense the cold atmosphere that swoops through the house. I can't even bear to close my eyes. At least when I do finally decide to allow myself to rest, I'll wake up in a few hours. Ivy will never wake up.

Miss Towers suggested that I look at some of the articles surrounding Ivy's past. She thought it might bring some closure for me. At first I couldn't even bring myself to type her name into Google, but now I feel like I have to, for both our sakes.

Boyfriend from Hell?

Notorious troublemaker Simon Wilson drives recklessly, costing his life and nearly his girlfriend's …

The Truth, the Whole Truth and Nothing but the Truth!

The death of a troubled youth has broken the local news recently. We all know about the tragedy with Simon Wilson and Leonora Towers, but do we really know the whole truth? Ms Meghan Sykes, a neighbour of the Towers family, tells us her view of the situation.

'He didn't crash that car. I know that girl, and I know how she operates. I've heard the commotion coming from next door every night—the screaming, the fights, the door slamming. Simon Wilson was a very troubled young man, but he didn't do it. I've seen him driving under the influence many times, and he always managed to drive properly. He had a knack for it; it's what he was good at. I'll go on record right here and say that car was crashed by Leonora Melanie Towers.'

I want Meghan Sykes to be wrong. I want Ivy to have helped Simon, or to just not have gone to the party in the first place. But that isn't what happened.

And now, for the rest of my worthless life, I have to live with that.

I fell in love with a murderer and I had no Idea.

Acknowledgements

To be honest, I never actually read acknowledgements in books, but I have so many people to thank that I couldn't not write an acknowledgement section.

To Winston Forde, my grandpa and my editor. Thank you, because without you, this book wouldn't even be published. If it weren't for your encouragement and your sheer belief in me, I wouldn't have had the motivation to complete this novel.

To Steven and Beverley Forde, my amazing parents. From the moment I decided to become a writer, you never doubted me. You understood when I wanted to write alone, and you were always happy to read my horrendous first drafts. For that I'm forever grateful.

To Alicia and Tamsin Forde, my beautiful sisters. You always took the wrath of my anger when my storyline just wouldn't come together or I felt like giving up. Again, thank you for reading my first drafts. (They really were awful.)

To Phyllis Ebanks, the nana to beat all nanas. Thank you for your undisputed belief in me and your never-ending river of encouragement. Your kind words and your personality that brightens up the darkest of rooms helped me through the hardest times.

To Hannah Appleton, Jaimie Farquharson, Emma Foster and Batool Al-Awsi, the best friends I could've asked for. Thank you for helping me with the storyline, for laughing with me at my thousands of failures, and for just being there for me. I couldn't ask for a better group of people to spend every lunchtime in the library with.

Finally, I'd like to thank the people that didn't believe in me. You made me even more dedicated to making this book the best it could be. You thought I was ludicrous for wanting to write a book, but look at me now!

Lightning Source UK Ltd.
Milton Keynes UK
UKHW010649300621
386396UK00001B/81